GUY HATER

A ROMANTIC COMEDY

ETHAN ASHER

For everyone who hates walnuts in brownies
as much as Charleigh....

PROLOGUE

Charleigh

I HATE THIS town.

I hate its expansive mountain views and all the *oh-so-happy-and-in-love* couples who Instagram said views. I hate the disgustingly fresh air. I hate the verdant evergreen forests and every single one of the crystal-clear, snow-fed tributaries that meander through them. I hate everything about this sleepy mountain town, from its tiny woodland critters down to its dumb name.

I know what you're probably thinking by now...

What are tiny woodland critters and how could anyone hate them? And fresh air? Wow, girl. You must be a blast at parties. And also: WHY. DO. YOU. STILL. LIVE. THERE?

You probably think I have some unresolved issues that I should work through with a therapist. Scratch that—a whole team of therapists working around the clock to make sure I'm not a threat to society.

You'd be right, somewhat.

However, when it comes to Whispering Pine (see? PINE TREES CAN'T WHISPER. Dumb.), Colorado, I only have one unresolved issue: Guy Finch.

Guy "My Farts Make You Flinch" Finch.

Guy's the type of—well, *guy*—who leaves less than a spoonful of ice cream in the container before putting it back in the freezer. He's the type of person who, if he does replace the toilet paper, puts the roll upside down like a savage.

Guy Finch wears socks with sandals.

Okay, I went a bit too far with that last one. I don't know if he wears socks with sandals. And to be honest, I don't know if he does any of the other things I've accused him of.

I know… I know…

But here's the one thing I do know for certain about Guy Finch. He made my life hell when we were kids. And when I extrapolate from what I know about him then, I'm sure my previous accusations are accurate and well within an acceptable margin of error.

And now that he's back in Whispering Pine, it's enough for me to hate everything about this town. He should've been turned away at the city's limits, but instead, the friendly folk of Whispering Pine opened their loving arms and embraced the monster that is Guy "I'm As Sharp As A Wrench" Finch.

But I won't be so welcoming.

CHAPTER ONE

Charleigh

AS I WALK through the oversized board-and-batten door of The Lookout, there are three things on my mind: taxidermy, Guy Finch, and a hard, stiff drink. To be clear, as much as I hate Guy, I don't want him dead, stuffed, and mounted on a wall. Unless...

No, Charleigh. You'd never get away with it. He's a cop!

It's the first time I've stepped foot in here and the decor is killing me. Dead eyes stare down at me from the wall, judging me as I pass by them on my way to the bar. Interior design tip number one: Swaths of oversized trophy kills lining every wall do not a rustic lodge make.

As I'm navigating through the packs of men (and *only* men), I feel like I'm in The Prancing Pony or Green Dragon Inn. The men may not be as small as Hobbits, but they're certainly as hairy. All that's missing from the ambiance is said group of men breaking into a rousing song about gold, dragons, or elvish lords while a few of the shorter ones dance a merry jig on a table.

Every breath I take is filled with alcohol, stale air, and burps. Mostly burps. And with the amount of testosterone circulating in the air around me, I'm pretty sure I'll have a full-grown mustache à la Tom Selleck or Ron Swanson by the time I leave.

When I find a stool at the bar, I check my phone and find a text from my brother.

Jamie: Where are you?!

Not there...

And by *there* I mean the dinner I should be attending— the one where all threads of conversation will weave together into a single strand: my brother's upcoming wedding. It's not that I'm not happy for him. Or that I don't want to hang out with his fiancée. Believe me, the more I hang out with Marissa, the more I respect her for being able to kiss Jamie without gagging. And I'd love to watch Jamie squirm as I recount how he wet the bed until he was twelve.

Kidding! Kinda.

No. The reason I'm *here* and not *there* circles back to the two things left on my mind: Guy Finch and booze.

Guy Finch and my brother are best friends. Which means that Guy is my brother's best man. Which means that he's going to be at the dinner. Which means that I'm *here* and not *there*.

Charleigh: My ceiling sprang a leak again! It's being fixed. I'll be there soon.

4

It's not a complete lie. There is a leak in my apartment but I plugged it with paper towels and duct tape. It's all up to code, I swear. Well, it will be once my landlord finally fixes it. Hopefully.

"What can I get you?" asks the only other female I can see in the bar. Her black hair and blunt bangs contrast starkly with her pale complexion and cornflower blue eyes.

"Tequila and lime, please," I say, staring at her shiny septum piercing.

She smiles. "That kind of a night, huh?"

My phone vibrates. I glance at the message and groan. "Yup." I let the 'P' really pop. "That kind of a night."

She raps her knuckles twice on the bar and then retreats to grab my drink.

Jamie: Guy's not here either.

Yet.

Is what I'd say if I wanted to be confrontational. Instead, I feign ignorance, which I'm sure will go over just as well.

Charleigh: Oh, he's supposed to be joining us tonight? I didn't know. I'm just waiting for them to finish up.

I'm such a bad liar. I've heard that you either cut close to the truth or deviate as far from it as possible. I settle on a middle ground between the two that seems plausible never of the time. Yes—never of the time. Neverytime. It will catch on, I swear.

Jamie: I know you two haven't always gotten

along. I know you're avoiding him. And I know he's changed.

Charleigh: You seem to know a lot of stuff, Jimbo, but do you know how to fix a leak? These guys are taking a really long time and I don't think they're accredited contractors. Is there some sort of accreditation process for contractors? Remind me to Google that later.

Jamie: Charleigh...

Jamie knows the history between Guy and me. He knows how Guy teased me. But he also knows that Guy wasn't always an asshole to me. We actually got along once upon a time.

"One tequila and lime," the bartender says, setting it down in front of me.

"Thanks," I say, snatching the glass and bringing it to my lips.

"You sure you don't want anything to chase it down?"

I pause, the glass rim grazing my bottom lip as I look at her pretty blue eyes staring back at me with such misplaced concern. I'm Charleigh Holiday. I know how to take a motherfu—*phleagh!*

I sputter and cough, shaking my head as I set the glass down and push it away. You know those videos of toddlers tasting lemons for the first time? That's my face right now. It's staring at me from the mirror behind the bar and it's not pretty.

After a few seconds of gasping for air, I mutter a semi-decipherable command that I hope will turn my drink into something that won't burn the lining of my esophagus the next time around.

Eyes watering. Nose running. Throat still throbbing. The bartender, trying hard not to laugh, takes my drink and leaves, her hair bobbing triumphantly as though to say, "I told you so."

What am I thinking? I don't like tequila. Hell, I don't even like alcohol. I'll have an occasional cider or glass of wine, but straight tequila?

Once the burning sensation in my throat subsides, I look around me, hoping that no one saw that. Thankfully, everyone else is too busy smashing pints to notice. Except for…

Oh, hello.

One of the only men at the bar with more hair on his head than his face stares at me with an amused grin. His lips move slowly as he speaks with the bartender but his eyes focus on me. From this distance, I can just make out his features.

Dirty blonde hair. Dark eyes. Prominent jawline and brow ridge.

This guy looks like an LL Bean cover model but without the hunter-green down vest, braying blonde wife, two kids, and a golden retriever named Kingsley. Some women might describe him as dreamy, but not me.

Nope. Not me.

The bartender leaves, but Mr. Not-So-Dreamy keeps his eyes locked on mine as he raises a glass to his lips, swallows, and then sets it back down. I turn away and focus on my phone just as he smiles at me, sending a fluttering sensation through my chest.

Charleigh: I swear I'm not avoiding Guy. I didn't even know he was going to be there.

There's a long pause between my text and the next one Jamie sends. But when it hits, it hits no harder than a bullet train.

Jamie: I expected more from you, Charleigh.

My brother sure knows how to hit me right in the gut. Ugh. This is awful.

"Here you go," the bartender says as she places down something that I definitely didn't order.

I glance at her with raised eyebrows. "What is this?"

She motions with her head at Mr. Not-So-Dreamy, who has a shit-eating grin plastered on his much too handsome face. "Chardonnay. Compliments of the gentleman over there. He said it might be more your style." Her cheeks redden as she turns, trying hard to mask the laugh itching to come out.

"More my style?" I sputter as she heads over to another customer.

I stare at the glass in front of me, take a breath, and groan. Okay, he may be right. I do like chardonnay, but I hate how this guy thinks he knows me based on absolutely nothing at all.

If I weren't already preoccupied, I'd tell him as much. Instead, I stand up, make a face at him as he waves at me, and then surreptitiously ask the bartender as I pass by her to have someone bring the glass of wine over to me in a few minutes. I don't want to give Mr. LL Bean the pleasure of knowing he was right.

I find a cozy spot in front of the floor-to-ceiling stone fireplace away from the noise, but the noise in my head is still raging. And my phone is still beeping.

Jamie: How's that leak?

Charleigh: If I were on a boat, they'd be calling for women and children to head to the lifeboats now.

With each lie I tell, I feel worse. I should bite the bullet and go. It's been years since I've seen Guy, and maybe Jamie's right. Maybe he outgrew his jackassery and cleaned up his act a little. The thought nearly sends me into a fit of laughter: Guy changing?

"You forgot something."

The gritty masculine voice hugs me like a fleece blanket. It warms me from the inside out like a steaming mug of hot chocolate (mini-marshmallows included, of course). It's deep and rough and—*oh my God!*

It's him. And wow, Lieutenant LL Bean is far more handsome at this distance. He looms over me with wide, strong shoulders and a smile that could drop a thousand panties. But definitely not mine. His rugged charm and masculine features and heavenly scent have absolutely no effect on me.

None. What. So. Ever.

I glance at the glass of chardonnay that looks like a child's cup in his large hands. "No, I don't think I did."

I turn around, pick up my phone, and begin texting my nonexistent friend who will totally save me from this situation. The heat from his gaze spreads all over my body me as I type gibberish into a note app. Jesus. I'm a plate of food under a heat lamp ready on the pass. Order up and get me out of here!

He leans over, setting the glass on the small wood stump table next to me. "You know," he says, his warm breath tickling my neck, "it's usually more convincing to open your Messenger app, rather than your note app, when you're pretending to text someone."

Every breath is filled with his scent. It's spicy and masculine and doing things to my brain that usually happen *after* I'm a few glasses of wine deep.

Blood rushes to my head and pounds in my ears. My heart thumps faster and faster as my mouth dries. Before I have a chance to respond, he takes a step back, tells me to have a good night, and then walks away, leaving every inch of my body sizzling.

That's IT?!

I'm no longer thinking about Guy. I'm no longer thinking of Jamie or the dinner I'm not attending. All I'm thinking about is the short, frustrating encounter with Mr.—o*kay, fine!*—Dreamy.

I'm not sure how long I've been stewing in my thoughts, grudgingly drinking my chardonnay—which is delicious, by the way—when I'm interrupted.

"Beautiful night isn't it, Red?"

I love it when creepy, drunk old men try to grab my attention by using one of my physical attributes as my name, said no woman ever. My gag reflex is fully charged as I slowly twist my neck to gaze at the monstrosity looming next to me, panting as though he's just finished a marathon.

The cloying smell of alcohol on his breath mixes with his Axe body spray and sweat, creating a scent that makes my nose want to shrivel up and die. But as soon as his greasy meat mittens grip my shoulder, I say, "Nope," and make my exit, finding another seat at the other end of the fireplace.

It takes a few moments for my departure to register

on Mr. Clueless's face. When it finally does, he comes stumbling after me with the grace of a newborn elephant on ice.

"Oh, come on. Give us a smile, Red," he says when he finally makes it to me.

Okay, it's official: I'm in *The Lord of the Rings* because not only does this guy talk like Sméagol, his bloated face with bulbous eyes and gnarly, slimy teeth bear a striking resemblance to him too. It's uncanny, but I'm not his *Precious*. And I swear to Gandalf, if he calls me Red one more time, I'll unleash hell.

I stand up, grab my empty glass, and head toward the bar. But as I pass by him, he snatches my arm and I can't help gaping at him, stunned. What in the hell is going on?

"Emma!"

I turn toward the voice, still dazed. It takes me a few moments to register the person's face, but when I do, I've never been so thankful. Mr. Dreamy's rushing over to me.

"Sebastian," I call back.

Sebastian?!

Sméagol releases me with a grunt just as Sebastian— whatever the hell his name is—reaches me. "There you are," he says, grabbing me. I assume he's going to drag me away, but instead, he kisses me.

And holy hell, is this a kiss.

11

CHAPTER TWO

Charleigh

HAVE YOU EVER been to outer space?

Me neither. But whatever the hell Sebastian's doing to me with his lips makes me feel weightless, as though at any moment I could float away into a vast nothingness if not for his arms tethering me to him.

When I finally come down from the euphoric high of making out with him, I have two things on my mind: Who the hell does he think he is, and why can't I stop myself from kissing him?

His lips are so soft and meld perfectly against mine, and he tastes sweet like cinnamon and sugar. My mind feels like a live wire, flopping and flailing and spinning wildly as sparks of electricity arc. I can't remember the last time someone's made me feel like this.

Has anyone ever made me feel like this before?

He grips the back of my head with one hand, deepening our kiss, while the other presses against the small of my back. My arms are bunched up against his hard chest as he kisses me roughly. I whimper as he pulls away for a brief moment, looking at me in a way that jolts all my baser instincts into overdrive.

My God, this man is something else.

He lifts an eyebrow. "Sebastian?"

I shake my head. "What?"

"You called me Sebastian. Why?"

Oh, right. I forgot about that. Could we just forget about it and go back to that whole kissing thing? Thanks.

"You looked like you just walked out of a Land's End or LL Bean catalog."

And Sebastian—Ryan Gosling—from *La La Land*...if he'd gained a few inches and thirty pounds of muscle.

He closes his eyes as he lets out a deep laugh that rattles in my chest.

I take the brief moment his eyes are closed to take a closer look at him. This man is so attractive I'm sure that if he lived during classical antiquity there'd be poems or ballads or plays written about him. Statues and paintings. I'm not saying that because he just saved me. Or because his mouth made me an amnesiac for a hot minute. It's all true. And all I can think about is what the rest of him could do to me.

When he opens his eyes again, my chest clenches as my breath leaves me. He's looking at me like there's no one else in the world. There's a hunger in his eyes, and I'm the only thing on the menu. A few more seconds under his gaze and I'm sure I'll pull a Katniss Everdeen and volunteer myself as tribute.

Then, for a brief moment, I see something oddly familiar in his eyes, but I shake myself out of it. "Why the hell did you kiss me?"

And what made you stop?

"Because I was drawn to you the moment you walked through that door."

Okay. I'm sure he's never used that line on anyone else before.

"And when that asshole touched you, I lost it."

I raise my brow. "You took it a whole lot further than that asshole."

He takes a step back and runs a hand through his thick hair, ruffling it before he lets his hand fall back to his side. "You're right. I shouldn't have kissed you."

Well, let's not get too carried away here...

"I wasn't thinking." He pauses for a moment, shakes his head, and then looks at me with those eyes. A look that I feel deep in my belly. "It's no excuse. I'm sorry. Forgive me for my lapse in judgment?"

I pretend that I'm thinking about forgiving him, but all that I'm thinking about is the possibility of those lips on mine again. It's strange. Under any other circumstances, with any other man, I'd be out of here. But there's something about Sebastian. I felt it the moment we locked eyes earlier, and it hasn't left me.

I offer my hand. "Apology accepted."

The right corner of his mouth pulls back slowly into a half smile as he takes my hand into his firm grasp. He shakes it a few times, and just when I think he's going to let go, he tugs me gently toward him as he leans in, invading my personal space once again, his scent hijacking my brain.

"But I don't regret it, Emma. And I think you enjoyed it," he rasps, his breath tickling the sensitive skin below my ear.

Ugh. Why can't he have a snaggletooth or unibrow? Something that would make it easier to be mad at him.

But I'm not. And he's right; I did enjoy it more than I want him to know.

"Maybe I did," I say slowly, trying to breathe as the air between us becomes thick. "But maybe I also think you're an asshole too."

He snorts as he pulls away from me. "I'll take it."

I sigh and shake my head, finally able to breathe again.

"Have a drink with me, Emma? Give me the chance to prove to you I'm not an asshole."

He's still calling me Emma. I kind of like it. It's like my alter ego. Charleigh wouldn't have a drink with this man. She wouldn't be taken in by his rugged charm, mouthwatering muscles, or (very) kissable lips. Charleigh's sharp as a tack. She'd turn around, walk out the door, and drive to her brother's dinner like an adult.

Emma? She's different. Emma definitely wants to see where this leads. Emma takes risks. Emma is all about exploring her sexuality.

"Fine," I say, channeling Emma.

"Don't get too excited now."

I jab his arm. "Don't make me regret this."

And I'm not regretting it. At all.

Sebastian (we've decided to stick with our nicknames for now) is more than a pretty face and an amazing kisser. He's funny and blunt and trouble, if I keep talking with him. Because I know exactly where this is going to lead. And no matter how much I'd enjoy where it's leading, I'm not interested in a one-night stand. Or a relationship. I have way too much to deal with right now, and I don't need complications. And everything about Sebastian screams complication.

Sex isn't complicated, Emma tells me. *Insert tab A into slot B.*

No, no, no. NOT happening.

Okay fine, slot C.

NO THANK YOU!

I'm not sure I like Emma right now.

"So why Emma? A few unresolved issues with an ex-girlfriend or something?"

He smiles at me with that same damn smile again. Two rows of far too perfect pearly whites. Crinkles at the corners of his eyes. A single dimple. Kryptonite.

"Not at all. You remind me of Emma Stone, only prettier."

Oh my JESUS. See? Trouble.

He brushes a stray strand from my face with his thumb. "I mean it."

Did we move back in front of the fireplace? Because my skin feels like it's being roasted like a marshmallow over a campfire.

Sebastian waves at the bartender. "Another glass of wine, Ms. Stone?"

I shake my head. "Thanks, but no thanks. I need to drive after this."

"I could take you home," he says, covering my hand with his.

YES, Emma screams, flailing her arms around like a toddler in the midst of a tantrum. GIMME! GIMME! GIMME!

"Oh no, I'll be fine," I say, ignoring the fluttering in my chest.

"What can I get you two?" the bartender asks, diverting my focus away from the maelstrom of feelings swirling inside me.

"A water, please."

Sebastian pulls his hand away from mine. "Make that two."

WHAT ARE YOU DOING?! Emma screams at me.

I don't know. I like him. I really do. And as much as I'd like to see more develop between us, the timing just isn't right.

TIME? IT'S ONE NIGHT! Emma isn't pleased with me right now, and I don't blame her.

He pulls out his phone and my stomach drops. "I'm sorry, but I need to take this."

"Sure," I say, trying to smile but failing miserably.

It's probably for the best. My life is a hot mess right now. And as if I need another reminder of that, I check my phone and see the mass of texts from my brother. I've been so engrossed with Sebastian that I completely forgot about both the dinner and Guy. I send off a barrage of texts begging for forgiveness, but each one is met with silence.

The bartender drops off the waters. I immediately guzzle mine, and when I fail to flag down the bartender, I guzzle Sebastian's too.

Charleigh: I REALLY am sorry, Jamie. I'll make it up to you, I swear.

Charleigh: I'll take Marissa out for a girls' night. We'll drink and dance and share embarrassing stories about you and—

I'm about to finish the text when I feel a hand on the nape of my neck.

"Emma," Sebastian rasps. The tightly corded muscles in my neck and shoulders unwind as I turn around and meet his gaze. It's strange how his touch puts me at ease. "I'm afraid we'll have to cut our evening short. I have a fire I need to put out."

"So you're a firefighter?"

He laughs. "A metaphorical fire."

My grip tightens around my phone. Tell me about it.

He retrieves a couple of twenties from his wallet and places them on the bar next to me. Then he grabs a card and sets it in front of me. "I hope we can continue our conversation later."

How about we skip the conversation and head straight to the bedroom, Emma tells me. *YOU'RE RUINING THIS FOR ME.*

"I'd like that," I say, palming the card. Just as I'm about to put it into my clutch, something else takes over. "Do you believe in fate, Sebastian?"

And there's the look. Brows pushed together. The uncertainty rising in his eyes. He's wondering what he's just walked into. And whether he's just dodged a bullet.

He tilts his head and then slowly, his smile returns. "Not particularly. Why?"

"Well, I do believe in fate."

Do I? I don't even know. I don't know what I'm doing.

NOOOOOOOOOO! Emma wails as I tear up Sebastian's card. "And if we're meant to see each other again, it will happen."

Sebastian laughs. "Is this some kitschy romance novel stuff?"

"No." I shake my head. "If we were in a romance novel, we'd already be sleeping together."

Sebastian runs a hand through his mussed hair. "You're a strange one, Em." His smile is slowly returning to his lips, and then his eyes draw back up to mine, sending a frisson of excitement through me. "Strange, but I like you."

Emma's stomping her feet in the corner of my mind, seconds away from flipping a table.

Sebastian lowers himself so that we're eye to eye. And what fine eyes they are. Green flecks on a backdrop of rich brown. Intelligent and piercing and kind. "If that's what you want. Alright."

"Alright?"

"All. Right."

He presses his lips against my forehead. The wet skin tingles as he pulls away, and I suck in a deep breath of his scent.

"I'll see you soon," I say as he turns to leave.

He smiles at me over his shoulder. "Or not."

Right…

What am I thinking? What am I *doing*?

THAT'S WHAT I'VE BEEN ASKING YOU THIS ENTIRE TIME, Emma screams as she flails on the ground.

I watch Sebastian as he reaches the door. He turns

around, waves at me as he flashes another smile, and then disappears. There's a strange sense of familiarity in his movements, but I can't place it. Probably the alcohol. My stomach drops as I see the door close behind him. It flies through the floor when I read my brother's next text.

> **Jamie:** I'm not the only one you need to apologize to. You haven't visited Mom in months. What's gotten into you?

It's the perfect one-two punch that has me reconsidering my life choices.

CHAPTER THREE

Guy

"**NEED SOME COFFEE** with that cream, Finch?"

Maddox's words hardly register, as though my head's underwater and he's standing above me, his form rippled and blurred. They're distant and distorted and—

"Dude, what the fuck you doing?"

Maddox grabs my wrist, shaking me out of my stupor. I look down at the mess in front of me. A pool of coffee and cream covers the area surrounding my paper cup. I have no idea how long I've been pouring the half-and-half but judging by how light the container is, it's been at least a minute.

"Shit." I drop the container of half-and-half on the counter, and both Maddox and I grab bunches of paper towels to prevent the coffee from becoming a miniature Niagara Falls.

Maddox tosses a soggy clump of paper towels into the trash and turns back to me, arms folded across his barrel chest. "You sure you're okay?"

"Yeah," I say with a shake of my head. I toss the drenched paper towels in the trash and grab a few more handfuls. "Fine."

Maddox slaps my shoulder, giving me a good shake before he turns. "I'll be in the cruiser."

As I finish cleaning up the mess, there's only one thing I'm thinking about. It's the only thing that I have been thinking about for the past twelve hours: Emma.

Emma, whose name isn't Emma. Emma, whose lips taste like honey. Emma, whose kiss has the power to bring me to my knees. Emma, who made me forget all about dinner with Jamie. And Charleigh.

Charleigh…

A clump of nerves twists and tightens in my gut. I've been back in Whispering Pine for a few months now but I haven't even seen her yet. We haven't talked. I tried to reach out to her through Jamie but that was a dead end. If she doesn't want to talk, I won't force her.

When I finally make it outside, Maddox is already in the driver's seat.

"No driving for you today, pal. I don't need you driving us off a cliff."

I collapse into the passenger seat. "There aren't any cliffs to drive off, Maddox."

"My point exactly. After seeing you in that weird trance back there, I'm pretty sure you'd find one. Shit, you spent fifteen minutes making that mess and you didn't even bring your coffee."

Damn it.

I grunt as I buckle up. "Point taken."

"Let's go!" Maddox revs the engine and then peels out, squealing out of the station and swerving onto the road, nearly flipping the car in the process.

This is why Maddox never drives.

CHARLEIGH

I'm fifteen minutes late to my coffee date with Jamie. My phone's been beeping nonstop for the past five minutes, but I refuse to look at the messages because I know exactly what they'll say: Where the hell are you? Or some variation thereof.

When I finally open the door to Common Grounds, I can feel Jamie's eyes home in on me. I glance right and find him at our usual table next to the window. He's in his weekday attire—a suit, navy today, paired with a white Oxford and patterned tie—and his light blonde hair is neatly combed, parted, and styled.

Red tie, huh?

My mother thinks I'm crazy, but I've discovered that I can judge Jamie's mood by the color of tie he wears. Jamie isn't one for pops of color in his outfits, so when I see the red hanging from his neck, it's like a beacon warning me of the danger ahead.

"Morning, Charleigh," Jamie says as I approach.

"Sorry I'm late." I'm not going to offer an excuse because it wouldn't matter. Besides, Jamie has every right to be mad at me.

He slides a paper cup in front of me, and I eye it warily. He's acting far too nice to me right now given the circumstances. I take a tentative sip, watching Jamie closely.

He shrugs. "Look, I'm not going to berate you."

Then why are you wearing that tie? Maybe my mom's right after all. Or the latte's poisoned…

"I don't hold onto grudges."

"Ouch, Jameson." I glare at Jamie and take a huge swig. I'm going to need all the caffeine in this decaf to get through this conversation. "I'll have you know," I say, setting my cup down, "I don't hold grudges either. I'm over Guy. Seriously o-v-e-r. Over."

The expression on his face tells me he's everything but convinced. Maybe I tried to sell it a little too hard.

"You know he didn't show up either."

I cock my head to the side for a moment and then take another long drink. "Really?" I try to sound indifferent but instead I sound more like a squeaky mouse.

"Yeah." Jamie nods. "He met someone and lost track of time talking with them. At least that's the story he told me."

If I'd been drinking my latte, I'd have sprayed it all over him.

"Was the other person chained to a wall? Because I don't see how anyone would willingly spend more than a few seconds talking to him."

I glance at my drink, and then push it away. Something doesn't feel right…

Jamie shrugs. "It seemed genuine. I don't think I've ever heard Guy talk about anyone like this before. Not even some of his past girlfriends." Jamie stands up. "Want a refill?"

"No thanks," I say. "My head's already spinning from this decaf."

"That wasn't decaf."

My eyes bug out. "What the hell, Jamie? You know I don't drink caffeine." I knew something was up. My theory about Jamie's ties still stands.

"I guess I forgot." A grin slowly forms on his face. "Like how you forgot about dinner last night."

I groan. And I'm supposed to be the one in the family who hasn't grown up.

"Sorry, I couldn't resist, Chuck."

"Don't call me Chuck ever again."

Jamie is way too pleased with himself as he turns around and heads to the counter.

Guy used to call me Chucky. You know—that redheaded doll that the soul of a serial killer inhabited. Wild red hair. Freckles and overalls. Yeah. That Chucky. I got so sick and tired of it that I tried to dye my hair. Tried being the key word here.

I learned the hard way that red hair isn't exactly the easiest hair color to dye. My bright red eyebrows looked like high beams in comparison to the odd blackish-purple bands that striped my head. When I finally came out of the bathroom, eyes blood-red from crying, snot dripping from my nose, Guy was the first person I ran into between the bathroom and my room.

Chargrilled Charlie was my new nickname because he thought the stripes looked like grill marks. It was such a low point. I came close to shaving my head, but thankfully my mom intervened and dragged me to a stylist, who, after overcoming her initial mortification, fixed the damage I'd done.

I. Hate. Guy.

But not nearly as much as I hate myself for not getting Sebastian's number. Or his real name. Or anything that would help me contact him.

For the past twelve hours or so, he's been all I thought about. Hell, I dreamt about him last night. His lips… His tongue… His…

A chill streaks up my spine as I recall the dream. He made me forget about Guy. When I was with him, it felt like I lived in a world in which Guy didn't exist. I don't know what came over me back at the bar. I finally met someone I connected with, who kissed me like a champ, and I sent him on his way.

My name is Charleigh Holiday, and I love to self-sabotage.

Jamie checks his watch. "I've got to head out, Charleigh, but I think we should reschedule the dinner. If not for me, do it for Mom."

I raise an eyebrow. "Who taught you how to lay it on so thick?"

He matches my brow raise with one of his own. "Who do you think?"

There's no doubt my mother prodded Jamie. Don't be fooled by that small, unimposing stature with a voice to match. She's the queen of getting what she wants without directly asking for it. And I love her for it, even when those skills are used on me.

"I'll talk with Marissa," I say. My vision begins to recede into a purple-spotted blackness as I stand up. I nearly faint, but Jamie grabs me just as my vision returns.

"Are you okay?"

I shake out of his grip. "Fine. This is why I don't drink

caffeine. It makes me loopy." And way too on edge. I can already feel my heart palpitating in my chest, and my pulse is pounding. This is going to be a long day.

Jamie apologizes and keeps his hand on my back as we weave around the rest of the tables and head outside. "Don't forget to reschedule dinner," Jamie says as he walks backward in the opposite direction from me.

"Jesus, I won't—I'm not—look." I reach into my purse and grab my phone. "I'm calling Marissa now. Happy?"

"I will be once I hear a firm date."

I groan and listen to the ringing.

"And Charleigh," Jamie says, stopping in the middle of the sidewalk. "You're going to have to see Guy again sometime. Why not just rip the Band-Aid off?" He shrugs and then turns around.

"Rip the Band-Aid off," I mutter just as Marissa answers the phone.

"Hey, Charleigh!" Her bright voice lifts my slowly souring mood. "How was coffee with Jay-Jay?"

I try my best not to laugh at her name for my brother. "Coffee with Jay-Jay went A-okay…'kay."

I catch her up on my conversation with Jamie as I walk back to my car. After apologizing for missing dinner last night, we come up with a tentative date in a few weeks.

"Again, I'm sorry I missed dinner."

"Really, it's not a problem. Jamie explained your history with Guy and I completely understand. It's not a big deal at all."

"I know, but I still feel bad." I open the door to my car and hop inside.

"Well, you can stop. We're going to make it all up in a few weeks."

"I really was going to come," I say, but my voice sounds a little too whiney. I chew the inside of my mouth for a moment and then say, "But then I met someone and just lost track of time."

There's a sharp intake of breath followed by a brief pause. "You met someone, Charleigh?"

"Uh-huh. Sebastian."

"Sebastian? That's a dreamy name. What's he like?"

I fill her in on everything that happened last night, from the botched shot to the chardonnay, Sméagol, and the kiss.

"Shut up. He kissed you?"

"Yup. But I'd hardly call it a kiss. A new word needs to be invented to adequately describe what that man's lips did to me. My body was on fire for the rest of the night. I couldn't think straight."

Marissa lets out a short squeal of delight. "I'm so happy for you, Charleigh. It's been so long since you've been with someone. And there's nothing wrong with that," Marissa adds hurriedly. "You've been so busy with work. I know what that's like."

"It has been hectic to say the least," I say with a sigh. And now that I think about it, I've spent more nights at my office in the past year than I have in someone else's bed.

"Well, I'm so happy for you, Charleigh. And you know what? You should invite him to dinner. He can be your sinfully sexy buffer between you and Guy."

"I like that."

But then I remember that I don't have his number. That I refused to keep his number.

I told you so, Emma says, scoffing at my stupidity.

"I don't have his number. I kinda tossed it."

"Kinda tossed it? How does that work?"

I tell her the rest of the story.

Marissa hums. "Then Google his ass and find him. I'm sure he has a Facebook profile or something."

"I'm not going to cyberstalk the man."

I've put that phase of my life behind me. Mostly.

"Anyway, I couldn't find him if I wanted to. His name isn't really Sebastian."

I explain the whole Sebastian and Emma dynamic, and even though she finds the whole thing adorable, I can tell she thinks I'm crazy for ripping up the card that had his actual name and number on it.

She's not the only one, Emma tells me.

"I'm sure you two will run into each other again. There's only one grocery store in Whispering Pine. You're bound to bump into each other in the produce section. Reaching for the same bunch of bananas. Your hands brushing each other's as—"

I laugh as Marissa recounts her imaginative fairy-tale version of how I'm to meet my mystery man again. She goes on for another minute or two, outlining everything from our first date down to his proposal and the names of our children. Finn and Karina.

"Okay, first of all, I hate bananas. And second..." I pause, trying to figure out how to phrase the next part. I take a breath. "That's some future you've detailed for Sebastian and me."

"I'm sorry," Marissa says with a sigh. "I got carried away. With the wedding coming up soon, I've just been so—I don't know. I just want everyone to be as happy and in love as me. It's so silly, I know."

I laugh. "No, I get it. How's the wedding planning going, anyway? I can't believe I haven't asked yet."

I start my car and head for work as Marissa gives me the full rundown. It's just as detailed as her vision of my prospective meeting and eventual marriage with Sebastian. By the time I make it to the parking garage, Marissa's finally winding down.

"So to recap." Oh dear, please don't. "Joint bachelor/bachelorette party in three months. Wedding the week after."

Wait. That's it? Thank Jesus. And thank GOD I'm not in the wedding party, but that's for Marissa's sake, really. I'd be horrible with everything going on in my life right now.

I shut off my car and grab my purse. "Wow, it's all happening so fast."

"I know!" I can feel Marissa vibrating with joy through the phone. "Now you've got to find your mystery man. For the good of your children."

I hop out of my car. "Frank and Karen, right?"

"Frank? Karen? What decade do you think this is, Charleigh? Finn and Karina. They're going to be fraternal twins."

Oh lord. This wedding needs to happen sooner rather than later. We say our goodbyes, and as I'm walking toward the offices of Florence + Foxe, my mind meanders back to Sebastian, to his body, and then to gallons of hot fudge dripping all over said body.

AKA my dream last night.

CHAPTER FOUR

Guy

I NEVER THOUGHT coming back to Whispering Pine would be this difficult. It's taken ten years for me to drum up enough courage. Add a few months to that count and that's how long it's taken me to step back inside my childhood home.

I pause for a moment on the porch. My breath puffs in the air in front of me as I stare at the door. After living here for over a month now, you'd think it would get easier. But each time I head up the steps to the porch I'm flooded by memories, the good and the bad. And right now, an especially strong one is hitting me hard in the chest.

The details in my memories have grown hazy over the years but the emotions have sharpened into a fine point. I don't remember what my parents wore that night. I don't remember what they said to me before they left. But I do remember how I felt when I learned I'd never see them again because I feel it right now. It's a stabbing pain in my core, twisting and aching and spreading through me.

I take in a deep breath, turn around, and cup my hands in front of my face, exhaling warm air into them. I follow the narrow, winding path that weaves through the trees, connecting the house to the road. I make a mental note of the landscaping work that needs to be done once the snow finally stops. It's been an unseasonably cold April, a new snowstorm nearly every week. Although each one has been weaker than the last, we're due for a big one tonight. The final, violent death throe of a winter that's gone on for far too long.

I force the unpleasant memory out of my mind with a few deep breaths and then turn around and head back to the house. The brushed metal doorknob is icy cold as I wrap my palm around it. The lock clicks and the door creaks open. A small cloud of dust puffs into the air and then rolls along the floor.

The floorboards shift and moan as I shut the door behind me, the thud of the door echoing through the empty room. I'm in the process of clearing everything out. Furniture, forgotten clothes and knick-knacks, dishes, cups, and mugs—I'm donating all of it. There are too many memories attached to these things, and I need to put them behind me.

The orange light from the setting sun spills onto the floor in long wide streaks. This house is nothing if not beautiful. The ceiling soars high above me, buttressed by large, exposed timber beams. There's so much open space that it feels like an extension of the forest of evergreens and pine trees that surround the property.

My parents started construction on the house when my mom was pregnant with me, finishing it a few years after I was born. They put their heart and soul into making this house a home, and I'd be lying if I said I don't sense them in it even now. That's why it's so hard to come back. They left their mark on this house, and now it's time to leave mine.

After neglecting to take care of it for years, I've decided to renovate it. I can't stand to see the house my parents built fall into disrepair by no fault other than my own.

I drop my coat on the island in the kitchen, fill a glass with water, and then head upstairs. I pause in front of my old bedroom. The door is closed and has been since I left Whispering Pine when I was a teenager. I reach out and grab the knob but I pause, staring at the door for a few moments before my phone rings and jolts me from my trance.

Jamie greets me when I answer. "Guy! What are you up to?"

"Not much. Just about to pack up the last of my stuff."

"When's the reno supposed to start again?"

I turn around and rest my forearms against the railing, glancing down at the great room below. "Next week, hopefully."

"Hopefully?"

"Well, my designer's fallen off the face of the earth. We were supposed to meet earlier today to go over some of the scheduling details but she was a no-show."

"Seriously?"

"She hasn't returned my calls or emails."

"What are you going to do?"

"I'll give her another day. I really don't want to go through this whole process again with someone new." Just thinking about it makes me nauseous. But then again, do I want to go through this process with someone who vanishes without a word?

The railing begins to creak and buckle under my weight, so I pull myself away and walk down the hallway toward the spare bedroom I've been staying in for the last few weeks.

"I talked with Charleigh today." Jamie pauses. I can hear the light sound of his breath. He's dangling the words out there like bait, hoping I bite.

"Yeah?"

"Yeah."

"Why are you telling me this?"

Jamie laughs. "No reason. Just wanted to let you know. Oh, by the way, she had the same excuse you did for why she missed dinner."

"It wasn't an excuse. I met someone and lost track of time."

"Yeah, small world because so did Charleigh. Imagine that, two people who haven't so much as dated another person in the past year met their perfect match on the same night."

I don't respond. I don't need to. Jamie can believe me or not—it doesn't matter to me. I close my eyes as I lean against the doorframe, remembering the way her lips felt against mine. The way she tasted. Her scent and every little detail, from how she traced the edge of her wine glass with her fingertip to how she sucked in her bottom lip before she laughed. I'd do anything to find out her real name.

"Whatever," Jamie says finally. "It doesn't matter. I'm calling to let you know that we're re-scheduling dinner, and I'm making sure that you'll be there."

I run my hand through my hair as I push off from the doorframe and head for the cot in the middle of the room. "I'll be there."

"Charleigh will be there too, you know."

"She's the one with the issue of being in the same room together."

"Just—okay, fine. I'll text you the details."

We hang up and I lie back on the cot. My living arrangement is nothing if not spartan. There's a single cot in the middle of the room. Next to it is a makeshift nightstand with a camping lantern placed on top. My dresser is comprised of a beat-up old suitcase that I still haven't completely unpacked. I have a few tattered copies of Raymond Chandler novels to keep me company, but that's it. I probably should've rented an apartment until the reno's over, but a part of me likes roughing it after having it relatively easy for much of my life. Financially, at least.

I close my eyes, and my mind inevitably drifts back to Emma. I've replayed that night over and over in my head ever since I left the bar to try and calm Jamie down about missing the dinner. I've never felt so strongly about anyone before, but something tugged at me the moment I saw her sit down at the bar. I knew I'd talk to her. A part of me knew I'd kiss her, although not as quickly as it happened.

I'm deep in my revery when my phone rings again. I let out a sigh, but when I see the name on the screen, I smile.

"Deanna! How are you?"

Deanna is Jamie and Charleigh's mother. She's essentially my second mother, and she's treated me like a second son for as long as I can remember.

"I'd be better if you'd get out of that old house of yours until you're done with the renovation. It's just not safe. And to be breathing…"

"Deanna."

"Who knows what's in that house after all these years? Just last week I heard on the news that…"

"Deanna!"

"Yes, dear?"

"It's fine." I sigh. "I'm fine, really."

"Well, I just want to make sure. You didn't come over for dinner last night, and that's just not like you. I wanted to make sure you were okay."

I shake my head. "I met someone. That's it. There isn't some deadly fungus or mold circulating in the air that's making me an amnesiac."

"You know carbon monoxide is the number one silent killer. It could be—wait. You met someone? That's wonderful! You're going to have to tell me all about her." She hums for a moment and then says, "How about breakfast tomorrow? You've got to eat, right? If you aren't going to stay here while you're renovating, then you have to at least let me feed you."

"I'll be there tomorrow morning bright and early." I'll make sure to be the one to cook, though. Deanna isn't exactly known for her prowess in the kitchen. I spent nearly two years eating her food when her family took me in after my parents' accident, so I know what I'm up against.

"Great! Make sure you bring your appetite. And your uniform. You look so handsome in that."

I grin into the phone. "I'll be leaving for work afterward, so I'll be wearing it."

We say our goodbyes, and I fall back against my cot. After a few minutes, I grab one of the Chandler novels and page through it. I set it down after reading the same paragraph four times. My mind is still stuck on Emma, and it won't be unstuck until I find her again.

CHAPTER FIVE

Charleigh

MY TOES DIG into my bedspread as I strain my arm reaching for the ceiling above me. *Almost there. Just a little bit more.* Finally, I manage to press that last bit of duct tape against the ceiling with my fingertips.

I hop off my bed to admire my handiwork. Strips of duct tape span an area about the size of a basketball. It faintly resembles a star, so long as I blur my vision. I'm no engineer, but I'm at least fifty percent sure that the new paper towels I've wadded underneath the duct tape will stop the constant drip of water from the ceiling.

I make a mental note to follow up with my landlord again and then grab my coat and purse. My phone lights up as I reach into my purse for my keys. After locking the door, I check my phone and find a text from my mom.

GUY HATER

Mom: Are you still coming over for breakfast?
Mom

"Shit!" I yell at my screen. And then once again as I look at the time: 8:47 a.m.

Eleanor, the elderly woman who lives a few doors down from me, *humphs* and gives me a look that says, "Well, I never!"

"Sorry, Eleanor!" I say as she passes by me toward the stairs. She shakes her head, waving me off as she mutters something about "kids these days" and "respect."

Whatever, Eleanor. You're not as wholesome as you want everyone to believe. I've seen the revolving door of men going into your apartment.

But then I remind myself that she's getting a whole lot more action than me. You know your love life's abysmal when you're jealous of your geriatric neighbor.

I type that I can't make it to breakfast, and that I'm sorry, and that I just don't have time. But then my stomach twists in on itself, coiling tightly. I can't back out, not after missing dinner. I promised my mother that I'd come over for breakfast. Even though I'm going to be late for work, I know I have to at least show up for a little bit. I sigh.

Charleigh: Of course! I'm on my way now.
Mom: I'm so glad! We're having pancakes!
Mom

I can't help but laugh. I've told her that she doesn't need to sign every text she sends—I know it's her—but she keeps it up without fail.

I shove my phone back into my purse and head to my

car. As I hop into the driver's seat I spot Eleanor and one of her suitors hugging. He's dressed in a vintage tweed suit and cap that I'm sure he's had for decades. He's an adorable grandpa. My heart flutters when I see the roses he's hiding behind his back. And when I see the look on Eleanor's face as he hands them to her, my cheeks get sore from smiling so widely.

He opens the passenger door for her, helps her inside, and then shuts it. The look on his face as he walks back to the driver's seat nearly brings me to tears. The scene is just so adorably romantic. But then my beautiful mind reminds me how completely and utterly single I am, and that no man will ever make any sweeping romantic gestures toward me, not in a million years plus infinity because that's what brains do.

I'm happy for you Eleanor. REALLY. HAPPY.

And then to add insult to injury, my car won't start. "Come on…" I coax Franny, my fifteen-year-old Forester. She whines and whirrs and screeches at me but refuses to start.

I sigh, letting my head knock into the steering wheel. I glance over and watch Eleanor and her man drive away. I could've had that if only I'd saved Sebastian's number. I could call him up right now, and he'd come over to fix Franny…

He'd be shirtless, of course, even though it's below freezing. There'd be grease smears all over his body. Sweat. Muscles galore.

I see the problem, he'd tell me.

Oh yeah? I'd ask, batting my eyelashes.

You need to let her warm up. You can't just crank it when

she's cold, he'd tell me as he leaned against the hood. He'd talk about spark plugs and carburetors and I'd nod along, pretending to know exactly what he's talking about.

And then we'd somehow end up in bed together because it's my fantasy and I don't care how unrealistic it is.

I take a deep breath and try Franny again. She doesn't sound as bad, but she still won't start. I give her another minute before trying one last time. *Click, click, vrrrrrrrooooom.*

I squeal with delight and then promptly reverse out of my spot before Franny decides to die on me. Fifteen minutes later and I'm at my mother's house.

"Mom!" I call out as I open the front door to the house.

"In the kitchen, honey," my mom yells back at me.

Jackpot.

The smells from the kitchen float down the narrow hallway toward the front door, and strangely enough, they actually smell appetizing. When it comes to my mother's cooking, appetizing usually isn't in the same sentence. I feel like a cartoon character who has just smelled an apple pie, sniffing the air as they float toward it. I have no idea what my mother is making, but I know it will be in my mouth shortly.

"What in the world are you—"

I swallow the rest of my sentence as I turn the corner. My mother's sitting at the kitchen table, reading a magazine as a mountain of a man in a frilly, flowery apron stands in front of the stove.

Holy hell. Those arms. His triceps look like horseshoes as they poke out from under his shirt. And his back. It's all

ETHAN ASHER

hard bumps and edges. I want to scale it like a rock wall and then plant a flag on top of his skull. You see this? This is mine.

"I'm so glad you stopped by, Charleigh. Guy was—"

A record scratches in my head. No. No. NO. NO. NO.

NOnonononononononoNOOOOOOO!

YES! Emma squeals as Guy turns his head, a smile on his lips.

My jaw drops and smashes against the floor.

"Sebastian?!"

His smile falters, giving way to the most confused look I've ever seen. He drops the wooden spoon, pancake batter splattering on the floor.

"Emma?"

"What now?" my mother asks, thoroughly confused as she glances up from her magazine.

I don't know what to think as I'm staring at Sebastian— scratch that—Guy. As my eyes peruse his well-muscled body and sharp features, it's no wonder I hadn't recognized him last night. He hardly resembles the doughy boy I remember from a decade ago. At least the feeling is mutual. Guy's looking at me like I'm some mythological beast— scales, horns, and multiple fire-breathing heads included— unsure at how to approach me. *If* he should approach me.

The answer: No. No, he *shouldn't.*

The standoff drags on for what feels like eternity, both of us eyeing each other from head to toe, sizing each other up while my mother gapes at both of us, still wondering what in the world is going on. Slowly, the confusion and uncertainty of Guy's face fades as a faint hint of a smirk begins to grow. And then he opens his mouth and makes it abundantly clear that he hasn't changed.

"Would you like a pancake, Charleigh?" Guy asks in a tone that says he thinks this is just a game. "I made them from scratch."

I stare at him for a few moments, but the longer I have to look at his face, the more annoyed I get. "No thanks, I'd prefer not to go to work with food poisoning."

"Charleigh," my mother hisses at me. "Manners!"

She sets down her magazine and stands up. "Now let me help you clean this up, Guy."

Guy and my mother spend the next minute cleaning up the spilled pancake batter on the ground as I watch, still shocked. I can't believe I kissed Guy. But more than that, I can't believe I liked it.

You didn't like it, Emma tells me. *You loved it. So much so that your vibrator needs new batteries now.*

Guy's apron flutters as he spins around and tends to the pancakes. He looks absolutely nothing like the boy I remember. He's slimmed down and added muscle. So much muscle. His jaw and cheekbones are chiseled and masculine and dear Lord I need to get it together.

"I like your apron," I say. "The flowers and lace really do wonders for you. Is it from your personal collection?"

He ignores the question as my mother glares at me and mouths "Stop it!"

"You tricked me!" I mouth back, but she just shakes her head and walks to the sink to wash her hands.

My mother set this up. She thinks our relationship is confrontational because neither of us wants to deal with unresolved feelings for each other. But she's wrong. So, so wrong.

"It's so nice to have you two together." She's trying to dispel the palpable tension in the air, but it's not working.

Guy makes a noncommittal grunt.

I snort.

My mom sighs and then motions for me to take a seat. I fold my arms across my chest and shake my head at her before turning to Guy. I'm burning a hole in the back of his head with my gaze, but he's either ignoring it or doesn't care.

Forget this. I'm not playing this game.

"I'm late for work," I tell my mom. "I'll come over for dinner tonight."

My mother gives me one of her signature guilt-trip looks, but I'm too annoyed for it to have any effect on me.

"Have a nice day, Charleigh," Guy calls out to me as I leave.

I can sense a teasing undercurrent in his tone, so I don't humor him with a response.

As I hop into my car, I send a text to Marissa.

Charleigh: I found Sebastian.
Marissa: OH MY GOD THAT'S WONDERFUL!
Charleigh: Nope. It's Guy.
Marissa: Oh… OHHHH… Wow…

And so it begins.

⟋

The last time I was in this foul of a mood was July 18, 1998. Yes, I have it down to the date—to the exact time too: 7:17 a.m.

I'd woken up ten minutes earlier with what the doctor ruled, a few hours later, to be strep throat. Strep throat that I *knew* Guy gave to me because I shared a Dr. Pepper with him at lunch a few days before.

My mom refused to buy soda because Jamie and I would drink it all within a couple days. Guy was my hookup. He'd usually bring an extra soda for me, but July 15, 1998, he left me high and dry. It was worse because Guy had been on vacation during the previous week, so I was basically fighting withdrawal symptoms.

This was back when we were still friendly—before he moved into our house and made an about-face in his attitude. To Guy's credit, he refused to give in to my pleading at first because he wasn't feeling well after his flight back home. But when it comes to my pursuit of sugar, I'm relentless. There might have been some tears. And when it comes to hysterical girls, boys are clueless, so he had no choice but to give me a sip. Or the rest of it.

The tickling in my throat started the next day. Slight soreness by the end of the day. But when I woke up the following day with a throat that felt like it had been lit on fire, I knew I'd made a terrible mistake.

It wasn't the strep throat that put me in a foul mood. It's what happened at 7:17 am. My mother smashed my eleven-year-old heart into a million pieces when she told me that I would *not* be attending the Hanson concert as previously scheduled.

Thank you very much, Guy.

Even at eleven, I knew my anger with Guy for giving me strep throat was misplaced. But for the next month, I refused to sit with him at lunch or talk to him. Hanson was a pretty big deal for an eleven-year-old. Especially when the Baha Men were set to open. Eleven-year-old me was ready to rock out to "Who Let the Dogs Out?", but it wasn't to be. Much like my fantasy to marry Zac Hanson.

Now that I'm thinking about it, maybe it was for the best.

I'm trying to focus on work. I need to focus on work. I have a to-do list as long as the digits in π, all of which seem to be other people's problems. At Florence + Foxe, the interior design firm I've worked at for the past three years, I'm the veritable dumping ground.

Need someone to pick out the toilets for a project? Call Charleigh—she knows a good commode. Have a minute detail that should've been handled weeks ago, but instead needs to be decided on the night before a client meeting? You wouldn't mind staying late, right, Charleigh? It's not like you have a family or husband or dog waiting up for you. Gee, thanks for the reminder.

After three years of performing above and beyond my job description, I'm only a few steps ahead of coffee-girl. I'd leave if it weren't for the necessity of…you know, feeding myself. It was hard enough to snag this job, and I'm not exactly thrilled about the prospect of going through the same process again.

But as much as I need to focus on my work, it's impossible. I can't stop thinking about what happened less than an hour ago. I still don't want to believe the man who kissed me like I'd never been kissed before, who made me laugh until I cried, who has been stuck in my head for the past week is the person I hate most in this world.

But did you see those muscles? Emma asks, mouth watering.

Yeah, but so what? Guy might've packed on a few pounds of muscle and learned proper grooming techniques in the intervening years, but it's all a facade. He's still the same person underneath that well-manicured, athletic exterior. There's no fix for asshole.

Eventually, loud braying laughter disrupts my fixation with Guy. I don't even have to look up to know the culprit of the most obnoxious laughter. Andrea. I look up anyway and find her, along with our boss Christiana, laughing together, smiling together, and having far too much of a good time together this early in the morning.

After a few moments, they break away from each other. Christiana turns around and heads to her office while Andrea immediately locks her eyes onto mine and charges straight ahead. I jerk my head back and glance around, wondering if I have time to dig a makeshift tunnel out of my cubicle before she has the chance to reach me. I spot the used spork from yesterday's lunch—the perfect tool for the job—but before I have the chance, Andrea appears in front of me. Her ridiculously slender fingers slide across the top of my cubicle, wrapping around the edge like pale vines. Her blonde hair is immaculate, much like the rest of her, and she stares at me for a brief moment before glancing at the mess of papers and supplies and files on my desk.

"No donuts today, Charleigh?"

Andrea's the type of woman who'd offer you candy or pastries and then muse out loud about how she could never eat stuff like that without it going to her hips. But only after you're two bites deep.

I grit my teeth for a moment but then relax my jaw. I'm not going to get worked up over Andrea. Forcing a smile, I say, "Not today. I was running late this morning and didn't have the chance to pick any up."

She scans me slowly. "I can tell."

"What do you want, Andrea?" I say with a sigh.

Andrea smirks. "Christiana wants to talk with you."

"What about?"

She shrugs in response with a look on her face that tells me I'm absolutely boring her to death right now.

I close my eyes and take a deep breath, hoping that when I open them again, Andrea will have lost interest and wandered off. When I open them again, I find that my wish has been denied.

"You know you should really get eight hours of sleep. Studies show that a lack of sleep can do a number on your health. And with all those donuts…"

The rest of Andrea's soliloquy fades into the background as I push away from my desk and head for Christiana's office. Her office resembles a fishbowl, albeit trendier: floor-to-ceiling glass walls on all sides, with minimal, mid-century modern furniture arranged around a large glass and metal desk.

She's sitting at her desk, legs crossed with her clear-framed glasses perched atop her slender nose as she's perusing a paper in her hand. Although she's nearing sixty-five years old, she hardly looks a year past forty, apart from her silver hair.

I tap the glass door twice with my knuckles, waving as Christiana looks up from her paper. After removing her glasses, she motions for me to come in.

"Charleigh," Christiana coos. "Just the woman I wanted to see. Please sit."

I glance warily at the chairs in front of her desk. Although absolutely gorgeous, mid-century modern is not known for comfort. I choose the left chair because I've learned it's the one that least feels like a concrete floor when I sit on it.

Nope, still feels like concrete.

"Andrea tells me that you have something important to discuss."

She frowns. "Everything I discuss is important, Charleigh. You know I don't waste time with superfluous words."

"Umm…" I don't know what to say, but thankfully Christiana's smile returns.

"I called you into my office because I wanted to discuss your future with this firm."

My stomach drops immediately. *What did I do? Is it because I was late? Oh GOD please don't fire me.* My life flashes before my eyes in the half-second before Christiana speaks again.

"Lana quit earlier today…"

Oh. Ohhhhhh…. OHHHHHHH!

"…and we're looking to replace her as soon as possible. She has some very important clients." Christiana clears her throat. "Every client is important," she corrects herself, "but some of Lana's are especially important. We all need to pick up the slack so that there's no lapse in service. Understand?"

"Yes." Kind of. Not really, but at least I'm not fired. "What do you need me to do?"

"We have a new client. Initially, we paired him with

Lana, but after her departure, I spoke with him and we decided that both you and Andrea will present your vision for the space, and he'll select one of the two. If you're up for it, of course."

Holy shit.

HOLYSHITHOLYSHIT!

"Of course, Christiana," I say, trying to seem as calm, cool, and collected as possible.

"Great. I thought you would."

She briefs me on the rest of the details. I should be receiving an email from her introducing Andrea and me to him. Then we'll schedule a time to see the space, and after that, I'll have about a week to create a plan. Christiana won't have her hand in any of it, checking in only to ensure that the plans meet Florence + Foxe standards and that the project is completed on schedule.

"And Charleigh," Christiana says as I push open the door to her office, "we'd like to keep the search for Lana's replacement internal."

I nod. "Got it."

I would've accepted the task without the possibility of a promotion at the end of this. Free rein to actually create a design? Hell yeah!

When I sit back down at my desk, I check my email. After spending a half hour catching up, another email pops up.

To: Holiday, Charleigh; Robbins, Andrea
CC: Finch, Guy
From: Foxe, Christiana
Subject: Meeting

GUY HATER

Mr. Finch,

I'd like to introduce you to Ms. Holiday and Ms. Robbins...

I can't even bring myself to read the rest of the email. *You have got to be kidding me.*

CHAPTER SIX

Guy

I DIDN'T PLAN it this way, I swear.

When I mentioned to Deanna my plan to renovate my parents' house, she suggested Florence + Foxe. They had stellar reviews, and a quick glance at their past projects sold me. But then I scrolled through the team section on their website and found Charleigh Holiday staring back at me. Well, not exactly staring back at me. Her profile picture showed her standing on a rocky outcropping overlooking a deep valley with evergreens along its edges. Picturesque, but her back was to the camera so I never saw her face. If I had, I could've avoided the whole Emma/Charleigh situation.

After discussing it with Deanna, she convinced me that I wouldn't be working with Charleigh because she wasn't a project lead. She mentioned something about letting old dogs lie or burying the hatchet—some cliche—and then went back to reading her magazine. I didn't want to spend more time than necessary to find a designer. They were all the same to me. All I cared about was whether the firm I went with had a proven track record, and Florence + Foxe clearly did.

But I had no idea that my designer would quit the firm a week before she was to present her design. Or that Charleigh would be thrust onto this project. It wouldn't be so bad if it weren't for the minor detail that she hates me more than the unholy trinity of sugar-, fat-, and gluten-free baked goods. Her words—not mine; a golden nugget in the novel-length texts she's been sending me over the past few days. But apart from the texts, all of Charleigh's email communication with me is calm, composed, and businesslike. She knows how to keep a semi-clean paper trail, I'll give her that.

The receptionist, Heather, greets me when I push through the glass doors.

"Ms. Foxe is expecting you, Mr. Finch. Would you care for a coffee or water?"

"Water's fine."

She motions for me to take a seat and then disappears behind the desk emblazoned with Florence + Foxe. I sit in an uncomfortable but stylish leather chair that squeaks every time I move and sometimes when I breathe.

"Here you are," Heather says, handing me a bottle of mineral water. She jerks her hand back and then runs it through her hair as she quickly turns around and trots back to her chair. Her cheeks are a few shades pinker when she sits down, clearing her throat and shuffling papers around.

I sip my water, waiting for Christiana to appear. And Charleigh. My nerves finally catch up with me as my mind turns to Charleigh. She was pissed when she saw me in Deanna's kitchen a few mornings ago and even more pissed when she found out she'd be working with me. I'm not exactly thrilled either, even more so now that I see how difficult it will be to work together.

"Mr. Finch," a familiar voice calls out.

I look up and find Christiana smiling warmly at me. Her silver hair is pulled into a tight bun at her crown, not a strand out of place.

"Good morning, Christiana."

I stand up and offer my hand. She grips it, shaking it a few times. "I'm so sorry about Lana. We had no idea she was being headhunted by other firms."

"It's no problem. I'm in no rush."

She smiles. "You may not be, but I assure you we're going to honor the initial deadline."

"That's great."

"Come," she says, motioning me to follow her.

The main office space is an open concept with low-walled cubicles spread throughout the center. Exposed vents and ductwork weave around the lofted space. Artisanal lighting hangs from the ceiling, but most of the light streams through the large windows that surround the space. It's bright and airy and if it weren't for the patches of greenery and wood accents, it would feel a bit too cold and industrial. But then again, I'm not an interior designer.

As we walk toward the conference room on the other end of the building, it feels like I'm playing whack-a-mole. Heads of employees pop up, glance at Christiana and me, and then pop right back down as we pass by. But as we near the conference room, almost everything around me seems to fade into the background when I spot Charleigh.

She's sitting at the end of a long conference table with another woman next to her. She's chewing on the inside of her mouth as her left leg bounces up and down. Given our textual relations over the past few days, I find it difficult to believe that she's nervous. Maybe it's not nerves. Maybe she's trying to stop her anger from boiling over.

Both of them stand when Christiana opens the door. The blonde next to Charleigh almost imperceptibly elbows Charleigh before taking the lead. Christiana doesn't seem to notice as she begins the introductions.

"This is Andrea," she says, nodding to the blonde.

"It's so nice to meet you, Mr. Finch," Andrea says with an unusually high-pitched voice.

She offers me a limp hand. I glance at it, trying to figure out how to shake the curled, limp thing offered to me. I grab her hand tentatively and then proceed to have the most awkward handshake ever.

"Andrea," I say with a nod.

She reluctantly steps aside, allowing me my first full view of Charleigh since the awkwardness at Deanna's house. It's not difficult to see why I hadn't recognized her at The Lookout. Little of her reminds me of the girl I knew over a decade ago. Her hair is no longer wild and frizzy; it now rests on her shoulders in silky, straight tresses. The glasses are gone. The braces are gone. And now there's a confident air about her.

"And this is Charleigh Holiday."

I offer my hand to her along with a smile as an armistice.

She stares at it, arms folded beneath her chest. She's still chewing the inside of her mouth, and she's wearing the interior struggle on her face.

"Charleigh?" Christiana says, verbally nudging her.

"Oh, I'm sorry. I just blanked for a moment." Charleigh turns the charm up to a hundred as she reaches out to shake my hand. I've never seen her smile like this before. "It's so wonderful to finally meet you, Mr. Finch. I can't wait to help turn your dream into reality."

Her voice is so saccharine that if she keeps it up, I'll have diabetes by the end of our meeting. *Jesus Christ* is all I can think as I bear witness to this monstrosity in a Charleigh suit. I stare at her blankly, wondering how long she'll be able to keep up this charade.

"Great," I say with a snort, glancing at Christiana, who seems to be eating up Charleigh's performance.

But as soon as Christiana walks past us, the facade falls, and I see the Charleigh I recognize: pissed. She mouths something to me as I follow behind Christiana, but I ignore it.

Christiana sits at the head of the table, and I take the seat next to her while Charleigh and Andrea are opposite me. I don't even have to glance across the table to know that Charleigh's staring a hole in me. I can feel the heat of her gaze on my skin, bubbling and sizzling as she silently seethes.

Good to know after all these years she still holds a grudge.

"Now, Mr. Finch. I know we've already been through this with Lana, but I was hoping we could cover your expectations and goals one more time so Andrea and

Charleigh can familiarize themselves with them. Is that okay?"

I drag my attention back to Christiana. "Sure. There isn't much to it, really. As you know, it's been more than a few decades since there have been any upgrades to my house, and I'd like to breathe a little life to it. You know, bring it into the current decade. Century, really."

Andrea brays with laughter as though I'd said the most hilarious thing ever, and both Christiana and Charleigh slowly crane their necks and stare at her. Her cheeks flush and she mutters something as she sinks lower in her chair.

I clear my throat and continue detailing my ideas. I love the rustic feel to the house, and I want to ensure that the design captures that feeling. Nothing too modern with perfect, clean lines, and none of that gray color I see everywhere. Earth tones. Stone and wood and metal. I want the house to feel like it belongs in the mountains of Colorado.

I'm not sure how long I've talked, but by the time I finish, I notice that both Christiana and Andrea have multiple pages of notes and are rapt with attention on me. I glance at the pad in front of Charleigh as they continue to scribble away. It's empty, and as I draw my eyes upward, I see her arms are still folded across her chest. A few more inches upward and I find her eyebrows are raised so high that they look like they're trying to escape from her face.

"Again, I'm pretty easy to please, so I'm sure that any of the designs you come up with will be perfect."

Charleigh snorts, leaning forward. "I've found that the people who say they're the easiest to please are the most difficult people to work with."

Without skipping a beat, Christiana sets her pen down, removes her glasses, and turns to Charleigh. "Can I have a word, Charleigh?"

It's not a question that Christiana expects an answer to, and Charleigh knows it. Her face blanches immediately and Andrea does her best to contain her glee. They get up without another word and I watch Christiana march out of the conference room with Charleigh in tow.

"I'd like to apologize for my colleague," Andrea says, reaching her hand out as though I need comforting.

"It's no problem," I say as I lean back into my chair. I knit my fingers behind my head as I look over at Charleigh and Christiana through the glass. It's not my fault that Charleigh can't keep her cool for more than a few minutes.

Although I have no idea what Christiana is telling Charleigh, her message is clearly displayed through Charleigh's demeanor. She seems to have lost a couple inches as she visibly withers in front of Christiana, whose lips haven't stopped moving since the door closed behind her.

"I'm in love with your ideas," Andrea says, trying to draw my attention back to her. "They're absolutely brilliant, and I can't wait to see the property and get to work. I—"

Christiana opens the door and pokes her head inside the room. "Mr. Finch?" she says, motioning to me. "Could you come here for a moment?"

"Sure," I say, standing up.

I cross the room and step through the door Christiana holds open for me. Charleigh is staring at her feet as I approach, but when I finally reach her, Christiana clears her throat and Charleigh looks up.

"I want to apologize for what I said in there," she says. "It was rude and uncalled for."

"It's no problem." I'm pretty sure that later on tonight I'm going to get a novel-length text from her detailing everything I did in the meeting that annoyed her.

"Well, I'd just like a few more minutes of your time, Mr. Finch. Could you join me in my office for a few minutes?"

"Sure."

I follow Christiana into her office. It only takes ten minutes to finish my business with Christiana before I'm back in the main office space. I scan the room, looking for Charleigh, and I find her talking with a coworker on the opposite side of the building. Andrea attempts to lure me into a conversation, but I politely excuse myself after a few minutes and head back to Charleigh.

Unfortunately, she's nowhere to be seen.

Guy: Can we talk?

A few minutes go by and there's no response, so I try calling her. Almost immediately I hear a song playing. *Your phone isn't on silent? Bad office etiquette, Charleigh.* It sounds vaguely familiar, and I whip my head around to gauge the direction it's coming from. There are a few spurts of laughter, and I head in their direction, phone still in hand and ready to redial Charleigh's number.

I don't need to because there are multiple women poking their heads out of their cubicles, cheeks flushing as they try hard not to laugh. There's one cubicle, however, that doesn't have a head poking out of it. And when I reach it, I find Charleigh with her head down, phone in hand.

I hit her contact in my phone again, and this time the ringtone comes in loud and clear as Fergie belts out, "Shut up, just shut up, shut up. Shut up, just shut up, shut up."

"Interesting ringtone, Charleigh."

There are muffled laughs around us as Charleigh silences the call, takes in a deep breath and then looks up at me, her cheeks bright red.

"Thanks. I think it's fitting."

"Oh yeah?"

She nods exaggeratedly. "Yup."

"Are you always this charming around your clients?"

"Only when they deserve it."

I rest my forearms on the top of her cubicle. Her eyes narrow on mine. "I'm not the bad guy, Charleigh. And if I recall, you thought I was a pretty good guy not so long ago."

Charleigh turns an even brighter shade of red as she stands up and leans into me.

"Don't bring up that night ever again. It was a mistake."

"Some mistakes are worth repeating."

She sits back down and then swivels her chair so her back is to me. "If you'll excuse me, I have some work to do."

I stare at her back for a few moments, wondering if it's worth the effort. I pat the top of the cubicle a couple times and then walk away. I only make it a few steps before Charleigh says, "I think we should limit our interactions because it's clear that we just don't work together."

I pause for a brief moment, my back still facing her, and then start to make my way out of the office again.

GUY HATER

She wants so hard to believe that I'm a bad guy. Well, if that's what she wants, maybe I should indulge her fantasy version of reality.

CHAPTER SEVEN

Charleigh

"I CAN'T DO it. I can't work with Guy."

Jamie sips his coffee, eyeing me as though I'm a kid seconds away from a tantrum. He's not too far off the mark, but instead of a toy being snatched away from me, it's my possible promotion to lead designer because I know working with Guy is going to drive me to do something that will get me fired. I mean, it's happened already.

"I've already gotten reprimanded once because of him."

Jamie arches his brow. "Because of him? How did he get you reprimanded?"

I bite the inside of my mouth, which is now raw because I can't stop chewing it. It's a nervous habit that I thought I'd outgrown, but with Guy thrust back into my life, old habits seem to be popping up everywhere.

"He said something silly and I had to correct him."

My brother sighs, rubbing his fingertips into his eyes. I gawk at Marissa, hoping she'll back me up. Instead, she offers the rest of her cinnamon scone to me, which is just as good in my book.

"I think what Charleigh's getting at is that it's complicated between her and Guy."

I nearly choke on my scone as I laugh, crumbs exploding from my mouth. Both of them look at me with concerned expressions, and I raise my hand, letting them know I'm fine as I swallow the remaining crumbs with my decaf latte.

"How complicated could it be? Guy needs his house renovated. You're a designer." Jamie holds his palms out, shrugging as though he'd just laid out a simple addition problem, $a + b = c$. Except that he forgot the tiny part where if you mix a and b together, you create a nuclear explosion capable of wiping out all of humanity, or at the very least, Whispering Pine.

Marissa and I both glare at Jamie, but he shrugs it off. "I just don't get it."

"We know," both Marissa and I say in unison.

He stares at both of us for a moment. "I think it's time for me to get a refill," he says, standing up slowly before retreating from the table. Once he finally leaves earshot, Marissa jumps into the line of questioning she's been bursting to ask me this entire time.

"What the hell are you going to do?" she shout-whispers.

"I have no idea," I say, munching on the last of Marissa's cinnamon scone as I wonder why anyone in their right mind would ever bake a pastry without chocolate. And don't get me started on people who think nuts in ANYTHING is a good idea. Because it's not. There's a special place in hell for people who ruin a perfectly good brownie with walnuts. And an even more exclusive place for people who put raisins in their cookies.

"You're not going to quit," she says matter-of-factly. "You can't."

My financial situation is a step above what people would call dire straits. A half step, to be honest. But I know Marissa isn't hinting at that.

"Don't give him the satisfaction of knowing he's still under your skin."

I hum. She's got a point. Besides, it's not like I'll be working with Guy every single day. The work will be front-loaded, and then once everything is approved by him and Christiana, the process takes on a life of its own as our contractors take over. I mull it over as Marissa continues.

"It's an amazing opportunity. I know you've been feeling a little underappreciated at work, and this project could really help you shine. Show Christiana that you've got the chops to step into a lead designer role. I've seen what you can do, Charleigh, and it's amazing. Christiana will see that if you take this on."

I can feel my cheeks begin to redden. I've always felt awkward when people praise my accomplishments because they don't feel all that special to me. It's work, and I do the best that I can.

"You sure know how to lay it on, Marissa."

"You're a queen of design, and I'm surprised you aren't running your own shop yet."

"I've only been in the business for a few years. That sort of responsibility is waaaaay down the pipeline. If it happens at all."

Marissa sighs. "Don't shortchange your accomplishments. You'll be running your own place in a few years. And this job is your first step. Besides, Guy can't be that bad, can he? You kissed him, remember?"

How could I forget? My cheeks flush an even brighter red as thoughts of that night flood back to me. But then I remind myself who I'm dealing with. I'm conflicted, to say the least, about this whole situation.

"I think I still have that text describing him to me. Adonis incarnate? Hmm..." Marissa reaches into her purse. "I can check for the exact wording."

I reach across the table and place my hand on hers. "No, that's perfectly okay."

On a surface level, I understand that the advice Marissa is giving me is perfectly appropriate: I should focus on my future and not the past. But I don't know how I'll be able to pretend the years of Guy being an asshole never happened. Sure, he wasn't a completely horrible person, but when the teasing comes from someone who used to be your best friend, which Guy was for a time, it hurts a lot. More so when there never was an apology or semblance of guilt in the intervening years.

I tried to push it away, but as soon as I saw Guy pass in front of the conference room, the memories came right back. For most of the meeting, I kept replaying his greatest hits over and over in my head. And when I finally had the chance to speak, I snapped at him.

"So are you going to do it?" Marissa asks after a few moments of silence.

I mumble something unintelligible and then groan.

"Charleigh?"

I chew on the inside of my mouth again, but it's so tender and raw that I stop immediately.

Marissa bobs her head around trying to get me to look at her in the eyes. "Come on. Look at me."

When I finally look at her, she wiggles her eyebrows as though to ask the question again.

"Okay, fine," I rattle out quickly.

"Yay!" she squeals. "You're doing the right thing. And maybe…" She narrows her eyes as though concentrating on something. "Just maybe Karina and Finn will—"

"No! Nothing is going to happen between us, especially not that."

"Well…" She lets it hang in the air for a while before finishing it with, "You never know."

She may never know, but there's one thing for sure that I know: *that* will never happen. Never.

"You guys ready to head out?" Jamie asks us.

Marissa looks at me with the widest smile and then says to Jamie, "I think so, Jay-Jay."

He leans over and plants a kiss on Marissa's forehead. "I love you, Riss-Riss."

Oh dear Lord put me out of my misery now.

We all head outside and as we near the door, I whisper to Marissa, "You haven't told Jamie about, you know…" I mouth "Sebastian."

Marissa shakes her head as Jamie asks, "Tell me what?"

"Nothing!" both Marissa and I chime together.

The look on Jamie's face says "not this again."

"Forget I asked," he says, holding the door for us as we usher ourselves out. "Forget I asked," he mumbles to himself again.

As we're saying our goodbyes, an awful feeling hits me. "Oh God, Marissa, I completely forgot to ask about your wedding plans. I'm so sorry."

"No worries. You've got enough on your plate. We can talk about it at the dinner we rescheduled."

Oh no. I forgot about that. More forced time with Guy... "Okay," I say through a gritted smile. "Sounds good."

As I'm driving to work I get a text from Guy. I have to read it twice to make sure it says what I think it says. My knuckles whiten as I grip the wheel and force my eyes on the road ahead of me.

He's got another thing coming if he thinks I'm going to back down now.

CHAPTER EIGHT

Guy

HAVE YOU EVER sucked helium from a balloon and tried to talk?

That's exactly how Andrea sounds. I don't know if it's her real voice or if she's playing it up because she thinks it's cute. It's not. It's grating and sounds more like a chipmunk yammering than a human talking. I'm not sure how I didn't notice it during our meeting a few days ago, but then again, I'd been focused on other things. Now that it's just her and me, I can't ignore it. This will be the longest house tour ever.

"This place is gorgeous, Guy!"

Andrea twists so I can help her take off her coat. "Uh, thanks," I say, storing it in the closet. "As you can see, it's a little dated, but it has good bones."

Good bones. It's my new favorite phrase. Up until a few weeks ago, I'd never heard of it. But I'd also never watched a show on HGTV up until that point either. Deanna rectified that quickly once I mentioned that I would be renovating my house. She told me that the shows on HGTV were the best way to research renovations and see what might be in store for me. I wasn't sold and told Deanna as much, but she wouldn't hear it.

"I'm not sure how believable this show is, Deanna. How can a part-time goat milker and a professional ghost hunter afford $250,000 in renovations? How can they afford anything?"

"I'm sure she's going full-time now, Guy. And ghost hunting can actually be pretty lucrative. Have you seen Ghost Adventures*? We should watch that too. Now, would you look at the bones on this house!"*

I'm sure Deanna knows that most of the show isn't based on reality, but I think she just likes the company. I don't mind it either, and over the last week or so, the shows have grown on me, *Fixer Upper* especially.

"Very good bones." Andrea fixes her gaze on me, elongating each syllable as she unrepentantly checks me out. Her eyes are playful, piercing, and a shade of blue that teeters on the edge of green. There's no denying that Andrea's attractive. Straight blonde hair frames her vulpine features. Her understated makeup complements her pristine complexion. The color of her dress matches her eyes and hugs her in all the right places, something that I'm sure she's well aware of as she leans toward me.

"Charleigh's supposed to be here too, right?" I ask.

I'd scheduled both of them to be here at the same time so I wouldn't have to give the same tour twice. As much as I like this house, I'd rather spend my time off doing something more productive than being a tour guide. I wanted to give them a spare key during our meeting so they could do it on their time and also avoid another awkward encounter with Charleigh, but Christiana insisted I be there with them should they have any questions.

"She's running late. Typical Charleigh," she adds with a laugh.

The last comment garners an eyebrow raise. Charleigh was never the type to show up late to anything. Charleigh's not here because she doesn't want to be here. Specifically, not with me here. I'm sure she'll wait until we're all gone and then break in and give herself her own private tour.

"How about we start? I'll give Charleigh a tour when she gets here." *If* she gets here. Andrea holds her gaze with mine for a long beat before asking me to lead the way.

With the house empty, every step Andrea takes with her three-inch pumps is amplified. I was surprised when she stepped out of her car wearing them. Although most of the snow has melted in Whispering Pine, that's not the case for my house. It's located on one of the mountains that overlook the town, so there's still a nasty mixture of ice and snow everywhere, my driveway especially.

We stop in the middle of the great room. It's my favorite part of the house. The cathedral ceiling, wood trusses, and large natural stone fireplace have always had a soothing effect on me. It feels like home.

"My parents started construction on the house in the mid-eighties, just before I was born."

"Did they do it themselves?" Andrea asks, whipping out a pink notebook with sparkling gold embellishments along with a purple pen with a pink poof ball on top.

"They hired contractors. Although both of them were talented in their respective fields, they knew their limitations, and constructing homes was one of them. The house took a few years to complete. They were supposed to move in before I was born, but there were some complications that extended construction for an extra year."

"That tends to happen," Andrea says with a laugh, placing her hand on my forearm. "But I assure you it won't with this project. We'll take *very* good care of you."

I glance at her hand on my arm and make a noncommittal grunt. Fortunately, or unfortunately—I'm not quite sure yet—Andrea's attention ricochets from me and to the back of the house where the large windows offer amazing views of the evergreen forests that surround Whispering Pine.

"Oh wow!" she squeals as she shuffles by me and presses her hands and face against the windows. "It's so beautiful I want to die!"

"Yeah," I say, rubbing my throbbing temples. "It's a nice view."

"Nice view?" Andrea spins around and gives me a playful thump on my shoulder. "It. Is. Gorgeous." She exaggerates each word and leaves her mouth gaping and eyes nearly bugging out as she spins back around and presses her forehead against the glass. "Your parents picked the perfect spot."

I check the time. Only five minutes have passed, but it feels like an eternity. With Andrea's attention bouncing around like a pinball, I'm not sure how I'll be able to keep her focused enough to finish this tour in less than an hour. Eventually, I'm able to wrangle her attention away from the back of the house and continue the tour. We spend the next half hour walking through each room, Andrea taking notes while I ignore her not-so-veiled flirtatious comments.

It's strange how I'm not interested. She has all the makings of someone I should be interested in. She's clearly knowledgeable based on her questions and suggestions she's making for how to improve the layout of the house. Not to mention, she's incredibly attractive. And she's toned down the cutesy voice, so it's not as grating. But I'm just off. I have been for most of the tour, fading in and out, incapable of maintaining my attention on her for more than a few minutes at a time.

When we finish the tour and head back to the front of the house, I'm finally able to pinpoint what's up. I check my phone and see that Charleigh's more than an hour late, and I haven't received so much as a text.

I can't believe she'd skip out on the tour. This isn't some dinner; this is her career—something I'd expect she'd take seriously. I can understand her reluctance to meet with me in a personal setting, but if she can't put our past behind her for thirty minutes in a professional setting, then how can she expect to work on this project? If she continues down this path, I have no problem giving Andrea the reins and cutting Charleigh out.

"Are you okay?" Andrea asks, placing her hand on my arm.

"Fine," I say, forcing a smile. Apparently, I'm wearing my mood on my face. "Let me grab your coat for you."

After getting her coat from the closet, I help her into it. As I open the front door, a bitter rush of wind blows past the threshold, and Andrea gasps.

"It's so much colder up here!" she says, burrowing her chin into her coat. "I wasn't expecting it." She shakes her foot at me. At least she acknowledges how impractical her footwear is. Maybe it wouldn't be such a bad idea to work with Andrea after all. Even more so now that Charleigh's MIA.

"There's usually about a ten-degree difference this time of year. I should've mentioned that in my email," I say with an apologetic smile.

"It's no problem." Andrea blushes and then looks around. "Charleigh really dropped the ball, huh?"

"Any word from her?" After the initial burst of angry texts Charleigh sent to me that first week, she's gone radio silent, only contacting me through email.

Andrea reaches into her purse and grabs her phone. "Nothing," she says, dropping it back inside. "Should I call her?"

"No, that's alright. I'm sure she'll show up."

Andrea smiles sweetly at me. "I could stick around and keep you company."

I glance down at her. "I'm sure you have better things to do with your time."

"It's no problem at all, really."

She's beginning to lay it on real thick, and if I weren't so annoyed with Charleigh, I might indulge her and play along.

"Thanks for the offer, but I'm okay. You should get going before you freeze to death out here."

She laughs, playing it up, but finally relents. She reaches into her purse and pulls out a pen and a business card. After writing something on the back, she hands it to me. "I'll get a preliminary plan over to you in a few days. My personal cell is on the back."

"Thanks," I say, eyeing the card warily.

"Call me if you need anything." She steps toward me, her perfume enveloping my senses. "Anything at all. Day or night."

I thought she was flirting with me earlier, but that was nothing compared to this open invitation. Jesus Christ.

Before I have to chance to respond, Andrea rolls onto her toes and does that weird cheek-to-cheek kiss thing as she wraps her arms around me. After a few seconds, she finally releases me.

"See you soon," she says as she spins, her hair fanning out like she's in a L'Oréal commercial.

What just happened?

It takes a few moments to shake out of it. Although not exactly the most professional or appropriate behavior, I have to admire the confidence. She wobbles her way back to the car.

"I did it!" she shouts back at me as she reaches her car. Unfortunately, that quick jump with arms raised in the air causes her to go off balance and she slips, sending her to the ground.

Damn. I move toward her. "You okay?"

Before I have the chance to take more than a few steps, she rises back to her feet and waves me off. "I'm fine," she says, wiping off the front of her coat. "I guess I should've saved the celebration until after I made it into the car."

"Probably a good idea."

A few beats later, she gets into her car and heads out. I wait for nearly fifteen minutes on the porch, but there's still no word from Charleigh. I called her twice, but she didn't pick up. I left her messages and texts but there was nothing more than silence from her end. A part of me is actually getting worried.

I almost call Deanna but realize it would only make her worry, which would then lead to her calling Charleigh nonstop. And then lead to Charleigh getting mad at me for no real reason at all.

I sigh and try my luck once more. She picks up on the third ring.

"Helllooooo?"

"Charleigh, where are you? It sounds like you're a mile away from your phone."

"Yes, that's the jackerthinger!" I hear say, her voice even farther away. "Do you even know how to fix—" The sound gets muffled. I'm not exactly sure, but it seems like her phone was just thrown into a lake. There's a constant hum coming over the line that I can't place. Something metallic falls. Someone curses. Charleigh screeches. I catch bits and pieces but I can't form them into a cohesive whole.

"Hello?" I ask.

There's another muffled noise; it sounds like Charleigh is picking up the phone. "Look, I'm going to have to call you back."

My grip tightens around my phone. "No, you're not. You're going to tell me why the hell you didn't show up to our appointment. I've been waiting—"

"I really don't appreciate your attitude right now," she snaps.

"And I don't appreciate you not honoring your commitments. You obviously have your phone. You could've texted or called or, well, any number of things normal human beings do when—"

Click.

She hung up on me.

"Oh... Oh ho ho no..."

It takes a few moments for me to gather my thoughts, but when I do I know exactly what to do. It's time to fight fire with fire. I find the number in the email, click it, and let it ring.

"Florence and Foxe, this is Heather speaking. How may I direct your call?"

"Hey, Heather. This is Guy Finch. Could you connect me with Christiana, please?"

"Certainly, Mr. Finch. Give me one moment."

A few seconds later Christiana picks up. "Mr. Finch, I hope everything is going well. What can I do for you?"

Charleigh has no idea what she just started.

CHAPTER NINE

Charleigh

HAVE YOU EVER had one of those days? You know the kind I'm talking about. The kind of day where everything that can go wrong does go wrong. The kind that snowballs until there's an inescapable avalanche heading right for you. That's the kind of day I'm having right now.

It started with me sleeping through my alarm. No big deal. I figured that I could grab something quick to eat, get dressed, and then head out and make it to work right on time. But then I spilled orange juice all over my last clean work shirt. After a mini meltdown, I grabbed a scarf to cover it up. Not ideal but crisis averted. Until I locked my keys in my car. After waiting for an hour over the locksmith's estimated arrival time, I found them in my purse. Of course, I didn't learn that until after he'd already unlocked my car, so he still charged me.

Usually, these types of days only happen once in a while, but I've been having them every single day for the past week. Every single day since I learned I'd be working with Guy Finch.

So here I am, sitting in my car, trying my best to stop another breakdown because I know the worst is yet to come. And I've known that since yesterday evening when Christiana put an urgent meeting on my calendar for this morning. There's no agenda, no hint at what this meeting could be about. But given the events of yesterday, I know exactly what it's about.

I'm about to be fired. And it's all my fault.

I shouldn't have hung up on Guy, but I was pissed. I'd spent half an hour trying to fix my flat tire by myself because no one would stop to help me. I couldn't call anyone because my phone decided that it was the perfect moment in time to update itself for half an hour. I tossed it back into my car but it slid underneath my seat and vanished. When I finally did hear my phone ringing, the two scrawny high school freshmen I'd wrangled into helping me had just kicked over the container holding all of the nuts for my tire.

To say I wasn't in the right frame of mind is an understatement.

And now I have only myself to blame because there's only one reason why Christiana would call this meeting. I'm sure Guy told her that I didn't show up for the walk-through and that when he called to check in, I lashed out at him and hung up. And as much as I can't stand Guy, he had every right to do it.

Welp, no reason to delay the inevitable for any longer.

The thirty yards from my car to the doors of the office feel more like a mile. The world feels like it's at a standstill. All my senses are dull, as though they're lending their energy to amplify the single thought that's running through my mind: I'm about to lose my job. I've worked hard to get to where I am, but I threw it away for a petty grudge.

Heather greets me when I open the doors, and then lets me know that Christiana is expecting me. I don't even take the time to take off my coat and purse at my desk because I'm sure I'll be leaving the office again shortly, this time with a box of all my belongings.

Christiana is sitting behind her desk. She waves for me to come in before I even have the chance to knock. Her face is impassive, but I know she's probably livid underneath it. You see, there's nothing Christiana holds higher in this world than reputation, and I sealed my fate when I acted the way I did. There's no way Christiana doesn't see my actions as a reflection of her firm. She trusted me, and I failed her.

"Good morning, Charleigh. Please have a seat next to Andrea."

I didn't even notice Andrea was in the room too. Great, I've always wanted an audience during my termination. I turn to look at her as I sit down. Her hands are folded neatly on her lap, and she's wearing the biggest smile on her face.

I swallow but my throat is dry. I can't stop thinking about how I'm going to pay my bills. How I'll be living off ramen from now on—if I'm lucky. How I'll be homeless by the end of the month.

Christiana's chair creaks as she leans forward, her hands clasped in front of her. Although she's hardly an inch or two above five feet, Christiana is the most imposing woman I've ever met. She selects every word carefully and doesn't pull any punches. When she talks, you listen, and right now, she has every ounce of my attention.

Her eyes home in on me and I immediately feel a sense of impending doom cascade over me. It's like a cold, sopping wet blanket is wrapped around me, weighing me down. "Charleigh, Mr. Finch called me yesterday and—"

"I'm so sorry," I blurt out without even thinking.

Shit.

My eyes bug out as I start to mumble incoherently. "Ah-bwah-so-wah-uh-uh." No matter the situation, I always seem to make everything worse. And the longer I fumble, the deeper Christiana's apparent confusion gets.

Eventually, I collect myself. "I'll empty out my desk," I say, standing up.

Christiana holds up a hand. "Charleigh, hold on a second. What are you talking about?"

"You're firing me, right?"

Christiana's head jerks back as she shakes it. "Fire you, Charleigh? What are you talking about? Before you interrupted me I was going to tell you that Mr. Finch wants you to take the lead on this project."

What the firetruck? Cue my awkward, choppy laugh.

"No…" I sit back down and stare at Christiana like a modern art painting: what *is* this?

"Well, I'm not quite sure what prompted this outburst, and I'm not interested to find out. Just know—"

"I can tell you what—" Andrea interrupts Christiana but backs down when she finds a death stare being leveled at her.

Christiana turns her gaze toward me. "As I was saying, Mr. Finch was impressed by you during the walk-through and shared his desire to have you as the lead designer for this project."

Every bit of air is sucked out of my lungs. What in the world was Guy doing? I wasn't at the walk-through. Andrea knows this. And a quick sidelong glance at her lets me know that she is absolutely seething at this news.

"I told him that I believe it's a little premature at this point, as we haven't seen either of your designs. He was adamant, but I'd still like to see both of your project proposals before we move forward. Yes?"

Both of us nod, dumbstruck by the news.

"Good, have your plans to me by the end of this week."

I should be happy about this. This is exactly what I wanted: my very own project to prove to Christiana I'm capable of moving into the lead designer role Lana vacated. But I'm not. I'm annoyed that Guy would put me in this position. He's toying with me, flaunting his power. This is just like when we were kids, but this time, I'm not going to back down.

Before I have the chance to duck into the stairwell and call Guy to chew his ear off, Andrea corners me in the hallway.

"What the hell happened back there? You never showed up yesterday. You shouldn't be rewarded for that. You should've been fired."

Harvey, one of our accountants, walks out of the break room about to bite into his donut when he notices Andrea berating me. His eyes bug out and he immediately circles right back around and into the break room.

"Look, Andrea, I have no idea what Guy is thinking. Seriously. I'm just as surprised as you are."

She huffs, folding her arms across her chest. Two strands from her otherwise immaculately styled hair fall across either side of her face as she leans forward, her body vibrating with anger. I can't blame her. I'd be pissed too.

There are a few moments of silence. It's long enough that Harvey figures the coast is clear to come out. Unfortunately, just as he pops his head around the corner, Andrea lays into me again.

"You're sleeping with him, aren't you?"

Harvey pops his head back inside the break room.

"Seriously, Andrea?"

She snorts. "It all makes sense now. There's no other way he'd let something like that go. I can't believe it."

I'm pissed. Not only at Andrea for jumping to conclusions, but at Guy for feeding the conclusion. In this business, reputation is everything, and I'm not going to have mine tarnished for something that isn't true—that would *never* be true.

I raise my hands, palms up. "I'm done, Andrea." Turning to the break room, I say, "Harvey, we're done."

"Thank you!" I hear from down the hall.

I walk by Andrea and open the door to the stairwell. "Well, I'm not," she snaps just as I push through the door.

I want to scream. Thankfully, I have the perfect outlet. I take my phone out of my purse and press Guy's contact number. He picks up on the third ring.

"Good morning, sunshine."

I'll let that one go. Just this once.

"You need to explain yourself."

"What do you mean?"

"Don't play dumb with me, Guy. You know exactly what I'm talking about."

"Huh." He makes a few clicking sounds with his tongue. "Nope, not sure what you're talking about. But look, Charleigh, I'm at work now, so I can't really talk. You know, that whole protecting and serving thing."

"Stop playing games," I bite back. "You're really screwing things up for me—"

Click.

"Hello?" I suck in a harsh breath, jerking my phone from my ear. He ended the call. Mothertrucker.

A few seconds later he sends me a text.

Guy: How's it feel, Chucky?

My skin tingles as I stare at the text. I'm going to get back at him one way or another.

CHAPTER TEN

Guy

DO I FEEL bad? *Mmm…*a little.

I knew my call would set a few things in motion. It would cause friction between Andrea and Charleigh, but most importantly, it would send a wakeup call to Charleigh: I'm here to stay whether she likes it or not. She either needs to step up and focus on this project, or she needs to leave. I'm not going to deal with her wishy-washy behavior anymore.

Over the last few days, I've found my more direct approach to be more effective. Charleigh, after fuming at me for a few days, seemed to swallow her pride. We were able to make some headway with the project. We'll be meeting shortly so we can have the walk-through she missed. It will be the first time we've been alone together since the night at the bar, and I'm not exactly sure which

Charleigh I'm going to get: Business Charleigh, Explosive Charleigh, or Charleigh-Charleigh (i.e., herself).

I'm pleasantly surprised to see Charleigh's Forester turn onto the winding drive five minutes early. She parks her car but leaves it running. The headlights cast two cones of light across the graveled drive, speckled by the light mist that's falling. I'm watching her from an upstairs window. It's hard to tell what she's doing in her car but it looks like she's talking to herself. She flips down the visor in front of her and then flips it back up a few moments later. The headlights go out and Charleigh climbs out of the car.

Her red hair contrasts starkly with her heather-gray peacoat. Instead of her usual pair of heels, she opts for a more practical pair of tennis shoes. No slipping today. She clutches her purse by the straps and lets it swing as she confidently plants one foot in front of the other. The small moment of hesitation she might have had in the car is gone.

The doorbell rings just as I make it downstairs. I open the door and smile. "Glad you could make it this time, Charleigh." There's a flicker of annoyance on her face, but she masks it quickly.

She's wearing more makeup than usual, but it's not overwhelming. Some mascara and eyeliner and then some gloss on her lips. My eyes pause on her lips for a bit longer than they should.

"Good to see you, Guy."

Business Charleigh. Got it.

I catch a faint smell of cinnamon as she passes by me. She pauses a few feet away from me, her back to me as

85

she looks out into the great room. The door shuts with a heavy thud. I reach out to help remove her coat, but she stops me.

"That's okay. I won't be here long."

Charleigh doesn't skip a beat, pulling a yellow legal pad and blue pen from her purse. She walks methodically around the room, slowly turning her head as she surveys it. "It hasn't changed much," she says finally.

I cross the gap between us and stand next to her. "That's the problem."

Charleigh scribbles a few notes but doesn't respond, and then after a few moments moves toward the large stone fireplace to our left.

"Would you like the tour?"

"No thanks," she says. "I've been here enough times to know my way around."

Translation: You'll just be in my way, so please leave me alone while I do my job.

"Why are you always so combative with me? If you want to make this project more difficult for both of us, then by all means continue. But I just want you to know I'm not the bad guy, and to be honest, I'm probably not even close to as awful as some of the clients you'll be forced to work with."

Charleigh spins around, her hair fanning out behind her. She draws in a deep breath as though she's winding herself up for a long, drawn-out verbal assault, but she stops herself. The long breath comes out as a sigh instead. "Look. I'm trying to be practical here. You and I," she motions in between us, "we don't work well together."

"You're acting as though you've tried to work with me."

"I don't need to. I know from experience and that's all I need."

I scoff. "What a wonderful outlook. Ignore the present and fixate on the past. Let me know how that works out for you." There's no getting through to her. She doesn't want to listen. I'm done trying. "I'll be in the kitchen. Come find me when you want to act like an adult."

There are two cups on the island filled with hot chocolate. I'd picked them up from Common Grounds on the way here as a peace offering, but that's clearly not going to work. Nothing is going to work unless Charleigh lets go of this stupid feud.

I'm not sure how long I've been sitting at the island, but by the time Charleigh finally appears, my hot chocolate is cold. She sits down in front of me but doesn't speak. I grab the other cup and take it to the microwave. I can feel her eyes on my back as I wait for the microwave to finish heating up the hot chocolate.

I place the cup in front of her. "I thought you might like something to drink."

She picks up the cup, glancing at the Common Grounds logo for a moment before popping off the lid and inspecting the contents.

I stare blankly at her as she sniffs the drink. "It's not poisoned." She glances up at me, still uncertain. I fold my arms, a little annoyed. "I could taste it first if you'd like, *princess*."

She flushes as she sets the cup back down and replaces the lid. When she finally takes a sip, her eyes light up.

"Good?"

"Better than expected," she says, taking another sip.

I shake my head, sighing.

Charleigh sets the cup down and grabs her notebook. "I wanted to go over some of my ideas and get your feedback." She spreads out a few pieces of paper in front of me. They're rough sketches of various rooms throughout the house. I'm actually impressed at how good they are, much more detailed than anything Andrea showed me during her walk-through. But I'm more impressed that she actually wants my input.

She spends the next ten minutes or so discussing each of her sketches, describing the changes she'd like to implement. "My main priority with this design is to keep the rustic charm of your house intact," she says, finishing up her miniature presentation.

I'm still leafing through her sketches, awed by her vision for the project. It's more than I ever expected. My parents would be proud.

"It's wonderful."

"Great," Charleigh says. She grabs the papers from my hand. "We'll be in touch."

"That's it?"

Charleigh looks at me, confused. "Yes?"

"Okay," is all I can think of saying to that.

Charleigh stands up and heads out of the kitchen. She can see herself out. If she's not willing to put forth the effort to be somewhat friendly, then neither am I. If all she wants is a business transaction, then that's what she'll get. A few minutes later the door slams shut.

I reach into my pocket, grab my phone, and find a text from Deanna.

Deanna: Are you ready for our HGTV marathon tonight? Deanna

Guy: How could I forget?

I did forget, actually. This whole Charleigh situation has done a number on my head.

Deanna: I bought everything you need to make your famous tacos again. They were so good last time! Deanna

Guy: Great, I'll see you soon.

I'm not going to let Charleigh dampen my mood.

"You've outdone yourself again, Guy." Deanna leans back into her recliner.

"I'm glad you're enjoying them, Deanna."

"Enjoying them? Dear, these are heavenly."

I laugh, polishing off my last taco a few moments later. This was exactly what I needed after that terrible walkthrough with Charleigh. I talked to Deanna about it, but she didn't offer any suggestions because it all comes down to Charleigh. She's hardheaded and won't back down when she thinks she's right.

"You should make these for Charleigh. She'd have to come around."

"I don't think it's so easy. She's still hung up on what happened between us when we were younger."

Deanna waves her hand like she's batting off a fly. "That nonsense? Both of you were at each other's throat for a time. You were kids."

"I know, but that doesn't mean it was right."

Deanna nods. "Of course not." She rocks back in her chair for a moment, contemplating something. A few minutes later she speaks again. "It was a tough time for you. You weren't in the right mind for a while. She shouldn't blame you for that."

She might be right, but it doesn't matter. I can't take back the things I said, just like I can't fault Charleigh for taking them as harshly as she did. But just because I'm granting her that, doesn't mean it's okay for her to act so ridiculously now. If she doesn't want anything to do with me, then she needs to drop out and hand the reins over to Andrea.

"Well, like I've told you. She'll come around. I know her, and I know you. Now let's get this show on the road. Maybe you'll learn a thing or two—something to impress Charleigh." She waves a finger at the screen.

I laugh. "I don't think Charleigh thinks there's a single impressive thing about me." I reach for the remote and restart the episode of *Fixer Upper* we'd paused. Chip's in the middle of swinging a sledgehammer into the wall, and it looks like a hell of a lotta fun. I can't wait to get this reno underway. Charleigh would let me swing a hammer, right?

I think about it for a moment. It's my house. Why would I need her approval? It's not like she wants or is actively seeking my approval either. I sit back and let the thought formulate in my head.

We're a few episodes deep into our marathon when the front door opens. Immediately my instincts kick into high gear and I jump to my feet. But then I hear a voice.

"Oh my God, where are those brownies? You would not believe the day I had."

Charleigh.

I glance at Deanna and she shrugs, offering a sheepish grin.

Damn it, Deanna... is all I can think. I knew she was up to something when she started texting during the last episode. I could count the number of people she has available to text on one hand: me, Charleigh, Jamie, and Marissa. I knew Jamie and Marissa were out tonight, so that left Charleigh. I should've known.

"Aside from nuts in baked goods, I don't think there's anything I despise more in this world than people who think—" Charleigh turns the corner and her eyes bug out when she spots me.

"What were you going to say?"

She stares at me for a few moments and then looks to her mother. "Why didn't you tell me he was going to be here?"

Deanna shrugs. "I didn't think it would matter."

Both of us look at Deanna. She clearly knows the issues of putting Charleigh and me in the same room—I just spent half an hour talking about it—but she believes herself a master at feigning ignorance. "I just thought you'd like to have some of the freshly baked brownies Guy made."

"They're not poisoned either," I say, glancing at Charleigh over my shoulder. "You dropped in before I had the chance."

It almost draws out a smile. Almost.

"Why don't you take some for the road? You wouldn't want to leave on an empty stomach."

Deanna gets up, grabs Charleigh by the shoulders, and leads her back into the living room and onto the opposite end of the couch from me. Charleigh is rigid, refusing to lean back or even move her head. She's statuesque as she faces forward, doing her best to avoid contact or even acknowledge me.

Deanna retreats into the kitchen. "I'll be right back."

When Deanna's out of earshot, Charleigh whips her head toward me. "What are you doing here?"

I nod to the TV. "It's HGTV night."

"You watch HGTV? With my mom?"

I keep my eyes trained on Charleigh. After a few moments of silence, she scratches her neck and then turns her attention to the TV. "Do you think I should be embarrassed?" I ask.

Charleigh draws her gaze slowly toward me. "Well…"

I snort. "Where else could I research about renovations? My interior designer hates me."

She rolls her eyes. "Good one. Why don't you fire her, then?"

"Because she's rather talented." I take a sip of my water, watching Charleigh out of my periphery. Some of the tension in her posture begins to loosen. "And I have no problem working with disagreeable people."

"I'm not disagreeable," she retorts.

"Okay." I grab the remote and press play again.

"Guy. I'm the least disagreeable person in the world."

"Sure sounds like something a disagreeable person would say."

She huffs and falls back into the couch. We sit in

awkward silence for another ten minutes before Deanna finally appears. "Sorry that took so long. I couldn't find the right container."

"Second shelf on the right next to the sink," I say without skipping a beat.

Charleigh gapes at me. "How would you even know that?" she whispers.

I lean into Charleigh and whisper, "I visit Deanna more often than once every other month."

Charleigh's face blanches and I immediately feel bad. I didn't mean to be nasty, but it's hard not to meet nastiness with nastiness, especially when niceness fails. She stands up a few seconds later and walks toward the front door with her mother.

Not much later I hear a low but heated argument between Charleigh and her mother. I turn the volume up because I don't really care to listen in. The front door slams shut and Deanna returns, dropping into her seat with a sigh.

"Charleigh says 'Good night.'"

I snort. "I'm sure she did."

CHAPTER ELEVEN

Charleigh

I'm officially screwed.

There's an email sitting in my inbox from Christiana with the subject line "Proposal Update?" I first noticed it this morning but have yet to open it because I know I won't have an answer that she'll like. It's not that I haven't finished my proposal—it's done. I wish it were something like that. I could fix that with an all-nighter. My problem is out of my control. My problem is that Guy has dropped off the face of the earth, and as much as I hate to say it, I need Guy.

If I don't have his approval, then Christiana won't even look at my proposal, which will mean she'll go with Andrea's and more than likely let her take the lead. I cannot let that happen. Andrea as my superior? I'd take being waterboarded while listening to "My Heart Will Go On" on repeat over that.

I check my sent folder just to make sure I didn't imagine sending those dozen emails. They've been sent. Next I scan my call log and my text messages, and sure enough, I wasn't dreaming about sending those either.

I glance at my monitor and then shut my eyes, silently praying that he'll respond. *Come on. Give me something. Just one word.* My email chirps and I raise my arms to the sky as I mouth "Thank you." Unfortunately, I wasn't specific enough. I got an email, just not from Guy. It was another email from Christiana, resending her original email.

I smack my palm on my keyboard. A few people around me pop their heads out of their cubicles and glare at me. I raise my hands. "Sorry! Fly. Missed it, though."

My cheeks flush as I turn back to check my phone for messages again. No texts, not even from Marissa. I'd texted her earlier about my difficulties with Guy. I hoped she could shed light on this situation or force Jamie to do something about Guy. But she hasn't responded either.

I spend the next half hour catching up on other work, but it's rough going. Every email notification I hear sends my brain into a frenzy, even when they come from other people's computers. I've been tracking Christiana's movements, hoping she doesn't come over and talk to me in person. She's currently in her office, but that could change at any time.

I'm just finishing up another email when I feel a light chill on the back of my neck that makes my hair stand on end. I get up from my desk slowly, peeking over the top of my cubicle as I look around the office carefully. After a few seconds, I sit back down in my chair.

False alarm.

My body is in the preliminary stages of growing Guydar. I first noticed it last week, before Guy went dark. I was in the cereal aisle at the grocery store when I felt the same hair-raising chill on the back of my neck. But along with that chill, I felt a tingle run down my spine and spread across the back of my arms. I thought I'd just walked under an A/C vent, but after dropping a box of Cinnamon Toast Crunch into my cart, I walked out of the aisle and spotted Guy. Guydar.

He was still in his uniform, standing with his arms folded so that his biceps bulged even larger. It took a brief moment for me to notice him talking to Andrea. She was dressed to the nines, hair and makeup included. I mean, who goes to the grocery store on a Saturday night wearing *that*? I had on my go-to sweatshirt covered with stains of many sizes and mostly indeterminate origin. Most of them had been on it for so long that I don't remember whether they were actually stains or part of the sweatshirt design.

Andrea tipped back her head and let out a horrific, exaggerated laugh as she latched her grubby mitts onto Guy's arm. I laughed. But rather than a normal human laugh, I snort-laughed something that would be more appropriate during the rearing of a litter of piglets. And almost immediately I felt eyes turning my way, so before either Andrea or Guy could find me gawking at them, I performed an evasive maneuver. My cart nearly tipped, skidding onto two wheels as I spun it back around and down the cereal aisle.

Now, whenever I feel the hairs on my neck stand on end, I expect to see him. And for the first time, I wish it hadn't been a false alarm because I need to talk with him ASAP.

Thankfully, Marissa texts me.

Marissa: Maybe he's busy?

Not likely. Guy's been very responsive to my messages until our little fight at my mother's house. This is something different.

Charleigh: For nearly a week?
Marissa: Have you done anything that might've made him upset? Annoyed? Not exactly thrilled to talk with you?
Charleigh: What? Of course not.
Marissa: Are you sure? Jamie might've mentioned a few things that he heard from Guy...
Charleigh: Well...

I'd hoped to follow that text up with something that supported me, but there really isn't anything. I know I haven't been the easiest person to work with. I know I've been cold and confrontational. I'm not usually like this, I swear. I know that sometimes I can be hardheaded and forceful, but they're the same traits that got me this job in the first place.

And the same ones that will GET YOU FIRED!

I press my teeth into my lip and then replace the message I was going to text with the only thing I should respond with.

Charleigh: Okay. Maybe I haven't been the nicest person.

Marissa: That's a start. Have you apologized?
Charleigh: Apologize? He hasn't apologized for everything he put me through when we were kids.
Marissa: Have you given him the chance?

Well, not exactly…

Marissa: But anyway that doesn't matter. Do you want this job or not? Because if you don't fix whatever is going on between you two, you're not going to get promoted. Andrea will be your BOSS.

If Andrea's insufferable now, I can't even imagine what she'll be like when she's my superior.

Charleigh: What do I do?
Marissa: You should apologize.
Charleigh: Do you think it would even work at this point?
Marissa: Of course. Guy's not that bad. Jamie and I've been out with him many times. He's fun!
Charleigh: …
Marissa: Oh umm…but he smells bad.
Marissa: Sorry. Seriously though. Just apologize and move forward. Things will work themselves out once you get this project rolling.

It makes sense why Guy's not responding. A part of me knew it too, but I just didn't want to admit it. I've been prickly with him from the start and it hasn't done a single thing for me.

"Charleigh?"

Every cell in my body turns to ice when I hear Christiana speak my name. She never leaves her office to talk to anyone, so couple that with the unread emails in my inbox, this is not going to be a fun interaction.

Christiana pulls off her glasses. "Could we have a chat?"

I smile, but it feels like a grimace. "Sure. Of course. Right away." I stand up but forget to push my chair out. My thighs smack into the edge of my desk and I fall right back into my seat with a loud *thwack!*

"I'll be in my office," Christiana says, placing her glasses back on, scanning me once before she turns to leave.

My stomach feels like I'd just dropped fifty feet on a rollercoaster. Chat? Christiana wants to chat? That's basically the last thing I wanted to hear at this moment because the word "chat" has a very loaded meaning in this office. A "chat" is just another word for a one-way conversation that leaves one person in tears. And in the immortal words of Justin Timberlake: *It's gonna be maaaaay.*

Christiana doesn't say a word as I walk into her office. Her eyes are locked on me as I maneuver in between the two chairs in front of her desk and then take a seat on the left one. I press the wrinkles out of my skirt with my palms, doing my best not to let Christiana's heated gaze get to me. But as soon as I raise my head to look at her, it feels like my breath has been squeezed out of my lungs.

"What's the status of your proposal?"

"It's almost done. I'm trying to schedule a time to meet with Mr. Finch, but it's been difficult to reach him."

I can't believe I just called him "Mr. Finch."

Christiana rarely allows her emotions to show on her face. So when they do register, its effect is powerful. Something as simple as her brow raise makes my pulse pound even faster than it already is. "Really? He's been one of my more responsive clients. Andrea's already handed in her proposal. Is there a disconnect between you two? Is everything alright?"

I swallow hard. "Everything's just fine. We're just playing a little phone tag."

"Well, I don't think I need to remind you, but I need the proposal by the end of the week. We have a lot of scheduling to do, and we need to finalize which plan we're going with as soon as possible. Even though Mr. Finch wants to move forward with you at the head, I might have to persuade him otherwise if you are unable to meet this deadline. It wouldn't bode well for the rest of the project."

"I'm trying, Christiana. Really."

"Have you dropped by his house?"

I tilt my head. "No."

"Then you still have some avenues open."

"Yes, I do. I'll get right on it."

Christiana leans forward and opens a manila folder on her desk. She slides her glasses lower on her nose as she begins to scan the document with a pen.

Not another word is said as I stand up and leave her office. When I reach my desk I grab my phone and call Guy, hoping he'll answer, but of course, he doesn't. I send him a few texts.

Charleigh: Can you please grow up and stop ignoring me?

Five minutes later.

Charleigh: You're such a NICE GUY.

Five minutes and two granola bars later.

Charleigh: Okay. FINE. I'm sorry I've been difficult to work with. Could you please respond so I don't lose my job.
Guy: New phone. Who's this?
I want to be mad, but his response actually gets a chuckle out of me.
Charleigh: Real funny. Can we meet?
Guy: I suppose.
Charleigh: Just respond to one of the thirty emails I sent you with all the dates.

I set my phone down and no less than a minute later, I get an email from him and then a text a few seconds later.

Guy: See you soon.

With my job on the line, "soon" isn't soon enough.

CHAPTER TWELVE

Charleigh

I CHECK MY makeup in Franny's vanity mirror. It's the fourth time I've dissected my appearance in the last fifteen seconds. Lip gloss: a-poppin'. Mascara: a-rockin'. Eyebrows: uh, present? I have no idea what I'm doing when it comes to eyebrows. But the rest of my makeup hasn't looked this good in years. That doesn't stop me from still freaking out.

Deep breaths. That's all you need.

I close my eyes and fill my lungs with as much air as possible. I hold the breath for a few seconds because that's as long as I can manage. I'm the only person I know whose deep breaths cause her to be out of breath. And don't ask me for help inflating balloons. My record is four without passing out.

So no more holding my breath. I'm not usually this

nervous before meetings, but I need this one to go well. I need to be friendly. I need to be happy. I need to be the version of Charleigh that doesn't hate Guy with every ounce of her being.

I shut the vanity mirror and close the visor. After grabbing my purse off the back seat, I check my phone and find I'm five minutes early. Perfect. I hop out of Franny and head for the front doors of Common Grounds.

It's mid-morning so the morning rush has passed and the lunch crowd hasn't arrived yet. There's a motley crew of people from all walks of life scattered among the tables: hipsters in the back, a table of elderly men at the front, and a mother chasing a toddler hopped up on sugar while her infant wails in its stroller.

The toddler's looking over his shoulder at his mom, clutching his cookie in his raised hand. Unfortunately, he's too distracted by outmaneuvering his mother to notice the immovable wall in front of him. And by immovable wall, I mean Guy. The toddler plows into him, keels over backward, and stares up at Guy blankly. There are about four seconds of silence before the kid starts wailing.

"I'm so sorry," the mother says, bending over to collect her kid. Her hair looks like someone rubbed a balloon all over her head to build up a static charge.

"It's not a problem," Guy says as she retreats to her table, dragging her flailing toddler with her.

Guy dusts himself off, giving me a few moments to watch him. He's wearing his highway patrol uniform. It's just the right size. Tight enough that he can move around unencumbered, but not so tight that the buttons would pop off if he were to bend over. Which would be, uh, super gross.

Just as I finish taking him in, Guy turns to me and smiles. There's a jolt in my sternum, a swarm of nerves in my gut. He knew I'd been watching him the entire time. I push both feelings as far away as possible and head toward him.

"I see you've moved on to punting toddlers. I'm shocked that you didn't steal his cookie while you were at it." It comes out so fast I didn't even see it coming. I was supposed to be on my best behavior, but just the sight of Guy is drawing out the other side of me. The part that doesn't care about keeping her job.

Thankfully, Guy doesn't mind. He snorts—that half smile of his growing on his lips. His eyes are set on mine, and the hairs on the back of my neck begin to stand up again. "Good morning to you too, Charleigh." His half smile deepens into a full smile. I'm doing my best to force the flashbacks of our kiss out of my mind, but they keep rearing back up.

"What can I get you?" he asks, placing his hand on my back and guiding me forward.

"I've got this. You're my client, remember?"

"I suppose I am."

I order my usual decaf latte, and after a few moments of indecision, coupled with Guy's gentle prodding, I settle on my usual chocolate chip scone. Guy orders a coffee. Black.

We stand awkwardly at the counter waiting for our drinks—mine, really—to be made.

Make conversation. You want to keep this job, right?

"So…" I say, rocking back and forth. "How's life? Saving lives. Protecting and serving. All that stuff."

Guy doesn't respond to me right away. He's doing that thing with his eyes again that makes me feel naked. I grab at my elbow from behind my back as I rock on my heels and chew the inside of my mouth.

"It's fine. How's work?"

"It's fine."

Guy smiles at me. "Fine."

Wow, it's going swimmingly!

The barista gets our drinks out on the counter, and not a moment too soon. Now that I'm trying to be nice to Guy, it feels like I've completely forgotten how to interact with him. Everything feels unnatural and forced. I don't like it.

Guy walks toward a table in the back.

"Do you mind if we sit up front by the window?"

"Just in case you want to make a quick exit?"

Deep breath. Don't Snap. Deep breath. Okay.

"The light's better. And I like watching people walk by."

Guy motions with his hand. "Lead the way."

He's partly right. The choice of table is strategic. If we're out in the open instead of hidden in the back of the coffee shop, we'll be on our best behavior. I will be at least, because I'm not about to be banned from the only coffee shop in a twenty-mile radius that serves palatable baked goods.

I place my scone and latte on the table as I sit down. Guy sits down, coffee still in hand. He leans back, half his back against the chair while the other presses against the glass.

"I'm glad we could finally meet."

"Is that sarcasm, Charleigh?"

"No, why would you—never mind." I wave my hand and then take a bite of my scone. Guy hasn't taken his eyes off of me. It feels like he's dissecting me, as though I'm under a microscope.

"I like what you did with your," I make a circle in front of me, "hair. It looks…smooth."

Smooth? Was that even a compliment? What are you doing?

"Thanks?"

"I mean it. Have you been working—"

Guy raises his hand. "Charleigh. Enough. Stop pretending you enjoy my company and let's get this done with."

Alright by me.

"As you wish, Mr. Finch."

He shakes his head as he slowly closes his eyes. When he opens them again they seem to ask me, "Really?"

"But before we start, I want to apologize for my behavior again. This hasn't been easy for me."

Guy takes a sip of his coffee, his eyes still on mine. I know he can sense the sincerity in my tone. I'm not forcing the apology out like my sorry excuse of a compliment. I mean it.

Finally, he says, "That's big of you."

Don't push it.

"Ready to see the plan?"

Guy nods. I pull my laptop and a paper copy of my plans out of my purse. I hand Guy the paper copy and then open the plans on my laptop. I'm only a few seconds into my presentation when Guy interrupts me.

"I can't see." He taps the top of my laptop.

I tap the paper copy he set aside. "I gave you a copy. It's the same as mine."

I dive right back in, but Guy isn't having it. He stands up from the table and my heart leaps out of my chest and into my throat. "You're leaving?"

He raises a brow and pulls his chair around the table, places it next to mine, and then sits down. "Nope. Just had to come to you."

I swallow my heart, but now it just sits in my stomach, thumping away, making me feel all sorts of queasy. I'm trying my best to ignore how amazing Guy smells. What is with men's body wash? Is there actual crack in it? Because I, for one, can't get enough of the scent. He's so close to me that I can feel the heat coming off of his skin, and it's getting a little more difficult to breathe or think or talk or do anything, really.

"Carry on," Guy says, taking another sip of his coffee, which smells like the baristas somehow distilled Christmas in a cup.

Carry on? That's easier said than done. I clear my throat and try to refocus my attention on the screen, but it's not that simple when there's a six-foot-three-inch behemoth of a man sitting next to me, invading my personal space. "So..." I point to the screen but my mind goes blank.

"So," Guy repeats.

"These walls. They're coming down. And we're painting..." I start scrolling through the plan. "Yes, and that brings me to the kitchen. What we..."

Holy hell, this is embarrassing. I've never felt so discombobulated. I can't think straight. I can't believe this is happening right now. I pause, trying to gather some semblance of calm.

"You're really nailing the presentation, Charleigh."

"Yeah, well, I'm about to nail you in a second," I mutter reflexively.

Oh, God.

If souls exist, I can feel mine rapidly draining from me the moment the words leave my mouth. It starts at my navel and rushes through me, leaving a cold, uncomfortable tingling sensation in its wake until it finally bursts from the crown of my head.

"That's not—uh—I didn't mean—I meant with a hammer—nails—construction—not like—you know."

"I think you should stop while you're… I was going to say ahead, but I guess it doesn't really apply here."

"Excuse me for a second."

I push away from the table, knocking my chair into the table behind me, and hightail it out of Common Grounds. I spend the next couple of minutes pacing back and forth down a side street while talking to myself out loud like a crazy person.

I can't believe what happened in there. I've never felt so awkward or embarrassed in my life. Well, now that I think about it, I can remember another time: the time I tried to dye my hair, which led to Guy dubbing me Chargrilled Charleigh. It's hard to ignore the common theme.

After a few more minutes and many concerned stares from several passersby, I walk back to Common Grounds. Guy's still sitting in the same position when I return. I assumed he'd have a shit-eating grin on his face, but instead, his face is impassive if not a little concerned. I sit back down as Guy scoots a few inches away to give me a little more room.

"I'm sorry if I made you nervous."

"It's not you," I say reflexively, even though it totally is him. "It's been a long day."

"It's not even 9 a.m."

"I know."

He snorts and then motions to the screen. "Pretend I'm not here."

I take a deep breath and restart my presentation. Thankfully, I run through it without a hitch. It was a little slow in the beginning, but after a while, I was so completely focused on my design that I hardly noticed Guy next to me except when I paused for an occasional breath. That damned body wash is unrelenting.

"I feel if we add too many modern updates, then it will lose the warmth and rustic charm. The space doesn't beg for clean lines and edges. It wants natural flaws and imperfections. It craves jagged stones and earth tones."

"That last one rhymed."

"Is that all you got out of that?" It comes out sharper than I would have liked, but after spending the last half hour or so spilling my heart and soul out to Guy, I'd like something a little more constructive than a comment on unintentional wordplay.

"Easy, Charleigh. I love the design."

I feel a wave of relief crash over me. I'd spent so much time preparing the design, and I'm so glad that he likes it. It's nothing like the design Lana had made for him. I haven't seen Andrea's but I know she prefers more flashy designs that just wouldn't appeal to Guy.

He's a down-to-earth, no frills, meat-and-potatoes kind of man.

"It's much more in line with what I envisioned the project to be. It's an ambitious project, but I don't think I'd want to do this unless I was behind it one hundred percent."

"Are you?"

He smiles and my stomach leaps. "Where do I sign?"

I reach over my laptop and snag the papers Guy ignored, rip the top sheet off, and hand it to him. "I just need you to sign here and make a note of any changes you have."

"No changes for me," Guy says, clicking his pen. "It looks perfect."

I try hard not to smile too widely as I watch Guy sign on the dotted line.

"It's not your official contract. I still need to get the seal of approval from Christiana. Then, if she has any changes or suggestions, I'll run them by you and we'll finalize the design together."

"What's the timeframe? Do you think we can get started now?"

Guy takes another sip from his coffee. He shakes the cup—empty—and then sets it back down. Without skipping a beat, he snatches my half-eaten scone off my napkin and takes a huge bite. My emotions are in a delicate balance between ecstatic and enraged. He's lucky that I had half of it earlier.

"Another week at the earliest, but that would be pushing it. There's still a lot of legwork that needs to be done. Drawing up the contract. Scheduling contractors. Ordering everything."

"Fine, but I get to help with the demolition."

"No, you don't."

It's a snap reaction, but I don't want him to mess up my first project. Handing Guy Finch a sledgehammer? That's career suicide, and I'm not going to risk this project collapsing in on itself before it starts.

"Andrea thought it would've been a good idea."

"Yeah, well, Andrea thinks that dog nail salons are God's gift to humanity. You're not going to help with the demo. I can't risk anything going wrong with this project."

Guy leans forward. "Charleigh. I'm going to help with the demo. There's no room to negotiate here. It's my house. My reno. My decision. You can either get behind that or I can talk with Christiana and put Andrea in charge while still using your design."

He wouldn't.

"You wouldn't."

Guy glances at his watch. "My shift starts in fifteen minutes," he says, standing up in front the table. "I suggest you reconsider."

I study his face for a few moments, wondering why he's so stubborn. "Why are you…" A pause. "The way…" I tilt my head as I narrow my eyes. "That you are?"

Guy presses his eyebrows together as they rise. "What?"

"You could have Andrea take my spot. You could have her use my design. But I promise you one thing—Andrea won't know how to implement it. She doesn't understand the house the way I do. She doesn't understand *you* the way that I do."

Guy bends over, encroaching into my space *again,* and making it way too hard to breathe. But with the anger building inside me, I'm having no problems pushing it right back onto him.

"You think you know me," Guy whispers, "but you really have no clue."

His warm breath covers my ear and trails down my neck. He pulls back and just before he turns, I say, "You might have everyone fooled, but you haven't fooled me. I see through you. I see the person you're hiding underneath. You're the same person. You haven't changed a bit. You've just gotten better at hiding."

Guy shakes his head. "Keep telling yourself that."

He walks to the front of Common Grounds without another word or glance back at me. The door slams shut behind him, and it takes more than a few minutes for me to take my eyes off it and leave the table.

It's going to take a miracle for me to get through this renovation intact.

CHAPTER THIRTEEN

Guy

THUMP! CRACK!

Wood splits as I force the crowbar between the boards, pushing and pulling backward. Dust billows from behind the wall as I continue to pry boards. After a couple minutes, I step back, remove my goggles, and admire my work.

It's a thing of beauty.

Well over a week has passed since I signed off on Charleigh's plan. Since then, this entire project has been moving at a snail's pace. It feels even slower because each time I ask Charleigh for an update, she gives me very little in the way of information. Our last conversation on the phone pushed me over the edge.

"When are we going to get this demo going?"

"I'm still working on scheduling the contractors."

"I'm ready to go. Let's do this."

"Christiana said you can help with the demo, but I need an actual contractor to make sure you don't tear down your house."

"So, you think I need a babysitter?"

"Well... I don't know about that...but yes. Exactly that."

"I've seen enough Fixer Upper *to know what I'm doing."*

"That's what I'm afraid of."

"So no ETA?"

"You'll be the first to know."

What did she expect? Charleigh knows I'm not one to wait around. And after coming home to this empty house week after week without any headway, you bet I'm going to take it into my own hands. So after a particularly inspiring HGTV night at Deanna's, I dropped by the home improvement store for supplies and got to work.

Cabinets? Gone. Countertops? Puh-lease. It was so easy to demolish most of the kitchen that I moved on to one of the bathrooms. Anything attached to a wall is on the floor. It's amazing what you can do with a sledgehammer, a crowbar, and pent-up aggression.

After a few hours of work, I finally started on the wall we'll be removing to open the kitchen into the great room. It was a bit of an undertaking, but I'd seen Chip Gaines do it enough times that it came naturally to me.

As I'm standing in front of the wall admiring my work, I feel like a king or some military hero after a long, bloody battle. The type of scene you'd expect Napoleon to commission as a painting to commemorate his victory. But instead of my foes under my feet and a sword in my hand, I'm standing atop a large pile of debris with my trusty sledgehammer at my side.

And to think Charleigh wanted an entire crew to demolish this wall. Which reminds me…

Guy: Which wall are we demolishing again?

I wait a few minutes for a response, but my phone's silent. I check the time. It's late so she's probably in bed by now. Although, now that I think about it, I'm not sure if she'd respond if she were awake. I wipe the sweat off my brow as I look once more at the partially removed wall. It's not exactly a thing of beauty—splintered wood and exposed wiring abound—but I can't help but feel an enormous sense of satisfaction.

It's not done yet, but I decide it was enough work for the day. I'm hauling out debris to my trash area when my phone dings from the kitchen.

Charleigh: The one in the kitchen, next to the great room.

That's a relief because there was a moment there when I thought I'd started taking down the wrong wall.

That would've been another awkward conversation.

Guy: Good.
Charleigh: What do you mean by "good?"
Charleigh: Guy…
Charleigh: GUYYYYY!!!!!
2 Missed Calls.
1 Voicemail.
Charleigh: I need you to tell me that you're not doing what I think you're doing.
Charleigh: Guy!

I take a sip of water, watching as more texts pile up. I can feel the slow pull of my lips into a smile as I imagine Charleigh, red-faced and frustrated as she sits on her bed in PJs hammering away on her phone. I remove my goggles, toss my gloves to the ground, and then take a selfie of myself standing in front of an untouched section of wall.

> **Charleigh:** Why are you so sweaty?
> **Guy:** Just finished an intensive workout. Good night.

My phone dings a few more times, but I don't have the energy to deal with Charleigh right now. As I head upstairs, the only thing I'm thinking about is a cold shower and bed. I may be sleeping on a cot, but it's going to feel like heaven after a night like this.

After weeks of stagnation, things are finally moving forward. The contractor will be coming out early next week, and in the meantime, Charleigh and I are finalizing some of the materials. But to be honest, it's a bit overwhelming. She's been texting me nonstop for the past hour. I've seen so many pictures of color swatches and backsplashes and granite and stone and fixtures that everything is blurring together. Thank God Maddox is taking the lead on our shift today because it feels like I'm about to go cross-eyed.

> **Guy:** Why don't you pick your favorites and I'll look them over.

Charleigh: These are my favorites. That's what I'm doing.

Guy: I think you misunderstand the definition of favorites. Just look at the granite. There's at least four of them that look exactly the same. I might as well flip a coin.

Charleigh: Can'tyouseethedifferentbanding? The color differences in the striations? THEY ARE COMPLETELY DIFFERENT.

"What's so funny?" Maddox sets down the speed gun on his lap and cranes his neck to look at my phone.

"Nada," I say, putting my phone to sleep as I force myself to stop grinning. Although it's difficult dealing with Charleigh right now, I can't help but get some enjoyment at her getting just as frustrated with me.

"Bullshit, lemme see. Shit's so boring right now. I'm about to pull someone over for going a couple miles over the speed limit."

"No, you're not. That would mean paperwork. And you already have a backlog of it."

"Not if I give them a warning." Maddox flashes a shit-eating grin at me.

I snort, shaking my head. "You're not pulling anyone over out of boredom."

Maddox bangs his head against the headrest repeatedly.

"You begged me to let you hold the speed gun, Maddox. And drive. So do it and quit being such a baby about it."

Maddox glares at me for a moment but then grabs the speed gun off his lap and resumes business as usual, which consists of a lot of groans, sighs, and muttered curses.

"I didn't beg," he says a few seconds later, aiming the speed gun toward the intermittent traffic. This stretch of highway is always slow at this time of day, which is why I'm letting Maddox take the lead while I'm dealing with Charleigh.

> **Guy:** I'll take your word for it.
> **Charleigh:** If you'd actually come with me to these stores, you'd be able to see the difference.
> **Guy:** Schedule your visits outside my work hours and I'll come.

Charleigh invited me to join her today, but I couldn't because of my shift. I'm sure she scheduled it this way so she wouldn't have to be near me. After our last in-person interaction ended in not-so-veiled threats, I don't blame her. Although relations between us have been delicate, I think we're finally making a little headway.

But then there's that small detail of me starting the demo without her. I still haven't told her, and I'm not exactly looking forward to that conversation.

> **Charleigh:** Tomorrow morning?
> **Guy:** I'm off Saturday. Why don't we do it before our lunch with everyone?
> **Charleigh:** Okay. I'll meet you at your place and we can head out from there.
> **Guy:** Why don't we just meet at the granite store?
> **Charleigh:** Because we aren't going to just the granite warehouse.

Charleigh: We need to look at tile and paint and trim and stain and so so so much more.
Charleigh: It makes more sense if we drive together because I don't want to keep giving you directions.

Oh lord. I didn't think it would be this involved. Oh well, it will give me a nice break from my demo project.

Guy: Alright, my place is fine then.

I suppose she'll have to see my handiwork sometime. Might as well rip off the Band-Aid and get it over with. It won't be so bad. I saved her countless man-hours of work, not to mention money.

Guy: Think you'll be able to handle being in an enclosed space with me?
Charleigh: I'll make sure to keep my breakfast light. Wouldn't want it to come up and make a mess of your fancy interior.
Guy: Har har. I'm still driving Jonah.
Charleigh: That thing is still running?
Guy: Jonah would take offense to that. But yes. He's running just fine.

I've had the same Tacoma for over a decade. It was my first car. My parents bought it for me when I got my learner's permit. Over the years I've taken better care of my car than I have of myself. While I skipped out on regular physicals and exams, never going to the doctor unless I was on the verge of death, I made sure Jonah the Tacoma stuck to a regular maintenance schedule. Routine oil changes. Tire rotations.

Fluids. Car washes too, of course. Anything and everything to make sure he's running like the day I got him.

Although I could easily afford a new car, I'm not going to let him go until I have to. He's one of the last vestiges of my parents that still remain. The more I think about it, I think I'll let him retire into the garage.

"Fuck yeah! Let's do this." Maddox tosses the speed gun at me and then flips the sirens on. I'm nearly thrown into him as he peels out of the shaded area we're parked in and screeches down the highway.

"This shithead thinks he can go five miles over on my highway? Get out of here."

"Five miles over," I repeat, rubbing my eyelids after finally buckling in. These are exactly the kinds of stops I didn't want to make, but with Maddox in the driver's seat, I'm at his mercy. Just this once. Because that seat will be mine before the end of this stop. My phone buzzes one last time before Maddox pulls behind the black Camry in front of us.

Charleigh: We're taking Franny because I don't want to die.
Guy: Franny's just as old.

Charleigh texts again, but I don't have a chance to look at it. Maddox has the Camry stopped and is about to leap into action.

"Let's do this," Maddox yells after clapping his hands.

I groan, wondering what in the world I did in my past life to get a partner like Maddox.

GUY HATER

You know those moments when you have absolute clarity? It's like the whole world dissolves around you as a singular thought comes into focus. It's happening to me right now. I'm lying on my back on a bench, my elbows locked while I extend my arms in front of me as I try my best not to let the over 200 pounds of metal come crashing down on my chest.

The only thought in my head is this: This was a terrible idea.

I'm in the middle of my last set of bench presses, struggling to eke out the last reps. Maddox talked me into going with him to the gym. I tried to decline because my muscles were already exhausted from spending most of my nights at my house doing demo work. But he wouldn't stop whining about it for most of our shift. Eventually, I relented. Whatever. It's just one workout.

It's easy to think that when you're not holding 225 pounds over your head. I finish the second to last rep and move on to the next. Maddox is trying to motivate me in his own way, but being called a pussy or a little bitch isn't exactly helping right now.

"Oh fuck," Maddox says as I'm struggling to push out the last rep.

"Little. Help?" I cough. I sputter. I can feel pressure building in my face and neck as I strain myself. I've stalled out, which is a typical signal to a spotter that you need assistance. But Maddox isn't your typical spotter, or human being for that matter, but that's a whole other conversation. Right now his eyes are focused on something in front of him and not on the hundreds of pounds of steel that gravity is pulling down on my chest.

"Look at that hottie who just walked in."

"MADDOX FUCK!" is all I can get out as my arms begin to wobble.

"Oh shit." Maddox grabs the bar and helps rack it. "Sorry, bro."

"Holy shit," I say as I sit up, panting as I try hard to not only catch my breath but fight the urge to leap on Maddox.

"You can't blame me for that, though. I mean, just look at that chick. She's fine as fuck."

I need a new partner. I repeat the thought in my head like a mantra.

"I'm gonna go talk to her."

"Whatever." I head for the water fountain. After taking a few long, refreshing drags from the fountain, I look around for Maddox. "You've got to be kidding me."

There's a sharp feeling just below my sternum when I spot Maddox. He's talking with Charleigh. Although Maddox is routinely crude in the presence of other guys, he's capable of laying on the charm in front of women. I've seen him do it countless times at coffee shops, always getting numbers or casual dates with women in minutes.

And as I'm watching Charleigh's face light up, I can see he's laying it on real thick right now.

I continue with my workout alone, doing my best to ignore Maddox and Charleigh. I don't have my earbuds with me so it's more difficult to do, especially when my mind wants to single out Charleigh's voice and laugh. No matter where I go in this gym, her voice cuts through the noise.

I power through the last reps of my last exercise with ease. I don't know where this strength is coming from, but I feel adrenaline pumping through me like crazy. I was sore before, but now I hardly feel any pain in my muscles.

I hear Charleigh laugh once again as I head to the locker room. After showering, I head to my locker and change into my clothes. As I'm putting on my shoes, Maddox appears.

"Holy shit, dude. That girl is fire. And not because she's a redhead. Man, I wonder if the curtains match—"

"Maddox!" I raise my hand. "I don't want to hear it."

"Jesus, dude. What's up with you?"

"Nothing. I'm just tired from lifting actual weights. You know, that thing you were supposed to be doing?"

Maddox slinks down on the bench next to me. "I was working just as hard. Just in a different way. That girl is something else."

"You get her number?"

"That's the thing, man. She said some weird girl shit about fate or something. Wouldn't give it to me."

I smile. "You get a name at least?"

"Emma."

I laugh. I underestimated her. She saw right through Maddox.

"What's so funny?" Maddox looks at me as I stand up.

I grab his shoulder. "Nothing, man."

"She gave me her email, but I'm pretty sure it's fake."

"What is it?"

"Emmabammatheslammajamma@gmail.com."

Holy shit. How the hell did she keep a straight face while saying that? I completely lose my shit as Maddox's face begins to droop as the realization sets in.

"Damn it, dude." Maddox leans forward, covering his face with his palms.

I clap him on the shoulder. "Yeah, I think you're right about that."

I leave the locker room, letting Maddox stew over his rejection. As I scan the room, I find Charleigh on the treadmill. I grab my phone and send her a text.

Guy: I see you've had the pleasure of meeting Maddox.

Guy: Emma.

I watch her as she looks down at her phone, picks it up, and then looks around her. She turns down the speed.

Charleigh: You're here? And you know that person?

Guy: He's my partner, unfortunately.

Charleigh: I'm so, so sorry.

Guy: And yes, I'm here. Heading out though. Have a good workout. I'll see you bright and early tomorrow.

I walk by the treadmills on my way out and wave at Charleigh.

"Night, Emma," I say.

"Night, Sebastian," Charleigh replies.

Maybe things have finally reached a turning point between Charleigh and me.

CHAPTER FOURTEEN

Charleigh

WHY DID I think this would be a good idea?

We've spent over an hour at the granite supplier but we still aren't any closer to finding a match. Guy's acting more like a twelve-year-old kid with ADHD than a full-grown man. He's wandering off on his own, darting in between slabs of granite, and overall making this entire process more difficult than it needs to be.

"It all looks the same to me. Just pick what you like."

I will not get mad. I will not get mad. I will not. Get. Mad.

I take a deep breath to calm myself down before telling him, "We've tried that already. You told me, and I quote, 'They just don't speak to me.' I'm not sure if you think you're some granite whisperer, but I need you to make some decisions."

"Okay." He darts behind another slab of granite. Jesus Christ. It's like I'm playing whack-a-mole without a mallet. He pops out one side, disappears, and then reappears somewhere else a few seconds later. This is aggravating beyond words, and slowly, I'm beginning to reconsider my choice to suck it up and be nice.

"How about this one?" Guy raps his knuckles on an almost pure black slab of quartz.

"That's not granite. And it's not even close to the color scheme I'm going for."

"Well, it speaks to me."

"No, it doesn't. You just want it because it's the complete opposite of what I'm trying to do."

Guy looks at me, arms folded together under his chest. "I'm trying to get you to relax. You've been so tense this entire time."

"You're sure taking an odd route to make me relax."

"Well, you're an odd person, Charleigh. And that means odd measures."

I repeat the "I will not get mad" mantra in my head a few more times until I have a small epiphany. "Okay. How about this. We each grab our own samples, and then we'll take them back to the house and figure out which mixture works best. Sound good?"

"That's fine with me."

I should've done this earlier, but for some reason, I thought including Guy in the process would've been more fun for him. But as I watch him bouncing around between the various stones, it seems like giving him a task rather than having him follow me around was a much better idea. But after spending this long inside this store, I'm not even sure if I'll be working with granite anymore. I won't know until we're back at the house.

We spend the next fifteen minutes perusing the stone. I have my top three choices and Guy was able to come up with three himself, one of them matching a selection of my own.

"I guess it spoke to us," Guy says.

"Don't—" I stop myself. As much as I don't ever want him to say that phrase again, I bite my tongue because things are slightly better than where they were before this little exercise. So instead, I smile and say, "I guess so."

It takes us another hour to finish hitting up the rest of the stores, but finally, we're back in Franny. With paint swatches, granite, tile, and more in hand, we head back to Guy's house to see how they all look in place.

"I had a nice time today, Charleigh."

I smile for a brief moment before catching myself. I don't want to give Guy the satisfaction. Not right now.

Although frustrating at the start, this wasn't so bad. I've had much worse days at work and have dealt with much worse clients. If today is an omen of what's to come, then things just might turn out okay.

I park Franny in front of the house, and before I have the chance to turn her off, Guy tells me, "I can't wait to show you what I did to the place."

There are certain things designers love to hear from their clients. What just came out of Guy's mouth is not one of them. It's the sort of statement that fuels my nightmares, and I'm trying my best not to freak out right now.

"What?" My voice wavers as I look at Guy. I haven't seen him this thrilled with himself before. He's glowing, actually glowing from whatever he wants to show me. A few moments later he opens his door and heads to his house without answering me.

"Guy?" I call after him as I watch him run to the front door.

There's an uneasy feeling the size of a bowling ball resting on my chest as I remember those texts from the other day. *Which wall are we tearing down again?* Oh God, please tell me I'm wrong. I hop out of Franny, unsure of what I'm about to walk into.

Guy's leaning against the door, one hand on the doorknob, cracking the door open. It's not a large enough gap for me to look inside. My eyes jump back to Guy. He pushes the door open and aside to let me pass. "After you," he says with a bow and arm flourish.

I don't know what to say. I don't know what to do. I'm frozen in place out of fear for what I'm about to see. I look inside, but it's too dark for me to see much.

Guy prods me to head in, and eventually, I do. And what I see is the exact nightmare that flashed through my mind when Guy told me he couldn't wait to show me what he did. I can't believe the complete and utter destruction in front of me.

Floorboards are splintered and cracked. Dust and debris are *everywhere*. It's like a bomb went off, followed by a tornado, hurricane, and avalanche all at the same time. In other words—destruction in apocalyptic proportions. But the most astonishing part of it all is when I turn around to ask Guy what in the hell he did, I find him smiling like a five-year-old girl who has just been gifted an actual unicorn.

"I know demo isn't supposed to start until this weekend, but I couldn't help myself."

I open my mouth, but I can't bring myself to say anything. This is the reminder I needed. The teenage Guy is still in there.

"I made sure only to remove things we talked about. The sinks, some floor, countertops, part of the wall."

A record scratches in my head as everything around me freezes.

"Part of the what?" I ask, hoping I misheard.

Guy cocks his head like a confused puppy that can't understand how the ball I obviously threw a few seconds ago ended up back in my hand. I'm not sure whether I want to scream at him or curl up into a ball and cry myself to sleep. If Christiana finds out that I can't control my client—or worse, if Andrea finds out—I can kiss my chance at becoming a lead designer goodbye.

This *cannot* get out.

Guy shatters any hope that he misspoke as he leads me to the wall I knew in my gut he was talking about. Well, what's left of it. And as I stand there, staring at the rubble on the ground, I look up and find my worst fears realized.

"Get out!" I grab Guy's arm, dragging him back the way we came. He yelps as my nails dig into his forearm, but I don't care. We need to get out of here now.

When we're outside, I proceed to unleash a tongue lashing that will be talked about for years to come because what he did was one of the most dim-witted, idiotic things anyone could have possibly done.

"That's a load-bearing wall, Guy," I say, finally taking a breath. "What were you thinking? You aren't a contractor. You aren't handy. "

I level a harsh gaze at Guy. I've never felt so mad before. Guy's standing there like he doesn't know what to do, shifting uncomfortably every few seconds.

I reach into my purse and grab my cell phone. With my hands shaking from the adrenaline, it takes a few moments before I'm able to find my contractor's number.

I press my phone against my ear. "Hopefully, Ryder can fix this mess," I say as I turn my back to Guy and begin walking to the other side of the porch.

"Ryder? Ryder King?"

Guy doesn't deserve an answer. I ignore him and keep walking.

Ryder grew up with us—the youngest of the five that make up the King family. They're a wild bunch, but Ryder's the wildest. He and Guy were actually good friends at one point, but like almost everything in Guy's life, their relationship fell apart once his parents died.

It's ringing. Hopefully, he has his phone with him. Although he's a great contractor, he's difficult to reach because he hardly ever carries his cell phone, especially when he's out working on his family's ranch. And when I check the time, that's most likely what he's doing.

I'm about to hang up when he answers.

"Charleigh Holiday." Ryder's rough, raspy voice rings in my ear. "To what do I—"

"Ryder, I need you. Now." I cut in because there's no time. I turn on my heel and begin pacing.

"That's a little forward, Charleigh, but I like a woman who knows what—"

"Ryder, shut up. Just shut up and bring the crew to Guy Finch's place. I'm pretty sure he knocked down a load-bearing wall and I need you to get here before the second floor collapses."

"Seriously?"

"Hurry up. Bring *everything*. I have no idea what else he's done."

"Yes, ma'am. You got it."

Ryder hangs up and I sit down on the porch swing. What in the world was Guy thinking? Obviously, he wasn't, because no one in their right mind would do something like this. I don't pull people over or bust criminals because I'm. Not. A. Cop. But for some reason, Guy thought he was just as knowledgable as a licensed contractor.

I don't know what to do besides stare blankly in front of me. The view from the porch is usually calming, but it's not doing anything for me. I hardly even notice it with the tornadoes rampaging in my head. But the thing that's pissing me off more than what Guy did is what he's doing now. He's leaning against the porch railing stewing without any shred of remorse.

"In what world is tearing down a wall by yourself a good idea?"

He snorts. "What? I saved you time and money by doing that work. And it wasn't an entire wall. Only part of one."

I jump to my feet and charge over to him. "And you think that makes it any better? You think that saved me time and money?" I point behind me. "What you did was the complete opposite of that."

"It's not my fault you're uncommunicative. I waited for weeks to get an answer on whether I could help with the demo. And even longer to find out when it was happening."

"What, so it's my fault you took a sledgehammer to your house?"

He shrugs.

I laugh. The nerve of this man.

"I'm done."

I wave him off and head back to the porch swing.

Charleigh: Don't count on me for lunch

Guy leaves the porch and disappears around the house.

Marissa: ...so how'd everything go with Guy?
Charleigh: Imagine your worst day ever and then double that. Twice. That's how everything went
Marissa: ???
Charleigh: I'll fill you in later. I have so much to fix right now and Guy's being a baby about it all

Fifteen minutes later Ryder and his crew appear with their caravan of trucks and SUVs. Guy's still MIA but I could not care less right now. Ryder hops out of his truck, spots me, and waves. He's wearing his usual outfit: well-worn, light-blue Wranglers paired with boots—steel-toed, rather than cowboy—a red and black checked flannel.

Ryder saunters over to me, as much as a six-foot, two-hundred-something-pound man can saunter. "Howdy, Charleigh," Ryder says, flashing his megawatt smile.

I'm so mad that I can't even bring myself to speak. I just shake my head and motion to the open door. Ryder keeps his eyes trained on me for a few moments but then takes a few steps toward the door. The boards of the porch creak under each footfall. He places one arm on the doorframe and leans his torso inside.

"Sweet Jesus…" Ryder takes off his black cowboy hat and places it against his chest as he peers inside.

I close my eyes, hoping for good news but brace myself for the worst. I open my eyes and glance at Ryder's crew milling about outside their trucks, waiting for Ryder to fill them in and give them the go-ahead. There's five of them, each one burlier than the next.

A few moments later, Ryder plops himself down on the swing next to me. There's an easy, playful smile on Ryder's lips. It's the kind of smile that would probably make other women melt. But not me. Ryder knows it too, but that doesn't stop him from flirting with me at every opportunity. He's intrigued that I'm not head over heels for him like most every other woman in Whispering Pine.

"How is it?"

Ryder laughs. It's a deep rumble that I feel in my chest. He shakes his head, glancing at the ground as he collects himself. He tilts his head toward me, his smile still wide as ever. "We've got some work to do, that's for certain." He presses his palms against his thighs and stands up, whistling sharply and calling for his crew. "Grab the temporary supports and get to work. There's plenty of it for us in there."

Two men drag the supports from the back of a pickup while the rest of his crew bolts into action. They sprint up the steps and into the house, clearing the floor to make room for the temporary supports that will keep the house from completely falling apart.

We stand in the doorway, peering in at his workers. "How long do you think this will take?"

Ryder rubs the back of his neck as he looks at me. "Can't say for sure. It's a real mess. I can give you a call when I know for certain. But luckily most of the support structure for the wall is still in place, so there wasn't too much damage."

I sigh, watching as the temporary supports are raised into place. "I can't—I just—" I groan, rubbing my face.

Ryder wraps a rough palm around the nape of my neck. "It's going to be fine. I'll take care of everything."

I glance up at Ryder and smile briefly. "Thanks." I'm confident Ryder can fix this mess. I've worked with him on other projects, and he's always done work above and beyond expectations.

"Just promise me one thing."

"Anything."

He turns around and looks behind us. Guy's leaning against the hood of his truck, staring us down. It's a little unnerving that I didn't hear him come back.

"Don't let him back in here unless I'm here to supervise him."

"I can deal with that. In fact, I'll go ahead and break the news."

I can feel the anger building again. It's a warmth that's spreading from my chest, and the closer I get Guy, the warmer it gets. I'm not letting Guy off the hook for this. I'm not backing down. I'm taking control of this renovation whether Guy likes it or not.

CHAPTER FIFTEEN

Charleigh

SO THIS IS what a standoff feels like. My eyes are focused on Guy's and his on mine. Neither of our faces shows any form of emotion, but there's no need. Our annoyance with each other radiates from our bodies, the air shifting around us as though we've stepped inside a greenhouse. Neither of us has pulled the trigger yet, feeling each other out. I have a few choice words circulating in my mind, but I'm waiting for Guy to make the first move before I unleash hell on him.

"What?" Guy says.

An interesting choice given the circumstances.

"That's all you have to say?"

Guy keeps his arms folded across his chest as he pushes himself off his truck. He looms over me. "If you're looking for an apology, you're not going to get one. I saved you time with the amount of work I put in. What did you expect when you kept me in the dark for weeks?"

I square up to him. He might have nearly a foot on me, but I'm not backing down. "I expected you to be an adult, but now I realize how incredibly shortsighted I was."

He raises his eyebrows, looking at me as though he's thoroughly bored with me. If he wants to act like a brat, fine by me. I'll treat him like one.

"I'm telling you how things are going to be from here on out. First, you're not living here until the renovation is over. Both for your safety and my peace of mind."

"You worried about me, Charleigh?"

That one gets a dumbfounded stare, followed by a hearty chuckle. "Worried about you? I'm worried that the next time I drop by, the house will be in ruins and you'll be tap dancing over the rubble." I take a deep breath and then continue. "Second, you're going to hand over your keys to the house because from now until the renovation is done, this house belongs to me. You do not come near it unless I'm present. You don't so much as think about it without my permission."

"Can I dream about it?"

"No."

"Paint it?"

"Do you even paint?"

"No."

"Then why are you asking me?"

"I just want to make sure I'm following all of your rules."

What in the world did I do in my past life to deserve a client like Guy? Was I a professional puppy punter? Kitten kicker? Someone who took off their shoes and socks in an airplane? I hold in my sigh because I don't want to give him the satisfaction of knowing that he's successfully annoying me.

I reach out my hand, palm up. "Just hand them over." For a moment, I'm not sure he will. He seems to balk at my request, but finally, he obliges, taking the key from his key ring and placing it in my palm.

"Thank you. Now get your stuff and get out of my sight."

"My pleasure."

Guy brushes by me and heads up to the house, sharing an awkward greeting with Ryder before he disappears inside. Ryder gives me a shrug and turns around, following Guy inside to make sure he doesn't jackhammer the foundation or take a hatchet to a circuit breaker. You know, the kinds of things Guy seems to think are essential to keeping this project running on schedule.

I walk around the property to clear my head and remind myself why I'm doing this. This house has so much potential. It's the sort of project designers dream of, and I'm not going to let Guy ruin it for me. By the time I make my rounds and reach the front of the house again, Guy's truck is gone. And the house is still standing. Thank Jesus.

I head back inside to find Ryder and figure out the damage.

"Charleigh," Ryder booms when I walk inside. He's leaning against the stone wall that surrounds the fireplace, his black cowboy hat on the mantle next to him. He grabs his hat and heads toward me, crossing in between the steady stream of workers clearing debris with ease.

"So what's the damage?" I ask when he stops in front of me. That easy smile of his is on his lips again, and it reaches his eyes as he looks at me.

"It's not as bad as it looks, honestly. Certainly, there are a few snags here and there, but nothing major. Guy did a surprisingly good job. Saved us some time, to be honest."

"Seriously?"

Ryder holds his hat over his heart. "Seriously." There's a brief pause before he motions to me. "Follow me, and I'll give you a rundown." He sets his hat on his head, turns around, and starts walking.

We spend the next hour or so reviewing the damage and outlining a course of action. As much as I want to deny that Guy did a good job, I can't. Apart from taking down part of a load-bearing wall, Guy saved us time and money. But that doesn't change anything. He did it all without my approval.

"So," Ryder says as he leads me around a pile of rubble. "You and Guy. How's that working out?"

"Look around you," I say, twisting my body to take in the destruction at all angles. "Just swell."

"The immovable object meets the unstoppable force. I'm surprised there isn't more damage."

"Which one am I?" I ask.

"Whichever you want to be."

"I'll go with the unstoppable force. I like momentum. I hate standing still." I glance at my phone. "Speaking of which, it's time for me to go."

"I think we're done here for the day too. Everything else can wait until Monday."

I sigh. "Thanks for your help, Ryder."

He nods and then heads over to address his crew.

I walk to the porch and plop down on the swing, rocking myself as I watch Ryder and his crew pack up and begin to leave. Rather than focus on everything that went wrong today, I formulate a plan to make the rest of my day and weekend better.

I need to work out to get my endorphins going and improve my mood. Hell, I might even grab a scone on the way home too. That always does wonders for my mood.

Once everyone leaves, I take one last tour of the house. It's a mess, but it has so much potential. After taking my time looking around for more surprises, I head outside, lock up, and then head for my car. I'm in far less of a bad mood by the time I reach my car. There's nothing like a good plan to make things right in the world. Until that plan crumbles to pieces right before your eyes.

My car won't start, and no amount of coaxing or sweet talk will help it. I let my head fall against the wheel as I groan. Why? It's the only word that comes to mind as I sit inside my broken-down car. After a few moments of despair, I call Ryder, but he doesn't pick up. I call him a few more times, but again he doesn't answer.

Neither Jamie nor Marissa answer either. Great. Finally, I call my mom and she answers. "Oh, of course, sweetie. I'll be over shortly. And you can use my car until we get yours fixed. I don't use it much anyway."

"Thanks."

"But I have one request."

I sigh from exhaustion. "Anything."

"You're not running off as soon as you drop me off. You're going to have dinner with your mother."

"Sure. Fine. No problem." After a day like today, I could go for a home-cooked meal.

"Great! I'll see you in about half an hour."

We hang up and about twenty minutes later I see headlights appear on the road and then turn into the drive. There's an odd feeling in my stomach as I watch them creep slowly down the drive. That's not my mother's car. That's…

No.

I hop out of my car just as Guy pulls up next to me.

"I thought I told you not to come back here without me," I yell into his window.

He rolls it down. "I heard you needed a ride. Get in."

"I'm not getting in the same car as you."

"Fine. Stay here all night." He begins to roll up his window. When it's about halfway up I open the door and get in.

This is going to be the car ride from hell.

CHAPTER SIXTEEN

Guy

Why did I ever think working with Charleigh would be a good idea?

The ride back to Deanna's place is what I expect: awkward and tense. Every time I change the radio, she sighs. Each time I ask her a question, she closes her eyes. She might as well plug her ears and repeat "la la la" over and over while she's at it.

"This wasn't my idea. Deanna felt faint and couldn't come." The last thing I wanted to do is spend nearly half an hour in an enclosed space with Charleigh. "Fine. Don't respond."

I know she's pissed, but so am I. I need her to communicate with me. It's my house, and I have the right to know what's going on with it.

We spend the rest of the drive listening silently to the same terrible pop and rap songs every single radio station plays over and over. She damn near tucks and rolls out of the car before it comes to a complete stop. By the time I turn off the ignition, Charleigh's already in the house. When I reach the front steps I hear the tail end of her argument with Deanna.

"—force me into the same car? I've already dealt with enough today."

"Honey, I just couldn't make it."

"You seem fine now."

I can't help but agree with Charleigh. When I left, Deanna was sprawled out on the couch, acting as though she was on the verge of death. Right now, she's bouncing around the kitchen like a pinball.

"I am," Deanna says. "Now that my two favorite people in the world are here."

Charleigh groans. "I'll be in my room. Let me know when dinner's ready."

A few seconds and a handful of heavy footfalls later, Charleigh blows by me without a word. The door to her bedroom slams just as I enter the kitchen.

"So I see that dizzy spell of yours passed," I say to Deanna as I walk by her and resume the baking project I'd started before she sent me to pick up Charleigh.

"Oh yes," she says, ignoring my thinly veiled sarcasm. "They come and go like the wind. Strange, really. I should get it checked out."

"I think you should."

Deanna settles in her chair at the kitchen table and begins flipping through *Martha Stewart Living*. A few seconds later, she sets it down. "You know, Guy, this is nice, isn't it?"

I pause mid-air measuring out the vanilla. "What's nice?"

"Having everyone back in this house. Jamie and Marissa earlier today. Now you and Charleigh. It's been so lonely without Michael and—" She pauses for a few seconds. I look back and see her smiling at me. "I'm so glad to see you all together."

I take a deep breath, forcing the shitshow that is my relationship with Charleigh out of my head. "It's good to be back. For a few months, at least."

When Deanna heard that Charleigh forced me out of my house, she wouldn't hear of me going anywhere else but her spare bedroom. Which just so happens to be Charleigh's old room because the beds have been cleared out of every other room.

"Three or four months should do it," Deanna fires back. "You need to account for setbacks. There are always setbacks in renovations. You should know that by now from all of our research." Deanna hums to herself as she settles back into her magazine. "What are you making?"

"Chili for dinner. And then there are brownies."

"Brownies?" Deanna asks, eyeing me over her magazine.

"A peace offering for Charleigh." I clear my throat roughly. "I might've crossed a line."

Deanna turns back to her magazine. "Possibly."

I take the brownies out of the oven to cool a little early because I know Charleigh likes them slightly undercooked and gooey. Thirty minutes later, I cut out a couple of the center pieces and place them on a plate.

"Wish me luck," I say to Deanna as I grab the plate and head toward the stairs.

Deanna swipes a brownie off the plate as I pass by, takes a bite, and moans. "Oh, you won't need luck. These are divine."

I head upstairs, pausing in front of Charleigh's door for a moment. There's a little movement behind the door, but otherwise it's quiet. I knock on the door and the movement stops. I try the knob but it's locked.

"Charleigh," I mutter into the door. "I think we should talk." Silence. Each second that passes feels like a minute, stacking together into eternity. "If Charleigh's not there, could I speak with Emma then?"

A groan. Progress.

"I've got a brownie. Homemade. Triple chocolate. Still warm and super—"

The door cracks open. Charleigh reaches through the gap and snatches the brownie off the plate, shutting the door before I have the chance to finish. The lock clicks back into place.

"Gooey," I finish. Well, there goes my bargaining chocolate chip.

I knock on the door again. "You realize that we have to find a way to work together."

Charleigh says something but it sounds like gibberish with a mouthful of brownie. I sigh. This might be a little more difficult than I thought.

I lean back against the wall and slide down to the floor, one leg pulled toward my chest, the other flat against the floor. I look around, glancing down the empty hallway at the closed bedroom door in front of me, all of it triggering memories I thought I'd forgotten. I can't help but laugh when one in particular pops into my head.

"Do you remember the first time we met?"

Charleigh doesn't respond, but I don't mind. I know she's listening. She always eavesdropped when we were younger. It used to get her in trouble.

I drag a finger lazily along the smooth grain of the wood floor. "It was the first day of kindergarten. We were finger painting. You were sitting next to me. I was watching you out of the corner of my eye as you drew a dog. It was great. You were always great at drawing and creating.

"Anyway. Your finger painting reminded me of my dog Boomer, and I decided to add him into the whole green field and house I had going. I was so into it. Mixing all the colors just right. I remember I was so focused." I shake my head, a grin growing on my lips. "Do you remember what happened next, Charleigh?"

More silence.

"You turned to me and asked if it was a giraffe."

Charleigh lets out a muffled laugh.

"I was so mad that I grabbed your painting and ripped it to shreds. You stood there, glancing between me and the painting, your face growing redder by the second. I thought you were going to cry. I thought I was going to get in so much trouble. But then you grabbed a bottle of paint and dumped it all over my painting. You always had to one-up me. There was no chance of salvaging it after that."

I run a hand through my hair.

"That's when you started to bawl, and I joined you because I didn't want to get in trouble. We weren't allowed to sit next to each other for the rest of the year."

Even though we were separated, I always kept my eyes on Charleigh from across the room. She made me so frustrated, but I couldn't help myself. Even though I was so mad at her that day, I ended up fishing out the pieces of her painting from the trash and keeping them. I had no idea why I did it. It was like that with Charleigh, though. There was something about her that made me act in strange and irrational ways that only made sense a while later.

"I kept your shredded painting in a box underneath my bed. I'd look at it every now and again, wondering why I kept it. But then the night before our last day of kindergarten I took the box out and pieced the painting back together. I even spent hours making you a card. I gave them both to you the next day. You hugged me and then ran off, leaving me more than a little confused.

"I guess what I'm trying to say is that I know I've done some stupid things. And okay, fine, tearing down that wall is one of them. And I hope that someday you can find a way to forgive me. Or tolerate me. Or if not, that's fine. I just want to try to put all of this behind us and move forward because I want to work with you. It was wrong, and I won't do it again."

After a few moments of silence, I stand up.

"Would you like another brownie?"

I can hear her rustling around. After a few sighs, she responds in the affirmative.

"And a glass of milk." A brief hesitation. "Please."

I snort and make my way back down into the kitchen.

"How's it going up there? I think the chili's ready."

"It might be a few more minutes, but I think I'm whittling down her resolve with brownies."

Deanna laughs. "She's always had a sweet tooth."

"Like mother, like daughter," I say as Deanna chews her second brownie.

I pour a tall glass of milk, grab two more brownies because I know Charleigh well enough, and then head back upstairs. I knock on the door again. This time when she opens the door, I'm ready. I slide my foot in the gap and then hold onto the edge of the door.

"We're not doing this again. If you want these brownies—yes, plural—you have to let me in."

She groans but lets go of the door. I follow her into the bedroom, breathing in the light scent of coconut that trails behind her. She sits down on the bed, her body language as closed off as possible. Arms and legs crossed. Red lips pursed. Brow scrunched as she watches me set the plate of brownies on the bed beside her and the milk on the nightstand.

She waits until I step away before she reaches for a brownie and takes a bite.

"How do you like the brownies? I made them myself."

She spits out a mushy black clump onto the plate, dropping the brownie onto it seconds later. She claps her hands, wiping off any stray crumbs.

"That good, huh? I guess I should save them for someone else."

I reach over and grab the second brownie off the plate. She's trying hard not to show it, but I can see a little part of her die inside when I take the first bite and then another when I grab the glass of milk and down it to her shock and horror.

I wipe my mouth with the back of my hand and let out a satisfied sigh.

"I can't believe you just did that." She raises her hand. "Wait. I actually can, considering you tore down a load-bearing wall." She narrows her fiery gaze at me. "I don't think there's anything you can do that would surprise me."

"How about another apology?"

"That *would* be surprising."

"I mean it, Charleigh. I know we're not on the best terms, but I want to fix that."

Charleigh reaches out and grabs the brownie she'd taken a bite out of. A couple of bites and a few seconds later, she says, "You really made these?"

I nod. "I made dinner, too."

Her eyes light up for a brief moment. "Thank God, because I wasn't looking forward to my mother's cooking. You know she's forcing me to have dinner with her before she'll let me drive her car."

"That doesn't seem like a bad deal."

"So long as it doesn't involve her cooking."

I laugh. "Noted."

I focus my gaze on Charleigh. She's looking down at the plate, slowly chewing her brownie as she holds the rest in her hand. It's the first time since the night back at the bar that I've taken a hard look at her. There's a smattering of freckles across the bridge of her nose, extending toward her cheekbones on either side. She glances at me with her green eyes, which narrow for a brief moment before she looks away and takes another bite of her brownie.

"You're staying here now?" she asks, lightly kicking my backpack on the floor next to her.

"Yeah. Someone evicted me from my house."

"They probably had a pretty good reason."

A pause. "Probably."

"Why'd you do it, anyway?"

I shift uncomfortably. This is embarrassing. "Apart from being left in the dark about the renovation process…" I glance around the room, look down, and mumble, "*Fixer Upper.*"

"What was that last part?"

I mumble the same thing.

"I'm sorry, what?"

"I was watching *Fixer Upper* and I thought I could take on the wall." I shrug. "I mean Chip just makes it look so easy, and—"

I try to explain the rest, but I'm cut off by Charleigh's booming laughter. By the time she's done, she's on her hands and knees, red-cheeked and out of breath. I, on the other hand, want to crawl into a hole and die. Jesus.

"Laugh it up," I say when she finally stops.

She takes one look at me and says, "Don't mind if I—" Another fit of laughter. Finally, she rolls onto her back and looks up at me with the biggest smile on her face. I no longer care that she's laughing at my expense. I'm lost in that vibrant smile of hers—how it lights up her entire face.

"You done?"

She sucks in her bottom lip, fighting back her fourth wind, and nods. "Yup."

"Dinner's probably ready by now. Think you have enough air in those lungs to make it down the steps without passing out?"

"I make no promises."

"Come on," I say, extending a hand to help her up.

She looks at my hand, unsure whether to take it or not. Seconds seem to dilate into minutes with my hand outstretched, waiting for her to take it, wondering if she'll take it. Finally, she lets out a breath and takes my hand. My palm fills with an electric charge with her hand in mine, and for a moment, I forget what I'm doing as the current travels up my arm and into my core.

When I pull her up onto her feet, she wobbles for a moment and looks as though she's about to pass out. Without thinking, I pull her slowly into me, her arms folding against my body as she rests her head on my chest without a fight. In any other circumstance, she'd be out of my grasp in half a second, but something's changed, shifted between us. I felt it in her touch, and I see it in her eyes as she glances up at me.

"You okay?"

"A little light-headed," she says softly. She blinks a few times and then pulls away from me. A few awkward moments pass where neither of us moves or says a word, unsure about what just happened.

"You two alright up there?" Deanna calls up the stairs.

It's enough to jolt both of us awake.

"Be right down," I call back.

I grab Charleigh's arm as she passes by. "Let me take care of your car."

She shakes out of my grasp. "The same way you took care of that wall? I'll pass."

I shake my head. "I feel bad for taking down the wall. Call it my atonement. I have to head back to my house anyway and grab a few things."

"You won't be able to get in without the key, though." She whips it out of her pocket, dangling it in front of me for a few seconds before storing it again.

"You think I need a key to get into my house, Charleigh?"

She stares at me for a long moment. It's kind of adorable how confused she looks. "Um, yes?"

"Where there's a will…"

"There's no will and there's no way you're getting back in that house without me present."

"I'm just grabbing my clothes. That's it. I won't touch anything else."

I take a bite out of my own brownie, watching Charleigh as she mulls it over in her head. After a few moments, she reaches back into her pocket, takes out the key, and then holds it out for me.

I reach for it and she closes her hand around it. "Don't make me regret this."

I smile at her. "I won't, Char."

There's a flash of surprise in her face when I call her Char. I haven't called her it that in over a decade, back when we were still friends.

She drops the key into my palm.

"We'll see."

CHAPTER SEVENTEEN

Charleigh

OVER THE LAST week, Guy and I have reached a sort of equilibrium. Guy listens to me, pretends to be interested in crown molding, sconces, and all the other nitty-gritty, unsexy parts of this renovation. We've settled on nearly everything. And everything is moving smoothly. Too smoothly, to be honest.

Guy invited me to join him and Deanna for their HGTV marathon night, and I had to decline. We're beginning to get a little too comfortable, and I want to make sure we keep our relationship professional. I never see clients unless it's work related, and it shouldn't be any different between Guy and me.

Guy: You sure you don't want to join us for HGTV night? I'm making tacos.

Tacos? This is a new development. There's a short list of food, not including desserts, that I'd put my life on the line for. Tacos are at the top. So as much as it hurts me to decline…I have to.

> **Charleigh:** I can't. I'm really busy with work. Christiana's been on me since that whole wall debacle.
>
> **Guy:** Sorry about that. I didn't want to make trouble for you at work.
>
> **Guy:** I'll make extra in case you change your mind.
>
> **Charleigh:** Thanks. How'd the demo go this week?

After a little pleading, I'd talked Ryder into allowing Guy back into the house to help with the demo. It was my peace offering for Guy behaving himself.

"Oh. My. God."

I set my phone down and then glance around the office. I could definitely get in trouble for looking at that. After a few seconds, my phone buzzes again, reminding me that the picture Guy sent me is still waiting for me, and after a few moments of hesitation, I pick my phone back up and take a longer look at the picture.

I'm staring at a shirtless, sweaty selfie of Guy. His hair is a mess, tangles of brown splayed out in all directions matted with dirt and dust and debris. Cheeks tinged red. His smile is wider and more brilliant than any I've seen. And don't get me started on those abs. Jesus Christ, Adonis doesn't cover a fraction of it.

I don't even know what to respond, so I send back a thumbs-up. He doesn't respond, but that doesn't stop me from checking my phone nonstop for the next few hours. I'm not looking for a response. I can't keep my eyes off that damn selfie. What is he trying to do to me?

I've been trying to work, but every few seconds I catch myself looking at the picture that may or may not be the current wallpaper on my phone. Okay, maybe I'm staring at his photo for a longer than socially acceptable time. And maybe I've been imagining all sorts of things that those arms and lips could do to me. But it doesn't mean that I *like* Guy. I can admire the body of someone I don't like.

I start thinking about the night we kissed. I was so enamored with him back when I knew him as Sebastian. It seems like such a long time ago, but I still remember every detail about that night. The way his lips felt on mine. How he made me laugh. It was the most fun I had in a long time. I take out my phone and check the time, which then leads me to unlock it and check out the selfie again.

It's my last time. I swear. I can stop at any time. I just choose not to.

I'm in the midst of no more than a five-minute glance at Guy's selfie when Andrea interrupts me with a laugh. "Seriously, Charleigh?" Her arms are folded across her chest as she glares down at me and the shirtless picture displayed prominently on my phone.

"What? Nothing. It's—" I try to put my phone to sleep but I end up knocking it off the desk. Mission accomplished, I guess. I lean back in my chair, folding my hands across my lap as though to say, "No I wasn't looking at a shirtless picture of my client. How may I help you?"

"I knew something was up between you two."

"Who are we talking about, Andrea?"

I try to play it cool, keeping my face impassive even

though my brain is sending signals to the rest of my body to initiate sweating protocols.

"I saw that picture of Mr. Finch. I'm sure there's more of them too."

"I wish," I nearly say, but instead, thankfully, I tell her that I don't know what she's talking about and that there are some scheduling issues with the new cabinets that she needs to attend to. My wishful distraction. "I sent you an email about it." Unfortunately, she doesn't take the bait.

"You know the rules. And if you don't do something, then I will." Andrea turns on her heel.

"Okay, great, Andrea. We'll reconnect in a little bit," I say as she walks away, her hair bouncing against her shoulders with each step.

"Dear lord…" I mutter as I reach under my desk and grab my phone. As I'm hunched over under my desk, I notice a pair of Jimmy Choos enter my cubicle.

"I just saw Andrea leaving," Christiana says, "it's great to see you two working so well together."

I sit upright and then pump my arm in front of me. "We're definitely getting into the team spirit."

Christiana beams at me. "Good."

There's a brief pause, but it feels like much longer as I'm wondering why Christiana is inside my cubicle at 4:45 p.m. Thankfully, she puts me out of my misery a few seconds later.

"I need you to work on something for me. It's Priority One. And you should have plenty of time to finish it."

Two thoughts.

One, I didn't realize we were now using labels for priority levels. Because if I had known, I would've thrown in a few different options. "Priority Midnight" feels more important than Priority One.

Two, I can't list a single project that Christiana has given that has taken less than fifteen minutes to complete, which is exactly how much time is left until the end of the workday. I have a feeling this is going to be a long night. And once Christiana outlines everything she expects me to finish before the start of the workday tomorrow, I know it's going to be a long night.

Scratch that. It's going to be a horrible night.

"I'll get it finished, Christiana," I say, smiling as though I'm not dying on the inside right now.

"Thank you so much, Charleigh. I expect nothing less from you."

Kill. Me. Now.

"And other duties as assigned" has to be the worst phrase you can find in a job description. Because as I've learned, the only other duties assigned to me are the ones that Christiana doesn't want to do.

As I slink back into my chair and contemplate what foul thing I'd done in another life to deserve this, I get a text from Guy. And by text, I mean a photograph of him holding the most amazing platter of meat and veggies and taco fixings I'd ever seen. It's just hovering there next to his mouth, all delicious, and I can feel myself beginning to salivate. But to be honest, I'm not sure if it's because of the taco and fajita fixings.

Guy's usually mussed hair is styled back and parted to the right, not a strand out of place. His sharp jaw is covered in dark stubble. And that toothy, dimpled smile, paired with his form-fitting blue uniform, makes me want to…

GUY HATER

Stop. Thinking. Like. This.

Guy: No second thoughts?
Guy: I can hold off grilling some of the meat until you get here

No, no second thoughts—more like fifty.

I palm my forehead and sigh, still looking at the picture on my phone. I thought that the dumping ground—also known as my inbox—would cease to exist once Christiana gave me full control of a project this large, but I was mistaken. And now I'm second-guessing myself because it's hard enough to keep my head above water with all the work I have to do here. That plus a complete renovation on my shoulders? I'm not sure how I'll get through this.

I reach down and pull open the drawer stocked with chocolate and carbs. After deliberating between ramen noodles, a granola bar, or a packet of hot cocoa, I grab all of the above and place them on my desk. After snapping a picture of my dinner, I send the photo to Guy.

Charleigh: I've got it covered.
Guy: You're still at work?
Charleigh: Yup. Christiana dropped a huge assignment on me last minute, so I'll be here late.

I toss my phone on my desk, watch in slow motion as it skids across the surface, off the edge, and crashes onto the floor. The cracking sound, along with the deepening pit in my stomach, makes it clear that my phone is shattered.

Faaaaaantastic…

When I finally drag myself out of my chair to inspect the damage, I'm pleasantly surprised by the lack of a spiderweb cracking on the screen. And thank Jesus for that because I definitely do not have the budget for a screen replacement right now.

I should probably get off my hands and knees, but right now I'm lacking all motivation. Everyone else around me is leaving while I'm stuck here for the foreseeable future. I'm moments away from curling into a ball when Andrea passes by my cubicle, smirking at me.

Laugh it up…

Even though it's the last thing I want to do at this point, I stand up and then collapse into my chair as I gently place my phone back on my desk next to my depression dinner.

Christiana drops by for a brief moment, adding a few more things to my plate before she leaves, but at this point, it doesn't even matter anymore. I spend the next fifteen to twenty minutes mentally preparing for the marathon I'm about to begin, carbing up with a chocolate peanut butter granola bar.

I glance another half-dozen times at the picture Guy sent me, drooling at his rock hard—*ahem, the tacos*—before grabbing the hot chocolate mix and heading into the break room for hot water. It's a scientific fact that hot chocolate can get you through anything.

After the water finally boils, and after dumping as many miniature marshmallows as possible into my mug, I breathe in the delicious goodness and then promptly burn my tongue. And then my throat because I'm not a savage who lets hot chocolate go to waste.

I'm on my way back to my desk, feeling a little better from the chocolate and a little worse from the pain of scalding liquid sliding down my throat. As I turn the corner and trudge to my desk, careful not to spill the precious liquid from my mug, I catch a faint but familiar scent. My skin prickles as goosebumps spring up along my arms and neck. Guydar.

"Charleigh…" Guy's deep voice rumbles as he leans back in my chair, feet propped up on my desk. His arms are folded across his chest, biceps bulging beneath the sleeves of his blue uniform.

Yowza.

"Making yourself at home, I see." I walk toward him, shoving his feet off my desk as I maneuver around the desk. "What are you doing here?"

Guy doesn't say a word. He sits there, regarding me calmly while my body feels like it's in free-fall. Finally, he leans forward, the chair creaking as he reaches inside the large paper bag that's on my desk.

"It's Taco Tuesday," he says. Guy lays out two containers and a more cylindrical object wrapped in foil on the desk. "I wasn't about to let you eat this."

Guy grabs the cup of instant ramen from my desk and drops it into the trash can.

Normally, I'd fish that cup of MSG-laden noodles out of the trash, but right now Guy has rendered me both immobile and speechless. I'm floored by his thoughtfulness—that he'd drive all the way to my office to make sure I'm eating a proper meal.

I watch Guy as he opens up the containers. With each container he opens, a new delicious aroma swirls in the air.

Rice and black beans. Pico de gallo and guacamole. Strips of grilled chicken and ground beef. Fresh, homemade tortillas that are still steaming when Guy unwraps them from foil.

"Did you make this? Because I know my mom did *not*. I know you remember some of her creations. Tuna casserole surprise?"

Guy laughs. "The surprise was whether we'd be able to keep it down before we left the table."

I snort far too loudly, which makes Guy laugh, and by the time I'm done laughing, my stomach feels like I'd just finished a grueling abdominal workout.

I wipe the few tears beginning to roll down my cheeks as I try to regain my breath. To this day, I still don't know everything she put into it or how she was able to make the noodles both crunchy and mushy at the same time. It's a miracle I made it to adulthood eating my mother's cooking.

"Have a seat," Guy says, standing up. He reaches out and grabs my arm, guiding me to my chair, which is still warm from his body.

"And don't worry. I made everything here. Tortillas included. No surprise tonight," Guy says before leaving the cubicle.

I wouldn't say there wasn't a surprise tonight...

Guy returns a few moments later with another chair.

"Dig in," he says, handing me a paper plate and fork.

I take the fork and paper plate, but after that I just sit there, watching as Guy begins to add beans and rice and guacamole to his plate.

Not even fifteen minutes ago, I was dreading the night ahead of me. Christiana gave me more work in that brief interaction than she's given me all week. And to get it done before 9:00 a.m.? Impossible.

But somehow Guy has alleviated all my stress, calmed my nerves, and made me feel like all my second-guessing was silly. Of course I can get everything done.

"Not hungry?" Guy asks as he sits back in his chair.

"Oh, it's not that. I'm starving, actually. I'm…"

Blown away by your kindness. Your thoughtfulness. Words that I want to say but can't because I'm trying so hard not to move outside professional territory.

"Thank you," I say, offering a brief smile before grabbing a taco or three.

"It's no problem," Guy says in between bites.

When I finally dig into my first taco, there's a brief moment when I have no idea what's going on in my mouth. All my tastebuds are on fire—in a good way—and the only thing I can think to do is moan.

"That's what I like to hear," Guy says.

I nearly choke on the tortilla in my mouth as my mind races to a place it should not be going right now. Diverting the subject to safer spaces, I say, "My mom must love having you around now."

"Tasty?"

I take another bite. It's as though my tastebuds are blasting off into space, overwhelmed by the salty, savory flavors dancing all over my tongue. I nod.

"Good. But make sure you save room for dessert."

I stop chewing. "Deshburt?" I mumble through a mouth full of food.

Guy nods. "Brownies."

Again? YES!

I lunge toward the brown bag, but it's empty. I knew he was lying. I can always sniff out any and all baked goods from a mile away.

"Do you think I'd leave brownies out in the open when you're around?" He reaches behind his chair and pulls out a plastic bag filled with them. He dangles the bag in the air between us before setting them down on his lap. He pats them a couple of times. "I'll keep them here for safekeeping."

He thinks they're safe. How cute.

I swallow the remaining bits of food in my mouth.

"You have no idea what you got yourself into, Finch."

CHAPTER EIGHTEEN

Guy

CHARLEIGH'S RIGHT. I have no idea what I got myself into.

And this isn't about the brownies, either. Although she was right about them too. I left them unattended for a few minutes while I went to retrieve some paper towels at her request. That chocolate-filled grin told me all I needed to know. It was all a ploy to separate me from the baked goods.

This is about something else entirely—about what I feel is beginning to happen between us. Or maybe I'm just imagining it—I don't know. All I know is that I can't stop thinking about her. I look forward to any encounter we have, no matter how brief—whether she's mad at me or indifferent. It's about my inability to stop smiling each and every time I see her face.

I'm doing it now, watching Charleigh as her face alternates between grimaces and extreme focus. She's been working at this PowerPoint for the last few hours, going through various files and images and spreadsheets, creating a presentation from scratch.

I was supposed to be gone hours ago—drop the food off, make some small talk about the reno or Jamie's wedding, and leave—but once I saw Charleigh turn the corner, I knew I wasn't going anywhere.

"You know you don't have to stay here, right?" Charleigh says once again, as though it will make any difference this time around.

"I know," I say, watching her curl a finger around a strand of hair. She twists and tugs at it before pulling behind her ear. Patches of red appear along the pale skin of her neck. "But where else can I catch up on the newest trends in toilets, faucets, and shower heads?" I hold up the catalogue of bathroom accessories that I'd been glancing through.

Charleigh tries to pretend she's not amused, glaring at me, but when she turns back to the screen, she sucks in her lips, trying to prevent her smile from seeing the light of day.

It's been like this for most of the night: me finding weird stuff in the unending pile of catalogues on her desk; cracking jokes at said weird stuff; Charleigh pretending not to enjoy said jokes.

"Well, I'm almost done, anyway," she says.

I go back to browsing the catalogue. I scan the same page over and over again because my attention is still on Charleigh, even though my eyes are focused on a seven thousand dollar commode.

I want to know what's going on in that head of hers—what she's thinking, what she's feeling, and whether it's the same as me. But that's the rub. You can never really know what's going on in someone else's head.

Not long later, Charleigh finishes the presentation, emails it to Christiana, and then shuts down for the night. We make our way to the parking garage. Not a single car is left besides our two.

Charleigh opens the door to her car. She stands next to the driver's seat, her bottom lip tucked under her teeth as she's considering whether or not to get inside.

"Thanks for dinner," she says, her fingertips toying with the plastic casing on her door. "I really appreciate it."

She glances at me, but only holds my gaze for a brief moment.

"It was no problem."

Silence hangs in the air between us. Neither of us wanting to make the first move to leave. My stomach is tense and knotted as I stand next to her, clutching my keys in my hand. She looks at me with those watery green eyes, searching my face for something, but after a brief moment, she says, "I'll see you Thursday."

I suck in a deep breath. "Thursday," I say, closing the door to her car as she sits inside. Before I have the chance to open my car door, I hear a familiar clicking sound of a car not able to start.

Again?

I'd jumped Charleigh's car earlier in the week, so it shouldn't have died this quickly unless the battery needs to be replaced entirely. I turn around and walk back to the side of her car and tap on the glass. It goes on for a few seconds more before Charleigh opens the door.

"Do you have any jumper cables?" she asks, peering up at me.

I shake my head. "I don't. And I don't think jumper cables will really help. Your battery is probably fried."

She lets her head fall against the horn, sounding loud and clear for a few seconds before it slowly winds down too, like a balloon slowly being drained of air.

"Come on," I say, offering my hand. "I'll give you a ride home. We can jump it tomorrow, but I think we might have to replace the battery."

Charleigh slowly raises her head, looks at me, and then at my hand. She takes it, and I pull her to her feet. Her body brushes up against mine as she stands, and I have a momentary loss of breath as I inhale in her sweet scent.

I guide her into the front seat, shut the door, and then catch my breath as I walk to the other side.

Charleigh's in a solemn mood, eyes hooded as she fidgets with her hands.

"How am I going to get to work tomorrow?"

"I'll drive you," I say, starting my car.

She turns to me. "You really don't have to. You've already done so much, and I can't just have you drop everything for me."

"It's fine, really. I have a late shift tomorrow. I'm helping Ryder finish up the last of the demo tomorrow morning. He doesn't need me anyway. Besides, he'd probably prefer me not to be there."

She bites her bottom lip, considering it for a moment, but then relents. "Okay."

Her voice is low, and it's clear from her tone that she's beyond exhausted with today, so I reverse out of the spot and head for the exit.

She guides me to her apartment, a fifteen-minute drive that we spend in relative silence. When we make it to her apartment, I barely resist the urge to lock the doors and speed off to her mom's house. The apartment complex is dilapidated and downright scary.

"This is it?" is all I manage, but the concern doesn't seem to register with Charleigh.

"Yes," she says. "Can you pick me up at eight tomorrow morning?"

The expression on Charleigh's face hits me square in the gut because I've been there. Days when the universe seems to be at war with you. Murphy's Law.

"I'll be here," I say, placing my hand on hers instinctively. It's soft and cold, but she doesn't move it from under mine. "I'll bring donuts."

She tilts her head back up and looks at me. The exhaustion I'd seen in them earlier seems to lift. "Thanks." There's a hint of a smile on her lips, but she leaves before I can see the full thing.

I watch her as she disappears inside her apartment.

CHAPTER NINETEEN

Charleigh

I CAN SMELL the donuts before I hear Guy's knock on my door.

"Just a minute!" I call out as I put on the finishing touches to my makeup.

After the day I had yesterday, it's amazing that I woke up before noon, let alone look somewhat presentable. It's amazing what the power of makeup and the prospect of donuts in the morning can do for me. Caffeine? No, thank you. Sugar's my drug of choice.

Guy hasn't stopped knocking. The rap, rap, rap is grating on my nerves slightly, but I remind myself of what should be waiting right behind that door.

Thump, thump, thump.

"I'M COMING!"

The knocking stops, and I swear I hear a snicker from the other side of the door. Unfortunately, the silence is momentary. A few seconds later Guy unleashes a rapid-fire pounding that I'm sure, given enough time, would knock the door down. I'm sure Eleanor, if not the rest of the apartment complex, is outside trying to figure out why someone's jackhammering this early in the morning.

I groan as I dart out of the bathroom, snatching my shoes off the floor as I head into the living room. I hop around on one foot as I slip one shoe on and then repeat the same process with the other foot, all the while Guy is pounding away. He's got quite the stamina.

I wonder just how much stamina... the voice I've been trying to quiet says.

After donning my coat, grabbing my purse, and with Guy's incessant knocking beginning to bore a hole in my skull, I'm seeing red.

"Look, Guy," I begin before the door's even open. "I swear if you don't stop knocking this instant, I'm going to—"

Before I have the chance to finish, Guy pops a chocolate-frosted donut into my mouth.

I can't speak, which may or may not be an effect of having a donut shoved into my mouth. The look on Guy's face tells me that he has no idea whether to laugh or run for his life. After biting the donut, the sweetness dulling my nerves, he should consider himself lucky. And I tell him as much.

"If there weren't sprinkles on this..." I let the threat hang in the air as I munch on my donut, eyeing his annoyingly handsome smile.

As I turn around to lock the door to my apartment, I can't help but give him a quick once-over: well-worn jeans and boots, tan jacket with a red flannel lining. His semi-styled bedhead seems to say "I'm wild but not a complete animal." And his scent… Mmm…

"I wouldn't expect any less, Charleigh."

The lock clicks into place and we head out, Eleanor eyeing both of us from her doorway, bathrobe and all.

I'm completely ignoring the fact that his scent is having a dizzying effect on me, making my mind spin in circles. But by trying to ignore him, I completely miss the stairwell and continue walking down the hallway that leads to other apartments.

"Uh, Charleigh?" Guy calls out to me. "This way."

I circle back around. "I usually use the back stairwell," I say, trying to save face, even though it's clearly out of our way because we have to retrace our steps one level down.

Nerves flood my stomach as Guy places his hand on my back and guides me to the right of the stairwell. "I parked over here."

We walk in silence to his car, his hand still flush against my back, my teeth slowly working on the donut.

"Thanks for driving me to work," I say when we finally reach his car and get in.

Guy smiles, starts the car, and begins to pull out of his spot. "Toss me one of those apple fritters."

I oblige, but not before I rip off a part of it and pop it into my mouth. His jaw drops but I just shrug.

"Finder's fee."

Guy shakes his head, biting into the fritter as we head back to the office to fix my car.

"You'll pay for that."

I tilt my head toward him. "Game on."

CHAPTER TWENTY

Guy

"TRY IT NOW."

Charleigh pops her head back into the driver's side and twists the ignition. The engine clicks for a second but then starts up. She squeals with delight, hopping back out of the car, running around to the front—still squealing—and wrapping me up in a hug.

"Thankyouthankyouthankyou!"

I cup the back of her head, feeling her soft hair as she nuzzles my shoulder. She smells so good. The moment only lasts for a short time. She pulls away and then dusts herself off as she clears her throat. I remove all the cables and then shut the hood. Hopefully, the charge lasts for more than a week this time.

Before I have the chance to stop Charleigh, she hops back inside the car and turns it off. I cringe, closing my eyes as I bite down on my lip.

"What's wrong?"

"We're more than likely going to have to jump it again."

"Wait, what?"

"Usually, you need to keep the engine running for at least fifteen minutes or else the charge won't hold."

Charleigh hops back into the car and lets out a groan when the car refuses to start again. She pops the hood and then we begin the entire process over again. It only takes a few minutes from start to finish, but I can feel Charleigh's annoyance with the situation in the air between us.

"Why don't we get out of here for a little while?" I ask her when the car starts back up again.

"I have work."

"It could be work-related."

Her eyes narrow as she studies me.

"You wanted me to go furniture shopping with you. We're already in Boulder, so why not just drop by those stores you told me about. West Oak and Pottery Mill."

"West Elm and Pottery Barn.

"Exactly."

"I have a one-on-one meeting with Christiana about the presentation I made last night."

"It shouldn't take very long, right? Move it up, or reschedule for later today. Tell her you've got a client emergency."

I've always liked the way Charleigh looks when she's considering something. Her eyes get a distant look to them. Her lips press together into a thin line as her tongue peeks out of the corner of her mouth. And with a light shade of red on those lips, it has me thinking thoughts I shouldn't be thinking right now.

Her tongue stops moving and her eyes refocus on mine. "Okay," she says with a nod.

"Okay."

"I'll be right back."

Charleigh turns around, her heels clicking against the concrete floor as she heads toward the door at the end of the parking garage. Hips swaying, hair bouncing—it's hard not to gape, but I force myself to turn away and begin putting away the jumper cables.

It doesn't stop the thoughts, though. I can't get her out of my head. Everything about Charleigh is intoxicating and addictive. Her laugh. Her groans. The smattering of freckles along the bridge of her nose.

Even though it's been over a month since we kissed that night in The Lookout, I can still feel her lips on mine—their softness, the way they taste. I want more, but I'm not sure Charleigh does. There are moments when she's at ease with me. But that's all they are: moments. Fleeting.

"Guuuuuuuuuyyyyyeeeeeeyyyyyyy!"

Oh, sweet Jesus.

I don't even have to turn around. I could recognize Andrea's voice anywhere. I shut the trunk to my car as she comes strutting toward me, waving one arm as her oversized purse dangles precariously in the other. It's so large that I'm surprised she doesn't topple over. Maybe if there was a strong enough breeze. She's hardly fifteen feet away before her cloying perfume hits my nose.

"Hey, Andrea."

"Guy!" she repeats, keeping her mouth wide open as she approaches. "What are you doing here?"

Her entire body appears to vibrate as she talks.

I nod at Charleigh's car. "Charleigh's battery died."

She reaches out and places her hand on my arm. "And you came all the way out here? That's so sweet!" Her tone shifts to saccharine, but I can sense a tinge of annoyance under it. "We really should walk through your house again, Guy. I was looking over some of the elements of Charleigh's plans, and I think she missed out on some great opportunities to make your place really pop."

I don't want my place to "pop," especially if that pop means a pink and purple accent wall with glitter highlights— the kind of design I imagine is Andrea's specialty.

"Don't worry about it," I say, folding my arms across my chest, her hand falling away in the process. "Charleigh and I worked on the plan together, and I'm confident in it."

"Oh."

Andrea speechless. Imagine that.

I hear Charleigh's rapid gait behind me, and there's a slight twitch in one of Andrea's eyelids as she notices Charleigh too. The hint of her scowl is replaced with a wide smile as she turns her attention back on me. She leans in and places her arm on mine once again.

"Well, there's always room for improvement," she whispers into my ear. She pauses for a moment, her breaths still warm on my skin. The sound of Charleigh's heels against the pavement is growing louder and then stops as she stands behind us.

"Good morning, *Charleigh*." The shrill, saccharine, and not to mention faux-friendly tone reverberates in the concrete garage.

"Morning, Andrea," Charleigh replies bluntly.

Charleigh's face is impassive, but her fidgeting hands in front of her belie her otherwise calm exterior.

"It's so nice that Guy was able to come all this way to help you out."

"Yup."

I choke on a laugh at Charleigh's response. Andrea snorts, clearly wanting to escalate whatever it is that's going on between the two of them. But with me here, she decides against it.

"You two have fun together," she says, brushing by both of us.

"So when's the boxing match between you two?"

Charleigh snorts. "Is it that obvious?"

"No more obvious than a sledgehammer to the hand."

Charleigh makes a face at me. "I'm not sure I know what the means, but okay."

"Don't worry about it."

"We should probably drive separately. I don't want us to get stranded if my car dies."

"Probably a good idea. Where are we headed to first? The Elm Barn?"

Charleigh laughs. "The Elm Barn? In what world does that even make sense?" She shakes her head and I get to see that smile again. "I'll meet you at West Elm. I need to make a quick detour first."

"Alright, just remember to keep your car running."

She presses her lips together and then blows out air, making a flapping noise.

"Just making sure," I say before hopping into my truck.

Ten minutes later I get a text from her. She turned off her car when she parked in front of Common Grounds, and go figure, the battery died again. I'm not exactly sure why she needed to pick up scones after having eaten at least four donuts. But then I remember who I'm dealing with.

She's something else.

CHARLEIGH

I've read that the first step of recovering from an addiction is admitting that you have one. I don't. I could quit sugar anytime, but why in the world would I do that? Life without sugar is like living in a world without color. So I'll deal with the sideways looks Guy gives me when I go out of my way to pick up three decadent chocolate chip scones. He's getting one out of it, which if anything, shows how much I care about his kind gestures. I *never* share sweets with anyone.

Can I get some of those M&Ms, Charleigh?

Make a grab for them, and you'll lose a finger or two.

I'm not sure when my sweet tooth first appeared, but I know it's a part of me that will never go away. Not without a fight to the death, at least. Or a diabetes diagnosis. One of the two. But hey, I work out like a fiend, so it all evens out, right? Right?

After jumping my car battery for the millionth time, we finally head out for our day of furniture shopping. I'm amped up, not only because of the sugar rushing through my bloodstream, but this part of my job is my favorite. And I sort of enjoy spending time with Guy now. He's funny (kinda), sweet (kinda), and extremely easy on the eyes (oh boy…).

I'm not sure what happened in the intervening years between him leaving and returning, but it's obvious that he picked up a few weights. Repeatedly. His arms are a thing of beauty, both hard and soft at the same time, two opposites in conflict with each other. Sort of like my mind when I'm around him.

I don't know how I feel about him, but I do know that I can't get him out of my head.

⌒

"How about this, Charleigh? I think it would be a great conversation piece."

Oh. My God.

For the past fifteen minutes, Guy has picked up the most random objects he could possibly find and asked me whether or not they'd be good conversation pieces. He knows the answer: no. But he just learned the term, and he's on a mission to annoy me by using it *ad nauseam*.

But I'm not going to let it get to me because overall this day has been wonderful. I've browsed West Elm and Pottery Barn and World Market. I've hit up every single thrift store and flea market in between. I'm pretty sure that there isn't a single piece of furniture left in Boulder that I haven't laid eyes on. I've carefully noted each one—price, location, and placement for Guy's house—in my notebook for when we're further along in the project, and I'm one hundred percent certain that the pieces will have a home.

So now that I think about it, I'm surprised that Guy has lasted this long. I'm pretty sure any other man would've tucked and rolled out of their car long ago.

"I think we should have a conversation about never talking about conversation pieces ever again."

I finally drag my attention away from the steamer trunk in front of me and glance at what Guy's brought me this time. It's an octopus. It's purple and gold and very, very shiny. There are gemstone embellishments embedded along each tentacle—I think it's supposed to be a lamp, but I have no idea.

"*What* is that?"

"See? It's already working."

I glare at Guy, but it's not enough to remove that annoying smirk from his face.

"Do you think you could find a place for it?"

"Sure. We could test out how it fits in the new pull-out trash bin I'm going to install in the kitchen. Or maybe use it for fuel in the fire pit."

Guy puts on a mask of mock surprise. "You wouldn't do that to Octavian."

"You've named it already?"

It's clear that we've been at it this for far too long and Guy is on the verge of losing his mind. Or maybe I'm losing my mind, hallucinating this entire encounter.

"And what kind of name is Octavian anyway?"

Guy pets the bulbous head of the octopus. "Only the best kind."

Unfortunately, I'm unable to persuade Guy not to buy Octavian. I hang around the front of the store, browsing the random knickknacks and candy, pretending not to know Guy as he waits in line to purchase his newfound friend. I make the mistake of glancing up as Guy grabs one of the tentacles and waves at me.

GUY HATER

Dear lord...

"This will be perfect on your nightstand," Guy says as he approaches me.

I turn around and begin heading out of the store. "That thing is not going into my room."

Guy shushes me. "He's sensitive."

"Yeah, I'm pretty sure that you need to get checked out. You've got a screw or ten loose."

"It could happen to anyone who spends this much time with you." Guy ruffles my hair, leaving a tingling sensation across my skull, which then spreads down my neck and spine. I shake it off as we head to our cars.

"I had a good time today, Charleigh."

There's an easy smile on Guy's lips. That dimple on his left cheek is on full display, and for a moment, I remember that kiss we had. It feels so long ago, yet I can still remember every detail as though it's been imprinted on my memory.

"It wasn't so bad. It wasn't so good, either."

I can't let him know how much fun I had. Even with the whole Octavian business. It's kinda cute. A little scary but kinda cute.

"What's the plan now?"

"Ryder's supposed to be finishing the demo today. They'll be doing the cleanup for a few days, and then after that, it's just a matter of getting everything built, installed, and inspected. Everything's ordered and scheduled. It's just a matter of hoping everything arrives in time and in one piece."

"Anything I can do?"

"Not really," I say as I hop into Franny.

Guy rests his forearm across the top of the doorframe and leans in. His scent seems even more intoxicating now than it did earlier in the day. Thankfully, I'm sitting down. "Don't be a stranger. Deanna would love for you to come over one of these nights."

"I'll try. Work is going to be hectic. These next few weeks especially."

Guy smiles at me one more time and then pushes away from the car. I watch him walk away in the rearview mirror and disappear into his truck.

I grab my phone out of my purse and find a text from Marissa.

Marissa: How was shopping with Guy?
Charleigh: We need to talk.
Charleigh: Now.

CHAPTER TWENTY-ONE

Guy

COMMON GROUNDS IS packed by the time I arrive. The smell of coffee is so strong that I'm pretty sure I'm getting a caffeine buzz from breathing. I edge by a mother downing a double shot of espresso, her daughter in tow behind her, as I make my way to the counter.

Jamie waves at me from our usual spot in the back corner. I nod from the line and then glance at the display of pastries. I don't usually have a sweet tooth, but what can I say? The scones look good. I think Charleigh might be rubbing off on me.

I grab my coffee and chocolate scones—yes, two of them—and head for our table.

"Scones?" Jamie raises his eyebrows. "This is new." He reaches out to snag one, but I move it just out of his reach as I sit down.

"That's cute. You think one of them is for you."

He laughs. "You're just like Charleigh."

I raise a brow. "Because we both like scones? Not exactly a groundbreaking similarity."

He drinks his coffee, his eyes focusing on me from over the rim. "Okay," he says, setting the mug down. "Point taken."

I tear off a piece of the pastry and pop it into my mouth.

"How's it going between you two now? You've still got your head attached, so that seems like a good sign."

I take a sip of coffee. With my tastebuds primed for sugar, it tastes more bitter than usual. Maybe I should've cut it with some cream. "It's been going fine."

"Just fine?"

"Yep."

I take another piece of scone. Damn. These things are good. I don't know where these things have been my entire life, but I understand Charleigh's love for them. I wash it down with another drink of coffee, sigh, and then set the mug down.

"I heard something different from Marissa."

"What are you talking about?"

What is Marissa talking about? And what is Charleigh telling her? Are thing's *not fine* between us and I just don't know it? Shit. I thought we were on steady ground. Over the last few weeks of the renovation, things have been professional and friendly, both of us completely capable of interacting together without ripping each other's head off. Maybe I've had it all wrong.

"Nothing. I just heard a different story."

"A story that you seem reluctant to tell."

"It's not mine to tell."

"But it's yours to bring up?"

Jamie laughs. "Point taken. I'll say this." He leans forward, his shoulders hunched as he slides his forearms against the table. "Things seem to be better than you're leading me to believe."

"That's news to me."

I mean it, too, because Charleigh's the master of hiding her feelings from me. Unless they're on the opposite end of the spectrum, then it's right there in my face. Thankfully, there hasn't been another blowup like the one I endured for the wall mishap.

"Alright. I won't push. You're holding your cards to your chest. I get it."

I shake my head. "I'm not holding any cards to my chest because I don't have any. Seriously. I don't know what Marissa told you, but from what I can tell, things are just fine between Charleigh and me. Nothing more, nothing less."

Jamie shrugs and then moves on to a different topic of conversation. "So how's the renovation going anyway? Everything still on schedule?"

I chew on my scone while I chew on the previous topic: Charleigh. I want to know what she talked about with Marissa. What am I missing? I swallow it, along with my scone. I'll deal with it later.

"Yup. Ahead of schedule, actually."

I take out my phone and show him all the progress pictures I've taken since the start, including the ones of me tearing down the load-bearing wall. He's in tears when I tell him my reasoning behind tearing it down.

"Come on. I don't watch *COPS* and think I could be a cop. What in the world—"

I raise my hand to stop him. "I've already heard it all from your sister. I don't need to hear it from you."

Jamie's cheeks are bright red, puffed up as he tries hard not to laugh again. Thankfully, he takes a sip of his coffee and settles down, and I continue showing him the pictures.

"It's incredible how fast they're moving," Jamie says as I show him the progress they've made on the kitchen and a couple of the bathrooms.

"Ryder's got quite the team," I say.

"Oh yeah? I didn't realize Ryder was working on the project."

"Yup. Apparently, he's Charleigh's go-to contractor." I take a sip.

"I bet."

There's something about Jamie's tone that's annoying, and that grin on his lips tells me he knows it. "You know he's going to be at the joint bachelor-bachelorette party, right?"

"Am I supposed to care? Why are you bringing it up?"

Jamie leans back in his chair. "No reason. Just thought you might want to know."

"When is the party again? A few weeks, right?"

"You realize you're my best man, right?"

"Yeah, things have been a little hectic lately."

And thank God Marissa's sorority sisters are in charge of planning the party instead of me.

"Nothing's as hectic as planning a wedding."

"You're right. I'm sorry."

"No worries. Just messing with you."

He fills me in on all the wedding planning, from the color scheme to table arrangements and everything else in between. By the time he finishes, I've been done with my coffee for ten minutes.

He checks his watch. "Shit. I'm late. You ready to head out?"

"Yup." I wrap the second scone in a napkin.

"I knew you wouldn't finish it." Jamie reaches out to me, palm up. "Hand it over, Finch."

I shake my head. "It's not for you."

If Jamie raised his eyebrows any quicker, they'd have shot right off his face.

"Well, isn't that *cute.*"

CHARLEIGH

"Excellent work, Charleigh."

Excellent?

I'm not used to hearing that word come from Christiana's mouth. Good, fine, okay—sure—but excellent? I'll take it.

We're having our weekly one-on-one meeting. Usually, by this point, there's a sinking feeling in my gut, a general sense of dread or despair because my work has just been put under a microscope and dissected bit by bit. Mistakes laid bare. More work added to the pile. But this is different. *Excellent?* I could get used to this.

I've just finished showing Christiana the progress pictures of Guy's house, and she loves them. Well, she thinks they're *excellent* which is close enough because I don't think Christiana is capable of loving anything.

Maybe her cats. Yeah, probably her cats. Angelica (Angel) and Penelope (Penny). Two fluffy white cats featured in EVERY. SINGLE. FRAME. In her office.

"Ryder should finish installing the new island today, along with the rest of the cabinets."

"Should be?" Christiana looks at me over her glasses.

"Will be," I correct myself.

Christiana removes her glasses and then leans back in her chair. "Good."

She stares at me for a few brief but unsettling moments without speaking. "You know, I was worried about you at the head of this project."

There it is. The shoe that I've been waiting to drop for the entire meeting. And it does drop, right on my gut.

"But you've impressed me, Charleigh. Certainly, you've had some difficulties, but you've weathered them and moved on."

Okay. This wasn't where I thought this was going, but okay. I can work with this.

"I look forward to seeing the end result."

She pushes her glasses up the bridge of her nose, picks up a stack of papers, and then begins leafing through them. This is usually how our meetings end. Christiana moves on to something else, while I'm just sitting here, hanging around as I wonder if the meeting is over or if she'll remember something as I'm leaving.

"Thanks," I say, awkwardly scooting out of my chair.

Christiana hums in response, and I head for the door. As I leave Christiana's office, the air feels fresher, the sky seems bluer, and Andrea even seems less bitchy. She waves at me, smiling as I pass by. Everything is right in the world, and I couldn't be happier.

Or at least I thought I couldn't be any happier. There's a chocolate scone on my desk. Jackpot. I pick it up and take a huge bite, savoring the delicious goodness.

I pick up my phone and find a message from Guy.

Guy: Sorry I couldn't stay. Thought you might like a pick-me-up.

Charleigh: You did this?

Guy: If by this you mean hand deliver a delicious scone, then yes.

Guy: I did this.

Charleigh: You can't.

Charleigh: You're my client. People will start to talk…

Guy: About scones?

Charleigh: I'm serious. I don't want to be known as the girl who sleeps with a guy to get a client.

Guy: I think I'd remember something like that.

Guy: I guess I could use a refresher.

As much as I'd like that, and as much as I've *dreamed* about it these past few weeks, it can't happen.

Charleigh: I know we're not but they don't know that. Andrea sure seems to think it.

Charleigh: Rumors are more contagious than truth, especially in an office of women.

Guy: What do you propose?

Charleigh: I don't know. Can we talk about it at the house later today?

We're meeting with Ryder later today to get an update on his progress. It's been a week since I've been to the house last and I'm excited to see what's changed since then.

> **Guy:** Sure, but only if it's at Deanna's house.
>
> **Charleigh:** Why can't we talk after we see the progress on your house?
>
> **Guy:** I can't make it. I'm swamped here and won't be able to make it out there.
>
> **Charleigh:** I dunno… It's kind of a drive out there.
>
> **Guy:** HGTV
>
> **Guy:** Fajitas
>
> **Guy:** …and dessert.
>
> **Guy:** What more could you ask for on a Thursday night?

A few things pop into my mind in no particular order, but texting them to Guy would be counterproductive to my whole "let's cut out anything that might be misinterpreted by my co-workers as inappropriate" conversation I'm trying to have with him.

> **Charleigh:** What kind of dessert?
>
> **Guy:** You'll have to come over and find out.
>
> **Charleigh:** I'll think about it…
>
> **Charleigh:** And don't think you can weasel out on our conversation. We're going to talk about it.
>
> **Guy:** See you tonight.
>
> **Charleigh:** Maybe.

The rest of my day drags on at a snail's pace. I can't concentrate on anything for more than a few minutes before my thoughts inevitably drift back to Guy. I don't know what I'm going to say to him tonight. Every time I think about it my stomach turns to knots because I feel that no matter what I say, I'm going to mess everything up between us. Whatever that is.

I like how things have been going between us, but at the same time, there's a part of me that's shooting flares into the sky, warning me that something bad is just on the horizon. I need to pump the brakes for a little while so I can figure it all out.

I throw myself into work. I double, triple, and quadruple check and the budgetary items, delivery dates, and send off a slew of emails. By the time I look up, everyone in the office is gone. I lean back in my chair and my back cracks in ways it shouldn't.

Yikes. I need to do more yoga. Or do it at all.

I check the time and immediately fall backward out of my chair and crash hard against the floor.

"Shit!"

I'm late for my meeting with Ryder.

CHAPTER TWENTY-TWO

Charleigh

"GLAD YOU COULD fit me in." Ryder has a crooked half smile on his face as he watches me approach the house. There's a thick layer of construction dust covering his blue jeans, which makes them look a shade lighter than usual. The sleeves of his green-checked shirt are cuffed below his elbows and covered in the same dust. His hair is disheveled and matted, but Ryder is nothing if not calm, cool, and collected.

"Sorry," I say, jogging up the steps. "It's been real—" I nearly topple over as my toe clips the top step, but I catch myself, barely preventing a face plant. I expel a harsh breath, vibrating my lips, dust myself off, and have another go at my explanation. "It's been hectic today."

Ryder regards me for a few moments, leaning against the wall next to the door. It's open, but even if it wasn't I'd still be able to hear the chaos going on inside. After a few moments, he pushes off from the doorway. "Seems to be contagious. Guy's going to be late as well."

"Actually, he's not going to make it. Police business or something."

Ryder shrugs. "Well, let's get started then."

Before I have the chance to walk inside, Ryder hands me a mask. "There's construction dust everywhere."

"I'll be fine," I say, pushing it away, but Ryder insists nonverbally by blocking my entrance to the house and offering me the mask once again, his expression making it clear that I'm not to enter without it.

"Why aren't you wearing one?"

He shrugs. "I breathe this stuff in all the time. I'm used to it. You'll have a coughing fit without it."

I eye the mask as he shakes it and then snatch it out of his hand. "Fine, but it's just going to make it more…" the elastic snaps behind my head as I put the mask on, "diffacuh tahs beak."

"What was that?"

I pull the mask down. "I said it will be difficult to speak."

Ryder reaches for the mask and places it back over my mouth. "That's unfortunate," he drawls before turning around and heading inside, starting in without another thought.

I groan but he doesn't notice because of my muzzle/mask. He's lucky that he's good at his job. I follow him inside, clouds of dust puffing into in the air with every footfall. Hammers are hammering, drills are drilling, and everybody not working on something is moving purposefully through the nearly bare-bones interior.

"We're making progress," Ryder says as we move through the great room.

"Any issues I need to be aware of?"

Ryder mouths "I can't hear you" as he points to his ear and continues to tell me about the progress he's made. I rip off the mask and fling it to the floor. Sure, it's dusty, but I'm not about to spend the next half hour or so incapable of speaking. "Are there any issues I need to be aware of?"

Ryder looks back at me, brows raised for a moment before they fall back down into his usual relaxed expression. "You just won me five bucks."

"Wha...?"

"Marco!" Ryder yells. A few moments later, a man in well-worn clothes and matted black hair struts over to Ryder.

"Fifteen seconds," Ryder says.

Marco looks at me, laughs, and then reaches into his back pocket and hands Ryder a five-dollar bill.

"You guys seriously bet how long it would take for me to take off the mask?"

Ryder shrugs. "Don't take it personally, Charleigh. We take bets on just about everything. Keeps things interesting."

I sigh. "Whatever, can I have the tour now?"

"Certainly, madame." Ryder bows and extends his arm to me. "This way, if you would."

I roll my eyes and grab on to his forearm. "Such a gentleman. So any issues?" I repeat, trying to get this train back on the track.

"Nothing we haven't already handled."

All of the debris that covered much of the floor during my last visit is gone. The stone face of the fireplace is gone and being prepped for the newer stone that will rise all the way up to the ceiling.

"It might look like a mess now, but in a few weeks, a few days really, it will look completely different."

I nod, not doubting Ryder at all.

"Everything on schedule?"

Ryder folds his arms across his chest and eyes me with a playful expression. "Under budget and ahead of schedule. You know I never miss my deadlines, Charleigh."

Ryder treads the thin line between cocky and confident, but he always finds steady footing in the latter because he backs up his talk with results. That's why I chose him out of the multitude of contractors Florence + Foxe employs.

"The cabinets are installed. The island, too. The electrician will be around tomorrow to wire everything."

"Great."

"And we were able to cancel that countertop order and rush the new marble—"

"Hold up." I pause, mentally rewinding the last few moments in my head. I couldn't have heard what I think I heard. There's no way. How?

"What are you talking about—marble countertops?"

Ryder is as close to being nervous as I've ever seen him. He rubs the back of his neck.

"Andrea sent the request a few days ago. Said both you and Guy signed off on it. I'd called you and Guy to confirm. I didn't hear anything from you, but Guy confirmed it."

I don't know who I'm more pissed at, Guy or Andrea. But rather than blowing my top, I take a deep breath and tell Ryder to reverse whatever he did because marble of any kind does not belong in this house.

"I don't care what it takes or how long it will delay the progress because marble will not work with the rest of my design."

"I agree with you there. That's why I wanted to call and confirm. It seemed out of character."

"Did Andrea authorize any other changes?"

"That's it."

Thank God. I'm going to have a few choice words with her when I get back to the office. Did she think I wouldn't notice something as major as this? I'm not as mad at Guy because I'm sure Andrea made him believe that I was okay with it.

"Great, let's see the rest of the house."

"You've got it."

I'm surprised by how far along the renovation has come. At this pace, so long as there are no other unforeseen issues, we'll finish ahead of schedule. We pass by Guy's old bedroom, but the door's closed. I open it and pop my head in. It's still in the same shape as I saw it during the first tour I had with Guy: A time capsule from his childhood.

"What's going on in here? Why hasn't all this stuff been removed?"

"Guy's orders. He wants to keep it as is."

I sigh as I shut the door, making a mental note to talk to Guy about it later. It's not that big of a deal, the only change I had in the room is repainting and restaining the hardwoods. Basic stuff that could happen in a few days.

Once we make it back to the front of the house, I shove my notebook into my purse and then hand Ryder the mask. "Thanks."

He takes the mask. "Not a problem, Charleigh."

"If anything comes up, call me, but it seems like you have everything handled."

"Of course, Charleigh."

I turn to leave, but Ryder stops me. "There is…" he says, smiling, "one thing."

I sigh. "Ryder…"

I'm not in the mood to be forced to turn down another date. He's made it a point to ask me each time I've dropped by.

He laughs. "Easy, tiger. I'm not asking you on a date. It's not that. I found something that I think you'll like."

Ryder guides me outside to his truck. He reaches into the cab and pulls out a piece of wood and hands it to me. I glance at it and then back up at Ryder, back and forth one more time.

"It's a piece of wood."

"Very observant of you, *Charlock* Holmes." He motions with his hand for me to flip it over.

On the reverse side, there's a rough inscription that makes me *awwww*. Scrawled at the top in capital letters is THE FINCH FAMILY and underneath it are the names Gabriel, Anne, and Guy, dated June 4, 1984.

"It was in a wheelbarrow of debris. I found it yesterday just before it was tossed."

"This is wonderful," I say, clutching it to my chest. "Guy is going to love it." I lunge at him, nearly knocking him off his feet with a bear hug.

"Alright," Ryder says, patting my head. He gasps, taking a step backward. "Jesus Christ, Charleigh!"

"Sorry!" I release Ryder from my death grip of a hug. I didn't mean to grab him so hard. I didn't mean to grab him at all. It just sort of happened.

Ryder looks down at his arms as he rubs them. "No problem. Just promise me that you'll never hug me again."

"Deal," I say, tucking the piece of wood underneath my arm. "Thanks for everything, Ryder. We'll be in touch."

Ryder nods and then turns around to walk back up to the house. I can still hear hammering and drilling and yelling from down here.

"I'll see you at Jamie and Marissa's joint party if we don't see each other sooner," Ryder says over his shoulder.

Crap! I completely forgot about that. I need to call Marissa...

"That's right! The wedding's coming up so soon."

Ryder raises his hat in acknowledgment before disappearing back inside.

I turn around, clutching the piece of wood under my arm, brainstorming all the possible ways to surprise Guy with it.

You like him, Emma says.

Yes, I do.

And that's a problem.

Guy: Deanna's going to be disappointed if you skip out tonight.
Guy: I already told her you were coming.
Charleigh: You did what?!
Charleigh: I didn't say I was coming or not!
Charleigh: Why would you?

Charleigh: This is…
Charleigh: IT'S BLACKMAIL
Charleigh: WHY WOULD YOU DO THIS?
Guy: A little guilt-trippish, yeah. It's hard not to pick it up after living with Deanna for a few weeks.
Guy: Blackmail, though…
Guy: That would've been much easier…and effective.
Guy: I recall you spent the better part of a few years sleeping next to a cardboard cut out of Zac Hanson…
Charleigh: Yeah, same with every other Hanson fan. Dig deeper, Finch.
Guy: The brownie incident of 2001…

I call him twice, leaving a warning message on his voicemail. Although I'm not sure who he'd tell, I'd like to limit knowledge of said brownie incident to as small a list as possible. Ugh…even after all these years it still makes my stomach turn.

Look. It's my mom's fault for leaving out a batch—three batches, *tops*—of brownie batter on the counter. How was I supposed to know that she was making brownies for underprivileged children? I'm not a mind reader. I'm a brownie eater.

Yes. I ate brownie batter meant to be consumed by underprivileged children. The look on my mom's face when she walked in the kitchen as I scooped batter into my mouth with my bare hands. And yes. I'm a bare-handed, brownie-eating barbarian. I'm not ashamed of it. Most of the time…

It's not my proudest moment. And neither were the ensuing hours of me throwing up said brownie batter because of the sheer amount of raw eggs I'd consumed. How I made it this far in life without my mom disowning me is a mystery.

I still don't know what made me do it. I promised myself I'd only have a taste, wipe excess batter from the rim. You know, help my mom out. But that single finger swipe turned into two, increasing in fingers until finally I just went for it.

Bare hand and all.

I'm cringing so hard about it right now that my future children can feel it.

> **Charleigh:** Guy...
> **Charleigh:** You wouldn't...
> **Guy:** Of course I wouldn't.
> **Charleigh:** I want to go, really, but there was an issue that popped up during the visit today that I have to work on.
> **Guy:** I'm sure they can wait until tomorrow. You still have to eat, right?
> **Guy:** And a granola bar doesn't count.

I stop chewing the Nutri-Grain bar currently in my hand, glance at it and then around at the office. Does he have cameras set up in here or something?

Guy's right. All of this can wait until tomorrow, and I could use a breather after this hectic day. My conversation with Andrea went about as well as I expected, which is to say not well at all. After denying it for a few minutes, she discarded her act and made it clear what she thinks of my design, which coincidently matches my thoughts of her.

I didn't want to loop Christiana into the mess, because that would've made the whole situation worse. She'd already given me an earful for not keeping Guy under control, so not being able to keep Andrea under control would be another strike. Unfortunately, she'd overheard us arguing and brought us into the office to discuss the whole ordeal.

After we settled the dispute, Christiana pulled me aside and questioned whether I was up for the task of Project Manager. I assured her that I was, but she wasn't as confident. From here on out, I'll be forced to give her weekly updates. Lucky me.

Charleigh: It's not a granola bar.

Charleigh: It's a nutrigrain bar

Guy: So a candy bar.

Charleigh: IT'S GOT WHOLE GRAINS IN IT. A WHOLE SERVING.

Guy: Easy, caps-lock commando, I can hear you yelling from here.

Guy: So you coming over? I'm just about to pull the beef and chicken and shrimp from the refrigerator.

Guy: They've been marinating all day.

Charleigh: The trifecta…

Hmm. It does sound better than the dinner I had planned.

Charleigh: What was for dessert again?

Guy: Nice try, Charleigh.

Charleigh: It was worth a shot.

Makeup: Check

Hair: Done.

Dress: Hugging me in all the right places.

If I'm going to be treated to dinner, I might as well dress up. Even if it is Guy who's treating me to it. But as I'm eyeing my reflection in the mirror, I'm wondering if it's a bit much. Sending the wrong signals?

Whatever. I'm starving and there's no way I'm going to shimmy out of this dress and find something else.

I give my reflection a final once-over before heading to my bedroom. The floor outside my closet is a mess. Shoes and dresses and sundry outfits are strewn haphazardly. It took a little longer than expected to find my outfit because I haven't been on a date in a long time and had no idea what to wear.

It's not a date, I remind myself. *It's dinner. Nothing else. AT ALL. Besides, my mom will be there.*

After grabbing my purse, I do a double take of the perfume on my dresser. Might as well… A few puffs later, I'm smelling all sweet and citrusy. Not like I'm trying to smell good for Guy or anything. It's all for me and me alone.

But when Guy opens the door for me, I'm glad I took more time than usual to get ready.

"Holy shit."

CHAPTER TWENTY-THREE

Charleigh

DID I JUST *say that out loud?*

Guy's vibrant, expansive, so-white-it's-blinding smile tells me that yes, yes I did say that out loud.

"I'm glad you came, Charleigh."

Dear lord. I don't remember Guy's voice being this rough. This sensual. It warms me like a steaming mug of hot chocolate on a cold winter night, while at the same time it steals my breath. And that outfit. Holy smokes.

Sleek dark slacks hug his muscular thighs. A form-fitting white Oxford with thin, light-blue pinstripes, cuffed just below his forearms. A button or two left undone.

Tousled hair. *DO* care.

Basically, I want to devour Guy—in the most platonic kind of way, of course.

He steps aside, leading me inside with one arm. "Come in," he says, completely ignoring the fact that I'm drooling all over the floor. Or maybe he's just being nice and not mentioning it.

Phew. Get it together. You're supposed to be laying down the law, remember? Focus.

I attempt to shake myself out of it as Guy slips my coat off and hangs it up in the closet. But my breath leaves me once again when he turns back around, his heady scent trailing behind him as he steps around me and then places a single hand on my back.

"You smell wonderful," I blurt out, momentarily mortified as the words stream from my lips. "Uh—buh." The longer I fumble, the wider Guy's smile grows.

"The food," I say, trying to salvage what's left of my crumbling dignity. "It smells wonderful."

Guy maintains his focus on me for just long enough for my neck and face to heat up like a grilled tomato. He lowers his gaze, allowing it to rake down my body at an agonizingly slow pace.

"You look wonderful, Charleigh," he says once he finally draws his eyes back to mine. He grabs my hand and then urges me toward the kitchen. "And you smell wonderful too." A wink and smile. Oh lord.

If it weren't for the incredible smells wafting from the kitchen, hijacking my senses, the last bit of dignity I have left would crumble to pieces.

The island at the center of the kitchen is covered with bowls filled to the brim with a medley of toppings—pico de gallo, cilantro and onions, guacamole, and sour cream. A steaming mound of rice and black beans flank either side.

Although the food looks amazing, I can't help but notice what's missing from this picture: my mother. She's not in her usual spot in the kitchen, relaxing in a chair and reading a magazine.

"Where's my mom?"

Guys tenses for a moment, stopping mid-stride. "She's at Jamie's."

It's a simple statement but comes with a slew of complications, the most pressing of which is that I'm essentially on a date with Guy.

"It came out of nowhere," Guy says abruptly. "She was helping me prepare dinner one moment, talking about how she was looking forward to seeing you tonight. And then in the next moment, she had her purse and was on her way out the door. I sent you a text about it."

I check my phone and lo and behold, he actually did send me a text, multiple texts, actually.

Guy: Deanna just left

Guy: She says she's having dinner with Jamie and Marissa

Guy: I didn't plan this I swear

Guy: You can cancel if you want

Guy: I have no problem eating the feast I made

Guy: And the dessert…

I can't help but smile at the slew of texts. But if he thinks he's going to have the dessert for himself, think again.

"It's fine."

Not really. I'm a little annoyed at my mother, but

whatever, more dessert and fajitas for me. Guy walks over to the stove, where strips of beef, bell peppers, and onions are sizzling in hot oil. "Go ahead and help—" he begins, turning around mid-sentence to find me diving into the chips and guac.

My mouth about orgasms when the guacamole meets my tongue. I moan as the tortilla chip—three wrapped together—crunches in my mouth. I have to sit down before my knees give in to the pure ecstasy going on in my mouth.

"Yourself," Guy finishes his sentence. "Tasty?" he asks, seeming unsure whether to be happy or terrified that I'm devouring his guacamole like a monster.

"Ish ferry good," I somehow manage with a full mouth, swallowing it down without choking. I take a quick breather as Guy turns his attention to the stove, shaking his head as he stirs the meat in the pan.

It's like I haven't eaten all day. Wait. I *haven't* eaten all day. Yikes. Today's been an unending stream of mind-numbingly boring meetings fractured only by near mental breakdowns dealing with Christiana's demands.

"How is it?" Guy asks over his shoulder.

"Amazing." Not only the guac but the view. I've never had anyone cook me dinner before, let alone a man as attractive as Guy. Yep—I acknowledge that Guy is pleasing to the eye. His muscles. His phenomenal bone structure. I mean, how the hell can a jawline be that sharp? And those hands. I can only imagine what he could do to me with them. With all that said, it doesn't mean I like Guy.

"I'm glad. It's almost ready. Could you grab a platter for the meat for me?"

I hop off my stool and head for the cabinet where we always kept all the platters. It's strange how I remember where everything is. Or at least, I thought I did. I close the first cabinet, moving on to the next, and then again when I can't find the platters.

"They're on the other side of the fridge now." Guy turns around and points. "Things have changed a little since you've been gone."

I can't help but think he means something more than the location of pots and pans. The skin prickles on the back of my neck as I roll onto my toes to grab a platter from the shelf. When I turn around, I find Guy's eyes on me. They're kind but unnerving at the same time, as though there's something hidden underneath the surface.

I offer a fleeting smile before setting the platter down next to the rest of the food. "There you are."

Guy turns around, hot pan sizzling as steam licks the air. "And here we are," he says, dumping the strips of meat and veggies onto the platter. He turns around, setting the pan back on the stove and then removes the foil covering another plate.

"Homemade tortillas."

Um, what? Is what my face is saying right now because I can't even begin to fathom how much effort Guy has put into this dinner.

"It's not that difficult," Guy assures me. "There are only a few ingredients. The secret is in the spices and a good sear on the meat."

I prod at his arms for a moment and reach up and pinch his cheek, which is easier said than done because there's not a shred of fat on his face. After I tug at his black tresses, he finally asks me what I'm doing.

"I'm trying to figure out if you're really Guy or Martha Stewart dressed in a man suit."

Guy lets out a sharp exhale, turning around as he laughs. He catches his breath a few seconds later. "I'm going to ignore the incredibly disturbing image in my head right now and pretend I never heard that."

He grabs a plate, tosses a couple of tortillas on it, and then piles them high with meat and veggies and pico and guac.

"Seriously though, how the hell did you learn how to do all this?" I follow suit, loading my own plate up with fajitas, rice, and beans.

Guy sets his plate down and then sits down on the stool next to mine. "Google," he says, grinning at me for a brief moment before rolling up the tortilla and taking a man-sized bite out of it.

After a few moments of awkward silence, mostly because he's busy swallowing the gargantuan amount of food in his mouth, Guy says, "Seriously. It's not that difficult to learn how to do this." He motions to the food laid out in front of us. "There are recipes for everything you can imagine. Videos, too." Another bite. Swallow. "It just takes a little bit of effort to go looking for them."

"Well, I'll have you know I'm adept at pouring boiling water into cups of ramen. And I know how to properly heat up a frozen burrito." I take a bite out of my fajita. "So if you need any help on that—" *Holy shit.*

These fajitas are fantastic. MSG? Salt? Fat? All of the above? What sort of sorcery is going on in my mouth?

Before I have time to think about it, I'm one fajita deep and halfway through the next.

"I don't know whether to be impressed or afraid." I glance up from stuffing my face and see Guy gaping at me, his own tortilla hovering in front of his mouth.

I swallow what's left in my mouth, set the fajita back on the plate, and then clear my throat. "This might have been the first time I've eaten all day. I didn't realize how hungry I was," I say shrugging, digging into the rice and beans.

"You haven't eaten all day?" Guy sets his fajita down. "That's no good."

"You remember that whole issue with Andrea I called you about earlier?"

"The marble mixup?"

"Mixup," I say, using air quotes. "There was no mixup. Andrea point-blank said she hated my design and wanted to make changes to it. If I hadn't caught this one so early, there would've been more."

Guy wipes his mouth with his napkin and drops it next to his plate. "She told me you'd signed off on it. I just didn't think to mention it to you."

"Maybe you should've brought it up, but this is all Andrea."

"She must be a blast to work with."

"You have no idea."

Guy smiles, and there's that swirling feeling in my gut. Or maybe it's the beans. Probably the beans. Whatever it is, I kind of like it. But what I like most about this moment right now is the overwhelming sense of ease between us. It was only a few weeks ago that every interaction with

Guy felt like work. It doesn't feel like that anymore, and I'm not sure when it changed. Some things are like that. They happen slowly and then all at once, from drizzle to downpour with no in between.

"Is the voice real?" Guy asks me out of seemingly nowhere.

"The voice?" Welp, that sense of ease is gone. I look around us nervously hoping that the TV is on in the background because the last thing I want to hear now is that the person I'm sharing chips and guac with is hearing voices.

Guy laughs. "Andrea's voice," he says. "That chipmunk voice of hers. Is it real?"

After my own laughing fit, I take a deep breath. Thank God Guy hasn't lost his mind. "It's all show. She turns it on when she's trying to schmooze someone. Well, guys only. She switches into a Southern drawl when she's with a female client." I scrunch my brow. "I'm not exactly sure why, though."

"She's playing the role she thinks the client wants. Unfortunately for her, she's assuming all clients are alike." Guy scoops out a heaping serving of guacamole with a chip, so much so that the chip breaks and gets stuck in the green goo of deliciousness. He looks at me, raising a brow, and I raise one in commiseration. Nothing's worse than losing a chip in guac. Okay, there are a lot of things worse than that, but right now, this one's pretty high up on the list.

Guy selects a heftier chip to rescue its fallen friend and then crunches down on both of them. He claps his hands together, wiping the crumbs off of them and then swivels around to meet me. A trail of his cologne follows in his wake. Christ, he smells so good—like a forest of evergreens after snow, mixed with a crackling wood fire and cinnamon. Definitely cinnamon.

"Ready to take this into the living room? *Fixer Upper*'s about to come on."

"What about dessert?"

"What about it?"

"Where. Is. It?"

"Easy there, Chuck." Guy pats me on top of my head. "We'll get to it after *Fixer Upper*. Deanna would be disappointed if we didn't watch at least one show in her honor."

"A few things. One. Don't call me Chuck ever again." Guy smiles at this, which makes me pause for a longer time than I wanted due to that fluttering feeling just below my sternum. "Two. Deanna has no right to be disappointed in either of us. She's the one who skipped out on tonight for no reason at all."

"She forgot about her plans with Jamie and Marissa," Guy says.

I smile at his naïvety, pull out my phone, and hand it over to him so he can see firsthand the slew of texts Marissa sent me once Deanna showed up unannounced at her front door.

"Huh," he says, scrolling through them.

"She totally set this up."

Guy's silent, scrolling. Scrolling. SCROLLING. WHY IS HE STILL SCROLLING?

"Do you really think—"

I snatch the phone out of his clutches. "I don't know what you saw, but whatever it was, I didn't write it."

"You didn't text Marissa that my biceps are built like boulders?"

"I—*pfft*—like—come on…" The pitch of my voice is reaching Andrea levels as I unconvincingly walk back the texts that I sent to Marissa about Guy. I tell Guy a story about an escaped monkey from a traveling circus that stole my phone for a period of time, so I couldn't be held responsible for most of those texts.

"I wasn't aware that there were traveling circuses, or that a monkey belonging to one of them would know so much about me. How'd you end up retrieving it?"

"Strange, huh? Anyway, how about that *Fixer Upper*?"

Yikes. I focus my attention on the last of my fajitas, trying hard to ignore the feeling Guy's gaze has on me. After a few bites, the embarrassment subsides, giving way to annoyance. Unfortunately, I still have a mouthful of food, so what I want to say comes out horribly.

Guy raises both of his eyebrows, prompting me to try again. I swallow and resume.

"Rule number one of proper phone etiquette. When someone hands you their phone, you're to look at whatever they are showing you and no more."

"I wasn't aware," Guy says unconvincingly. "But I promise not to snoop anymore." He pauses for a few moments. "Does that include your room too?"

MY WHAT?!

Seeming to sense the storm brewing in my mind, Guy makes the appropriate decision to get up from the island and walk away. Unfortunately for him, I'm not going to let him go so easily now that I know he's been snooping in my bedroom. I hop off my stool and follow him out of the room.

"Guy you have no right to be—" I'm only able to get

a few words out before he spins around and bear hugs me.

"I'm kidding, Charleigh. You have nothing to worry about."

I grab his back reflexively and find nothing but pure muscle underneath my fingertips. Yikes. I don't think I've ever touched something so hard yet soft at the same time. I try to respond, but with my mouth being smothered by Guy's torso, each syllable comes out all wrong. I'm not complaining though.

He pulls away and I can't help but feel a little bit of loss. I'm not sure whether I should be ashamed at how good that hug—his touch, his scent, his voice—made me feel or embrace it.

"HGTV now. Dessert later." Guy's raspy baritone sends a chill down my spine with waves of tingling pinpricks in its wake, radiating outward.

I try my best to look menacing, squaring up to him with my hands on my hips. "Dessert now. Dessert later."

It doesn't work.

"You drive a hard bargain, Charleigh, but no."

He walks over to the sofa and sits down.

He has no idea just how far I'll go to get what I want.

CHAPTER TWENTY-FOUR

Guy

I CAN'T KEEP my hands to myself.

Every chance I have to touch Charleigh, no matter how fleeting it may be, I take it. I'm teaching her how to make a molten dulce de leche cake. She's never had it before—and I've never made it before—but I wanted to try something new. Something outside of my comfort zone. But I hadn't planned for this entire night to be outside my comfort zone.

From the moment I opened the door and saw Charleigh, I knew that any hope of keeping tonight simple was out the window. Charleigh's shoulder-length tresses fell like silk against her shoulder, framing her perfect alabaster complexion. When I saw her I had to resist every urge to reach out, run my hands through her hair and taste her sweet lips again.

"How's it look?" Charleigh asks as she focuses on stirring the caramel sauce on the stove.

"Gorgeous," I say, not taking my eyes off her. I finger a stray hair that fell across her cheek and pull it behind her ear.

"Thanks," she says, blushing slightly. I'm not sure if it's because of my touch or the heat from the stove.

"It's about time, too. What has it been, an hour?"

"Just about. Anything worthwhile takes time."

I brush the length of her arm with my hand as I turn around to focus on the egg mixture in the mixer. I'd started it already, but if I spent another second that close to Charleigh, there'd be no hope of finishing the dessert tonight. I need to divert my attention from her for a moment before another part of me takes over.

After a few minutes, she asks, "How's it look now?"

I take a sharp inhale of breath, turn around, and then look at the mixture.

"Perfect."

Charleigh looks ecstatic, bouncing on the balls of her feet while holding the spatula in the air as the thick caramel-colored mixture slowly drips down it.

My forearm brushes against her stomach as I grab the pot and take it off the heat.

"Now what?"

"Now we wait for it to cool."

She stops bouncing. Everything about her bubbly demeanor crashes to the floor. Spatula included. "That's a joke, right, Guy? Right? Guy?"

Okay. The crazy eyes are freaking me out a little, but I push through it.

"It needs to thicken. A few hours. Tops."

"Tops," she mimics, bobbing her head. "Tops."

And then it happens. She levels a gaze at me that I've never seen on her face before.

If looks could kill, not only would I be dead, but so would my unborn children and several generations thereafter. If there's one thing I've learned, never get in the way of Charleigh and sugar. Especially after having her work for the better part of an hour on a caramel mixture that won't be ready for double that time. I'm a dead man walking at this point, but I have a little something up my sleeve.

I reach into the cabinet next to her and pull out a store-bought jar of dulce de leche. I feel a little bad that I made Charleigh go through the entire process of making the homemade version, but only a little.

I offer it to her, but she just stares at it with a mix of shock and anger. Well, mostly anger. And by anger, I mean she's looking at it—and now me—with such ferocity that I'm surprised it hasn't been vaporized from being superheated.

"Do you think that's going to save you, Finch?"

Finch. Yikes. Maybe I underestimated how pissed she would be. It takes a few moments for me to squeak out a response. And when I do, I hardly recognize the uncertain, fragile sound that comes from my lips. "Yes?"

She edges close to me, finger prodding my chest over and over until she starts laughing. "Oh my God, you should've seen your face!"

I gulp, a little concerned but a lot relieved, and then laugh nervously. "You had me going there, Charleigh."

She snags the jar from my hand. "Serves you right."

I take a step forward, reclaiming the space between us. The self-satisfied smile on her face falters as her breath quickens, the air around us thick with tension. She takes a step back but I meet her step with one of my own.

"Can you blame me though?"

That hour gave me more time with Charleigh. If anything, the hour passed far too quickly.

She hadn't been that relaxed since the night at The Lookout. Christ. I still can't get that night out of my head. It's torture reliving it over and over again, unable to satisfy my hunger again. Even though the one thing that could satiate it is inches from me.

"I guess not." Charleigh's voice is soft, breathy. Her perfect bow lips part slightly as she meets my gaze. I can taste those lips, feel their softness. It's taking every ounce of restraint not to touch her.

"You're so beautiful." And for a brief moment, I regret saying it. Not because I don't mean it—it's true. I only regret it because the words can change the fragile dynamic between us. It's too soon. It's not the right time. My mind is out of control trying to figure out what's going on in that head of hers.

Her eyes narrow and then open, alternating between the two as she looks up at me. They give no hint of what she's thinking or feeling. And the longer we're at this impasse, the deeper my regret builds.

Fuck it. I don't care. I'm not taking it back because I meant what I said, and I know Charleigh won't take it the wrong way. She'll probably make some joke out of it. Lord it over me. I don't mind because I think she likes knowing how I feel about her.

"You're trouble, *Sebastian*," she says finally, a wave of relief rushing through me.

"I think you knew that when I kissed you, *Emma*."

I cup her cheek and she seems to melt away, her eyes closing as she lets out a shaky breath. I tangle my fingers in between strands of her hair and tug down gently, raising her chin as her lips part and her eyes meet mine again. There's nothing else in this world that I want right now more than to taste those lips again, and when I tell her that, she wets her lips in response.

I lean in, mere millimeters away from her lips when the front door opens.

"Guy! Charleigh! I'm back from Jamie's." Deanna stomps her boots on the mat as she enters the house.

You've got to be kidding me.

My lips are so close to Charleigh's that I can almost feel them. There's electricity crackling between them, but before I have the chance to breach the gap between us, Charleigh slides away.

"How was dinner, Mom?" Charleigh calls out as she grabs her purse from the table.

Shit.

I make my way after Charleigh. She's already talking with Deanna about something—I don't know what. My attention's on Charleigh. Her lips. Her face. The shape of her neck underneath those red curls. How close I was to tasting those lips again.

"I'm so glad you two had a good time." Deanna's voice finally registers. "But now… it's time for bed."

She turns around and gives my shoulder a light squeeze. There's a knowing twinkle in her green eyes, a content smile on her lips. "Goodnight, Guy." She winks, glances once more at Charleigh, and then heads upstairs.

The moment she leaves, the air around me shifts. It's hot and thick, and I'm trying desperately to catch my breath as the most beautiful woman in the world stares back at me. How the hell did this happen?

It's like the boiling frog metaphor, but with me in place of the frog and my feelings for Charleigh in place of the water. I'm not *falling* for Charleigh—I've *fallen* for her. It's a done deal. I thought I was in control the whole time, but the near-immobilizing feelings flooding through my body tell me I had it all wrong.

"I should go." Charleigh opens the closet door and retrieves her coat.

I want to tell her to stay, but the expression on her face tells me that it's not a good idea. I've already pushed her too far, and even though she reciprocated in kind, it's all happening too fast.

"Okay."

I help Charleigh into her coat and then hand her purse to her. She grabs it but I don't let go. I don't want to because that means she'll be gone too. I want to prolong our goodbye for as long as I can.

"I'm not playing tug of war with you, Guy."

"I think you're already playing it."

The push and pull—for every inch I seem to gain with Charleigh, she takes four back. She narrows her eyes briefly before relaxing.

"You can have it," she says, letting go of the purse. "But I'm not sure if it will match your uniform very well."

I crack a smile, pausing for a moment before I hand it

back to her. "You're right. It's not my style anyway. I need something with more heft. Something pink, maybe."

Charleigh mashes her lips together, doing a terrible job at hiding that smile as she fumbles with the door lock behind her.

"You seem to be leaving in a hurry, Charleigh. Are you sure you don't want to stay for dessert? After all that work?"

I'm not above a little bribery. Charleigh almost takes the bait, her eyes widening as she realizes she's only a few minutes away from fresh-baked molten dulce de leche cakes, but she regains control.

"No can do, amigo." The door lock clicks behind her, creaking as it opens.

Amigo? Confused is an understatement for how I'm feeling about Charleigh throwing her very limited knowledge of Spanish into the conversation. But that's nothing compared to her choice to pass on dessert.

"You sure you're feeling okay, Charleigh?"

I reach out as though to take the temperature of her forehead, but she ducks the back of my hand and hops through the gap in the front door. "Yup!" she calls back after as she takes the front steps two at a time. I'm surprised she doesn't fall flat on her face as she full-on sprints back to her car.

"It has nothing to do with—uh—what happened in the kitchen either," she yells before slipping into the driver's seat and shutting the door behind her.

"Well, that's a normal response," I mutter to myself, scratching my head as I watch Charleigh reverse out of the drive with as much grace as Maddox.

Nothing to do with the near kiss indeed.

CHAPTER TWENTY-FIVE

Charleigh

AMIGO?

What in the world was I thinking? Oh, that's right—*I wasn't.* I mean, I'd congratulate anyone who could act normally after nearly having their lips assaulted—in the most romantic way possible, of course—by a man like Guy.

My body was on fire from the moment he opened up the door and didn't die down until my mother walked through the front door. And thank God she showed up when she did. A few minutes later and she more than likely would've walked in on something she definitely would not have wanted to see.

My heart had been vetoing every objection to Guy that my brain threw at it all night, leading up to the moment our lips nearly met. It's still vetoing my brain, but thankfully my brain still has a firm grasp on my motor skills or else Guy would be receiving some embarrassing texts right about now.

I force my eyes closed. *Go. To. Bed,* I urge myself.

Easier said than done. I took a shower, changed into pajamas, drank a cup of soothing herbal tea—everything that usually forces my body to accept that it's time for bed, but I can't sleep. I'm tossing and turning and can't stop thinking about how close I was to kissing Guy.

How much *I wanted* to kiss Guy.

My spine tingles as I relive the moment for the hundredth time, its effect on me just as strong as the first time. Everything about it is engrained in my mind—his scent, the electric sensations that pulsed just under my skin, how maddeningly difficult it was to breathe with his lips so close to mine.

I wet my lips reactively as I picture him in my mind's eye. My body begins to come alive as I relinquish the last of my resolve and allow myself to focus on that moment. I should've kissed him. I should've tasted those lips again. And in my imagination, I do.

My center aches as I fantasize about what should've happened between us. Our lips crash together so harshly that our teeth nearly touch. But it doesn't even matter. All I care about is tasting Guy, feeling his rough, masculine hands all over my face, cupping my head, gripping my hair as he kisses me.

I slip my hand down the front of my pajamas, feeling the slick warmth already building. It hardly takes any time at all for me to come, and not long after that, I finally drift to sleep.

GUY HATER

"Guy, do you even know how to fix a leaky pipe?"

Streaks of black grease mark his jawline and forearms. His white t-shirt is ripped to shreds, hardly covering his tanned torso, which of course has patches of black grease on it.

A few questions come to mind: Why is there grease all over him, and why does it look like a mountain lion swiped his shirt multiple times? But more importantly, how did I get here? And where is here?

I look around. We're in the kitchen at his house, but at the same time, we're not. It's different, hazy around the edges as though I'm looking at it through a foggy lens. A Gaussian blur on steroids. The kitchen has somehow been renovated, but the design isn't my own. But when Guy opens his mouth, I don't care whatsoever.

"You can fix just about anything if you have the right tool," he says, whacking his wrench against the palm of his hand.

The smile on his face just about knocks me out of my socks, if only I was wearing socks to get knocked out of. I look down and I'm wearing bright pink, fluffy slippers shaped like baby elephants. Okay…

He kneels down and ducks under the countertop, and my eyes lock on that amazing ass. I swear I've somehow been flung into some low-budget porno flick. All that needs to happen is—

There's a loud grinding sound of metal on metal followed by jets of water spraying everywhere. Guy crawls backward from underneath the sink and stands up, turning back toward me.

"Oh no," he says, smiling at me. "It looks like I'm all wet."

Okay, that seals it. I am in some low-budget porno film.

But as I watch Guy slowly pull his shredded shirt over his head, I don't care. Yowza. Those rows of abs. The striations along his sides.

When in dreams…

I step into the spray of water, letting it soak me. And just as I'm about to utter my perfect, porny response, the world around me is sucked away.

"Looks like I'm all wet, too," I finish as I wake up.

And I am. I'm soaked.

"Shitshitshitshit!"

I roll out of my bed, barely dodging the waterlogged pieces of my ceiling as they fall onto my bed. Apparently, my paper towel and duct tape fix weren't up to code. I told my landlord about the issue a month ago but of course, nothing's happened, and I've been too busy to actually follow up.

I rush into action, trying to find the water turn off, but of course, I can't find it anywhere inside my apartment. After letting out a blood-curdling scream as my frustration reaches fever pitch, I burst through the front door of my apartment into the night, soaked and freezing and full-on sprint to my landlord's house across the road from the complex.

"I've got a gun!" he squeaks from the other side of the door.

"And my bedroom's about to have a lake view if you don't get out here and fix the broken pipe in my ceiling. I told you about it months ago."

After a few beats of silence, the gears apparently churning in his head, he says, "Two-two-three?"

"Yes. Apartment two-twenty-three."

A few minutes later I'm back in my apartment with my landlord. The water's off but the damage has already been done. My bed is soaked. The floors are soaked. The ceiling is falling apart. I'm in shock.

"It could always be worse," my landlord says, rocking back on his heels.

I'm at a loss for words, so I just glare at him. He almost shrivels underneath it.

"We'll have this fixed in a jiffy tomorrow," he says as he turns to leave.

"Tomorrow?"

"Can't do a thing now. It's three a.m. I need supplies. Men to do this. You understand, right?"

I don't even have the will to argue. I'm at my wit's end.

"Get out of my apartment."

He shrugs, turns back around, and heads to the front of the apartment. A few moments later the door shuts.

It takes a few minutes, but the cold finally registers in my brain. I'm freezing, soaked from head to toe. I'd been so fired up from adrenaline that I hardly noticed. But with it out of my system, I feel terrible.

I can't sleep here, so I grab a change of clothes, toiletries, and everything else I'll need to get through tomorrow. A few minutes later, I'm out the door, heading to the only place I can think of going at this hour.

The door's locked when I test the knob. *Shit.* I knock a few times, but there's no response, so I send a text.

Charleigh: Can you open up? I'm here.

The seconds tick by like minutes as every moment seems to stretch out longer and longer.

Charleigh: A pipe burst and–

The door swings open as I'm typing another message. Guy, naked from the waist up, answers the door. His hair is mussed, and the look on his face is adorably sleepy, making my stomach flip. But when I allow my eyes to wander to the rows of abs stacked one on top of the other, I feel the sensation flutter between my thighs.

My dream was realistic in at least one way: Guy's physique. He's shredded. Not an ounce of fat on him. He has more defined muscles than I've ever seen on anyone, and I'm pretty sure if scientists studied him, they'd discover entirely new muscle groups.

"This is unexpected," Guy says, rubbing his hair as he begins to yawn.

I force myself to look away from his torso. "So was the pipe that burst above my bed."

He closes his mouth, his eyes widening with raised brows as though to ask, "Seriously?"

I nod.

He steps aside. "Come in. Can I get you anything? Tea? Food?"

I sigh. "I'd just like to go to sleep."

"Of course. Take your old room. I'll sleep on the couch."

"No," I say, "you're living here. You can take the bed. I'll take the couch."

Guy laughs as though it's the most ridiculous thing I've ever said.

He leans in. "You're taking the bed."

My spine tingles as his warm breath strikes the sensitive skin just below my ear.

"I won't take no for an answer."

He snatches my bag and heads upstairs. I stand at the bottom of the stairs for a brief moment, watching as his muscles alternate between flexion and contraction. I could get used to this view, but a part of me doesn't want to. I want it to have the same effect every time.

"I'm sure I can find new sheets and pillowcases if you'd like."

"It's fine," I say. "I'm too tired to care and I just want to go to sleep."

"Then I won't keep you up."

Guy sets my bag on the desk. Just as he's about to pass by me, he stops. "Good night, Charleigh," he says, kissing the top of my head.

I can feel myself melting away as he leaves the room, shutting the door behind him. Why does Guy have to be so sweet?

Why does it matter? another part of me pipes in.

I've run around in circles about these same thoughts ever since I started hanging out with Guy again, but right now I'm too tired to give it any more thought.

But as I crawl into bed, the sheets still warm from Guy, all I can think about is him. All I can smell is his scent. With the sheets wrapped tightly around me and my eyes closed, it feels like he's holding me, snuggling me to sleep.

I don't know how I'll be to keep things professional between us anymore.

CHAPTER TWENTY-SIX

Guy

CHARLEIGH WAS THE last person I expected to see at the door at 3 a.m.—not that I usually expect anyone to knock at my door at 3 a.m.

She'd left in such a hurry after our near kiss that I figured I wouldn't see her for a few days, possibly a week. It tends to be Charleigh's MO. Two steps forward, twelve steps back. I feel like I'm Sisyphus, pushing a boulder up a long, winding hill only to have it roll right back to the bottom again.

Deanna rounds the corner and walks into the kitchen. "You're up early."

"Couldn't sleep, so I figured I might make myself useful and make breakfast."

Pancake batter sizzles in the skillet as I ladle a scoop of it in.

"You've been more than useful around here, and you know it."

She wraps her arms around me, resting her head against my back. "It's so good to have someone else in the house. It's been so long."

Deanna sighs and I know exactly what she's thinking because I'm thinking about it too—him, really. Michael, her husband, passed away nearly a decade ago. It happened during my junior year in college. I loved him as much as I loved my own father, and when he died it felt like I'd lost my dad all over again. But this time around, it wasn't as much of a surprise.

Michael worked a high-stress job—in-house counsel for a major oil company. He worked hard, so when he had time off, he played just as hard. His vices weren't hard drugs. He was addicted to heavy foods, sweets, and alcohol and overindulged in them on a regular basis.

In terms of vices, it may not seem sinister. In fact, most of his family never saw it as a problem until it was too late. Those extra pounds that were explained away by stress quickly morphed into ten, twenty, fifty and more. I know Deanna tried countless times to help him when his weight ballooned, but Michael was prideful. He wanted to take care of it himself.

And he did for a time, but with every addiction, there are always setbacks and false starts. And the moment you think you've killed it is the moment it all comes crumbling down because the addiction never completely goes away. It's always lurking, insidious with its twisted logic that's just believable enough.

Birthdays? Special occasions? Live a little. It's just a piece of cake. It's just a beer. But the vice knows the truth: It will never be just one. In the end, his vices caught up with him. Michael died of a heart attack at forty-six years old.

I take a deep breath, holding it for a few beats before releasing it. "It's good to be back."

I flip the pancake, but it folds in on itself and I spend the next few seconds unsuccessfully trying to salvage it.

It's a universal truth that the first pancake will never turn out.

Deanna releases me from her bear hug and finds her way onto a stool in front of the island.

"How'd your date with Charleigh go? I hope I didn't interrupt it."

Deanna's smiling so hard that I can hear it in her voice.

"It wasn't a date. It wasn't supposed to be just her and me. Someone else was supposed to be there but they vanished just before she arrived."

"Some things are just out of our control. But I'm glad your date went well."

"It wasn't a date. It was just dinner. "

"You know what happened with the last man I had *just dinner* with?"

I remove the misshapen pancake from the griddle and set it on the plate, but not before tearing off a piece and popping it into my mouth.

"What happened?" I ask, chewing as I turn to look at Deanna. It's not bad. A little undercooked but not bad.

"He put a ring on my finger less than a year later," she says, brandishing her ringed hand in the air.

Thankfully I've swallowed the pancake before she says this or else I'd be a coughing and sputtering mess. Charleigh and me? Married? Hell, me and anyone. Marriage is the last thing on my radar at this moment.

"I'm pretty sure that a year from now, Charleigh and I won't be married."

"I thought the same thing about Michael, but love finds a way."

I turn my attention back to the pancakes, grabbing the ladle from the bowl and pouring more batter onto the griddle. "Charleigh's not interested in me, Deanna."

At least, that's the way it feels sometimes.

"If she wasn't interested you, she wouldn't have had dinner with you."

Okay, she has a point.

"And besides, judging from the red cheeks on both of your faces, I think I interrupted something a little more than *just dinner*."

I sigh, turning my attention back to my pancakes.

"Give her time," Deanna says, getting up from the stool. She walks over to the coffee maker. "She'll come around."

"Who'll come around?"

Deanna shrieks, nearly dropping the pot of coffee onto the ground while I launch the pancake I'm trying to flip out of the pan and onto the countertop. The uncooked batter splatters against the countertop as it crashes against it.

"Charleigh…" Deanna says, clutching her chest. "What in the world are you doing here?"

I clean the pancake off the countertop and toss it into

the trash as I glance over at Charleigh. She's wearing a pair of my sweatpants. One of my shirts too. And with her hair pulled into a loose ponytail, I can't think of a more attractive sight.

Deanna pours coffee into her mug.

"Guy didn't tell you?" Charleigh asks, walking over to the island.

"He told me your date went well, but he didn't tell me it went *that* well."

"Wait. Hold—" Charleigh stutters. Pauses. "You don't think…"

"You don't have to explain a thing." Deanna's tone is reassuring. "We're all adults here." She brings her mug to her lips and takes a sip. When she finishes, there's a wide smile on her lips. She sighs deeply.

"I always knew…"

A deep flush colors Charleigh's cheeks.

"Always knew what?"

Deanna laughs.

"I'll leave you two alone," she says, gliding out of the room. "Give me a shout when those pancakes are done, Guy."

"Will do," I mutter as I ladle more batter into the pan. The back of my neck heats up from Charleigh's glare.

"Why does my mom think that we're dating?" Charleigh asks once her mom leaves. "And sleeping together?" She laughs.

I flip the pancake. It turns out much better this time.

"Do you remember what you're wearing?

She glances down at her outfit. "Right. But still. You and me? She can't be serious."

"What's so crazy about that?" I ask, turning around to face her. She's no more than a few steps away, one hand on the island, the other playing with the necklace dangling in the hollow of her neck.

I take a step forward and she takes a step back.

"Because we hate each other."

"Wrong, Char."

I take a few more steps forward and she takes the same amount backward, but now she's up against a wall. Her palms rest flat against it as she looks at me.

"I don't hate you. You know that."

I watch Charleigh's chest rise and fall as I close the gap between us. "And I'm pretty sure you don't hate me." I press my palm against the wall next to her, bracketing her in on one side.

"Yes, I do." Her voice is no louder than a whisper. I can feel the tremor in it.

I laugh. "You sure sound like you mean it."

She presses her palm against my chest and pushes me. "I do."

"Then why are you here?" I don't wait for a response. "You could've easily stayed at Jamie's. He's closer to your apartment. This house is out of the way. Why did you choose to come here?"

Her pink flush deepens to crimson. She won't look at me. She's embarrassed but doesn't need to be. I guide her head so she's looking at me.

"I like you. I always have. I know I was an asshole at times when we were kids, but that's just it. I was a kid. A stupid kid who'd just lost his parents and didn't know what to do. You didn't deserve any of the hurt I caused you. And I'm sorry. For everything I did."

Tears are beginning to well in her eyes, but they refuse to fall. Her lip trembles slightly and there's nothing more in the world that I want now than to kiss her. But I know it's not right. Not now.

"All I'm asking is that you give me a chance to show you that I mean it."

She drags her teeth against her bottom lip but doesn't say anything. I pull away but as I turn around, she latches onto my arm and tugs me back into her. My body presses against hers and I can feel her heart pumping frantically in her chest.

I slide my free hand beneath her curls and cup the back of her neck. There's nothing more that I want to do right now than to taste those lips again. I lean in close, lightly brushing her cheek with my nose, breathing the faint perfume left on her skin. She lets out a light gasp as her grip loosens around my forearm and then slides up my arm and onto my back.

My skin's on fire, tingling as she drags her fingertips across my body.

"You're beautiful," I whisper into her ear.

Her eyes narrow for a brief moment, and her hands pull me into her and our lips meet. It's soft and slow as though she's testing the waters and then all at once it shifts into something else entirely. All of our history, the good and the bad, comes crashing into one localized point. This kiss has years of pent-up anger and passion and frustration. It's nothing less than what I expect a kiss from Charleigh should be.

"I leave for one minute and look at you two lovebirds."

Jesus Christ. Both Charleigh and I separate from each other instantly as Deanna walks by us.

"Don't mind me," she says. "I forgot my coffee."

Both Charleigh and I look at each other in stunned silence.

"I always knew," Deanna says as she passes by. "I always knew."

Charleigh mouths *Oh. My. God.* And then laughs right as I lean in to kiss her again.

"Your pancakes are burning, by the way," Deanna calls out as she heads upstairs.

I look back at the stove and see a black cloud rising.

"Shit!"

CHAPTER TWENTY-SEVEN

Charleigh

"SPIT IT OUT, Charleigh," Marissa says.

"But I really do love that nail color on you!"

"I'm sure you do, but I know you didn't assault my phone with texts and voicemails to meet so we could talk about my nails. About the weather. The color of the sunset yesterday." Marissa pauses. "Should I go on?"

I know I'm avoiding the single reason I called this emergency meeting because avoiding it allows me to live in an alternate reality where my lips didn't meet Guy's lips. Although what happened wasn't a meeting of lips. It was more than a kiss, more than anything I'd felt before. And that's exactly why I'm freaking out right now. More so now that I see Marissa reaching for her purse.

"Okay, you're right," I blurt. I take a shaky breath. "Please stay. I'll tell you."

Marissa lets go of her purse, looking at me as though I'd better hurry up—this offer only lasts for a limited time.

Nerves swirl in my gut. I haven't eaten anything and the little bit of caffeine in my decaf latte has my head spinning. After a few moments, Marissa brings her drink to her lips, and I take a deep breath.

"So I—well—I kissed Guy."

Marissa's eyes bug out as she tries not to spit out her latte, setting it back down on the table. "Can we rewind that?" she says, motioning with her hands. "When did this happen?"

"This morning."

She raises an eyebrow. "This morning," she repeats. "And why were you there this morning? And..." She lets the rest of the sentence drop off, and I can see the gears turning in her head as she tries to piece everything together.

"It's a long story."

Marissa checks her watch. "Well, I'm already late for work. And if you don't tell me everything, I'll create my own version of it to fill in the blanks. And you know how vivid my imagination can be."

I try to laugh, but it comes out more like a growl. "How could I forget about my future twins?"

"Finn. And. Karina," Marissa says, nodding along with each word.

"Yeah, them."

"Spill."

I lean back in my chair and recount the last few days and how they led to the kiss this morning. From the scone Guy left on my desk to the impromptu date thanks to my mother, the pipes bursting in my bedroom, until finally this morning.

Initially, I skip over the dream I had about Guy, but when Marissa asks me why I kissed him, I blame it on the sexually-charged dream.

"Now, let me get this straight." Marissa's hands are clasped in front of her. She pauses for a moment, biting down on her lip as she tries her hardest not to laugh. I don't blame her. It's so ridiculous, but it's also my life. So, there's that. "You dreamed that Guy was a plumber."

My palms dig into my cheeks as I lean forward over the table. "Not a real plumber."

"A low-budget porn plumber."

"Yup." I cross my arms on the table and let my forehead crash against them.

"And you think this dream had something to do with why you kissed him?"

"Mmmhmm," I mumble into my arms.

Marissa finally laughs. "No," she says. "The dream, although I'm sure it was wonderful, had nothing to do with whether you kissed Guy or not. You kissed Guy because you wanted to kiss him."

"No way. I—" I pause for a moment, trying to gather my thoughts. Marissa watches me carefully, the expression on her face letting me know that I'll come to the same conclusion. And she's right. I wanted to kiss Guy. I wanted to kiss him, so I did.

"Okay. But what now? The whole reason I wanted to meet with him yesterday was to talk to him about slowing things down."

"Did you ever bring it up?"

"Well, no."

"Well, so it seems like you dumped gasoline onto a fire."

"Yeah." I smack my palm against my forehead and lean forward.

"What do you want, Charleigh?" Marissa asks after a few moments.

"What do you mean?"

"What do I mean?" Marissa motions to herself. "I think it's a pretty straightforward question."

Maybe to everyone else, but not for me. Not right now. There are a lot of things I want. I want to finish this project. I want to be promoted. I want to be taken seriously as a designer.

After a couple seconds of tense, awkward silence, Marissa reaches out and covers my hand with hers. I look down and see the napkin I'd been unconsciously shredding in front of me.

"Okay, how about this. How do you feel about Guy?"

I chew the inside corner of my mouth, let it go. "I don't know. I like him. But I also like baked goods, but that doesn't mean I should jump into a relationship with a scone."

Marissa sighs. I know I must be frustrating to deal with, but this is how I deal with uncomfortable things. I either run away or make light of them, minimizing them until they become so small that they go away. But I'm tired of it. I need to stop running.

"I'm sorry. You're trying to help me and I'm being annoying." I slink back into my chair, letting my hands fall into my lap. "I guess I'm just afraid."

"Afraid of what?"

"Of being hurt by him again."

Marissa's features soften as she looks at me. It's the truth. It's why I was so guarded and antagonistic with Guy when he dropped back into my life. I wasn't sure which Guy I was going to get: the friend he used to be or the foe I remember him being so vividly before he left. Rather than waiting to find out, I cast him as the foe without a second thought. It was easier that way. With our dynamic already determined, I didn't have to figure out how I felt about him.

"Has he given you any reason to believe he might hurt you again?"

"No," I say. "I know it's irrational, but that's me."

"And a little unfair to Guy, to be honest."

I start shredding the napkin again. "I know."

There's a long pause that does nothing but make me even more uncomfortable.

"You need to clear it up with Guy. Talk to him. Ignoring this won't make it go away. Figure out what you want, whether it's Guy or not."

"You're right," I say. It's the same conclusion I came to earlier but never followed through on.

Marissa pauses for a few moments. "And do it quick, because I'd prefer not to have an awkward party next weekend."

"Oh God, it's that soon?"

"And the wedding's not far from that."

We spend the next few minutes talking about the party and then the wedding. It's going to be a blast, and I can't wait to have a little time to unwind from this renovation, which is moving along at an incredible pace thanks to Ryder. He's running his crew like a well-oiled machine and even called in some favors from a few of his business connections to speed things up. There's no doubt in my mind that the renovation will be done by the wedding.

After wedding talk, Marissa weaves right back to Guy talk.

"No more ignoring texts or calls from him."

"But it makes things so much easier when I pretend things didn't happen."

"That's not how it works. You might feel better for a little while, but Guy's probably losing it right now trying to figure out what's going on. You two kissed, Charleigh. And you meant it. It wasn't an accident. That changes things."

"Does it really though?"

Marissa glares at me.

"I'll talk to him after work today. It's not like I can really ignore him anyway. I'm moving back in with my mom until my apartment gets fixed."

Marissa grimaces. "Just don't let Deanna make you anything."

"Oh, I know. Thankfully, Guy's taking on the role of home cook."

"Oh, yeah?"

"Flowery apron and all."

"I can picture it."

Oh, so can I. All the time. Him in an apron, and *only* an apron. I wonder if his butt is as cute as I imagine...

Marissa snaps her fingers in front of me. "Charleigh, you okay? You just zoned out for like fifteen seconds there."

"Oh yeah, just fine. Just thinking about work."

Or Guy working it…

Oh jeez. I really do need to slow things down between us, at least until this renovation's over. It won't matter then if we date or see each other. He won't be my client. Andrea won't talk. Everything will be right.

Marissa and I get up and make our way out of Common Grounds.

"No scone today," Marissa says. "You really were distracted."

"Thanks for the reminder," I say, looping around back to the front door.

Marissa laughs. "I shouldn't have said anything."

"Oh no, you definitely should."

"I'll see you at the party if I don't see you sooner. Text me how it goes with Guy."

We say our goodbyes, and I head back inside to get my morning scone fix. The rest of the day goes by in a blur. I double, triple, and quadruple check and the budgetary items, delivery dates, and send off a slew of emails. By the time I look at the clock, it's past 6:30 pm and everyone in the office is gone.

I check my phone. There's a missed call and voicemail from my landlord. I play the message and after hearing the words "We've got a problem," my stomach drops.

"Yikes."

Guy leans against the doorway to my bedroom, arms folded across his chest. He's still wearing his police uniform, and my brain is floating dangerous ideas—how to rip it off of him. Which is the complete opposite of what I should be thinking right now.

"Yeah, they found it everywhere."

Black mold. I couldn't believe it when my landlord broke the news to me earlier today. I thought they'd have everything fixed and patched up so I could move back in today, but that's not going to happen.

"How long until you can move back in? Not that I want you to leave or anything," he adds quickly.

I sigh, mashing my face between the palms of my hands. "I don't know. They won't know until they finish ripping out the drywall. Then there's remediation. Inspections."

"Sounds like fun."

"Yeah, it's a whole lot of fun living with your mom in your late twenties."

Guy smiles. "It's not so bad here. Besides, you've got me."

Yes. Yes, I do.

I let his statement die in the air for dramatic effect, and when it gets just uncomfortable enough, I say, "Oh, was that supposed to be a positive?"

He smiles at me, creased lines forming at the edge of his eyes. "I like you, Charleigh."

"I like me, too."

I cringe inwardly as soon as it leaves my mouth. Why am I such a weirdo around Guy? But for some reason, Guy doesn't seem to mind. In fact, it seems to draw something out of him that shifts the air around us instantly.

"We never finished making dessert from last night."

There's a change in his tone, all gravelly and sensuous, and it has an immediate effect on my body. My pulse quickens. My skin tingles. And my breath comes in choppy spurts.

I swallow. "I don't like dessert."

He takes a step forward and I take two back. We're back at it again. The same dance we had this morning. As much as I want to figure out how far we could take this, the timing is off. But I'm beginning to realize that timing is the least of Guy's worries.

He takes another step, and I take two, striking the edge of my bed with my calves.

"I think we should talk," I say.

"I'm tired of talking. As much as I'm tired of you running."

"I'm not running."

Guy's smile deepens. "It sure feels that way. Every time I move forward you step back. Why is that?"

He's in my space. Every breath I take is filled with him. I can't see anything but him. He reaches for my cheek, his fingertips dragging gently across my skin. The fine hairs on my neck and arms shoot straight up as he draws a strand of hair away from my cheek and hides it behind my ear.

I don't know what to do. The logical part of me wants to stop. I'm about to break so many company policies pertaining to client relations that I could kiss my career and reputation goodbye. But the other part of me is begging for Guy's lips again.

Forget company policy—do what's in your heart.

"I know what I want," Guy rasps, dragging his fingertips achingly slowly down my cheek. His touch is so delicate that it's giving me goosebumps.

"And what's that?" I whisper.

GUY HATER

"I want you."

And with those three simple words, something inside me switches on. All my doubts and worries fade away as what I want comes into focus for the first time. And before I have a chance to think, I'm on my back with Guy on top of me.

CHAPTER TWENTY-EIGHT

Charleigh

GUY'S HIPS PRESS against mine, pinning me in place. I'm double fisting his shirt, hanging on for dear life as his lips crash against mine. It takes a few moments for my mind to catch up, reminding me that I'm making out with Guy on my childhood bed.

Jackpot.

It's a whole hell of a lot better than I ever dreamed. And I have dreamed about it once, twice, or twenty times. Either or, really. But with Guy's lips mashed against mine, his tongue sliding against mine, and his hands all over me, my mind is drawing blanks.

Guy wraps a warm, rough hand around the back of my neck, pulling me closer into him, deepening our kiss as the other hand slides down my side and rests on my hip. Never have I ever kissed anyone like this. It's as though there's an asteroid the size of Texas on a collision course with Earth, primed to destroy humanity as we know it in a few hours. Heated, hungry, and hurried—we're getting our fill before either of us has any second thoughts.

But the only other thought I'm having is wondering how much better his abs are going to look up close. And as I let go of my grip, letting my fingertips slide across them, I know I won't be disappointed.

He lets out a deep groan as I take his bottom lip between my teeth. I let go and ask, "Did I hurt you, big guy?"

And it's taking on a whole new meaning right now. I can feel his big guy pressing against me. Wowza, he's big. Guy grins against my lips, his warm breath dancing along my skin.

"Not at all. It reminded me to breathe, actually. A few more minutes of kissing you and I'd have been a goner."

"That'd be a shame."

There's a small break. Silence. Breathing. My heart thumping. His eyes locked on mine. Every nerve ending in my body feels like it's firing on all cylinders with slow, rhythmic pulses. I make a move to slide back on the bed for a better angle and he gets up. HE GETS UP! And now he's walking to the door, and I'm pissed, my body still reeling.

"Guy!" I shout-whisper. "GET. BACK. HERE." I will not be denied my God-given right to have sex in my childhood bed.

He glances back at me. "You think I'm done? We're not close to being done, Charleigh." Guy shuts the door and then says, "I figured you wouldn't want Deanna to walk by the open door."

Point taken.

Guy turns back around and unbuttons his shirt, tossing it to the ground. He crosses the room as he pulls his white undershirt over his head like some underwear model in a commercial. And as I gawk at him as he looms over me, I realize that he *is* an underwear model. Pure muscle. Those abs, rows stacked on rows of pure muscle, are so tight that I'm sure they'll pop out at any moment now.

And all of it is mine.

I position myself on my knees in front of him, unbuckling his belt as quickly as I can. Which, as it turns out, isn't all that fast because my fingertips refuse to work together, fumbling every step of the way. What sort of sorcery holds this belt together?!

Hurry this up! Emma squeals at me.

I'M DOING THE BEST I CAN!

Is this how men feel when they can't unhook a bra? I'm about to say screw it and just unzip his pants when Guy reaches down and removes the belt for me in one smooth motion. Jesus, this is embarrassing.

"That's some belt you have there."

He smiles, placing his warm hand along my jaw, his thumb drawing light circles against my cheek.

"Standard issue. Who'd have known they could be so complicated?"

"Seriously."

"I'll make a note not to wear one next time."

"Or anything at all. You could just walk around naked from now on."

He laughs. "I'm not sure Deanna would appreciate that."

"Well, I would," I say, dragging a finger along his torso. "And that's all that matters."

I kiss him just below his belly button and he groans. I like that sound. I like the noises he makes and I wonder what else I'll be able to draw from him. I lean into him, my knees digging into the edge of the bed as I continue to kiss my way up to his face.

He weaves his fingertips into my hair, skimming across my scalp, which sends wave after wave of delicious tingles down the nape of my neck. Before I make it to his chest, he grips my hair and pulls back gently, forcing me to look up at him. His eyes are dark, hooded under his lids, and a few seconds later he's on me again.

My legs splay open, and he slides in between them. I can feel his length against me, rubbing and grinding. It feels so good. I wrap my legs around him and press him harder against me, angling my hips so he rubs against me perfectly.

I drag my hands along his chest, up his arms, and back again, feeling every firm mound and ridge as though I'm trying to commit all of it to memory. I've never been with anyone so athletic, so masculine, and I want to savor every second of this.

I nuzzle against Guy's hand as he cups the side of my face, breathing in his spicy scent. He guides my face back toward him, and then he kisses me again. His tongue glides across mine as our lips press together, both of us taking choppy breaths whenever we can.

Guy begins to unbutton my blouse as I reach for his pants, my fingertips regaining their dexterity and making quick work of the single button and zipper. I slide out of my blouse, unhooking my bra as Guy slips out of his pants.

Guy snorts when he sees my eyes bulge as I look at his bulge, but wastes no time unzipping the back of my skirt and sliding it off me. He's at the edge of the bed, my legs dangling off the side. His palms press against my thighs, edging farther and farther up as his head follows behind. His warm breath dances across the surface of my skin as he plants kisses along my inner thighs.

Our eyes lock just before his lips reach my panty line. I can hardly breathe. I can hardly think straight. But then Guy asks me if I'm sure this is what I want. There's not a single questioning thought left in my mind. This is exactly what I want. Guy is exactly what I want.

I nod, but Guy doesn't continue.

"I need to hear you say it, Charleigh."

I drag my teeth across my bottom lip, my center aching for release.

"I want you, Guy," I say in a breathy whisper. "I want you so much."

It's true. I feel it deep in my core with unwavering certainty.

And then his lips brush delicately along my wet center, barely covered by a thin layer of lace. His thumb follows shortly after, teasing me, rubbing gently. My hips buck against him, trying to increase the pressure, trying to take control, but he presses his forearm down against my hips, locking me in place.

I let my head fall back against the bed as I relent to the agonizingly slow circles he's drawing against me. He kisses the length of my inner thigh as his thumb continues to tease me. I moan and groan as I arch my back, writhe, and beg for him to continue. And then he slides his fingers beneath the elastic band of my thong and slides it off in one smooth motion, baring me to him.

He wastes no time, sliding one arm across my abdomen, locking me in place as his lips find my wet center. Sparks erupt in my head as my body pulses. Our eyes lock, and I don't think I've seen anything sexier than this. I can only hold eye contact for a few moments because whatever the hell Guy is doing to me is making me lose control—and quick.

My head rolls back along with my eyes as wave after wave of pure bliss rolls over me. Even though I'm writhing and twisting, Guy's firm grasp keeps me in place even as every part of me becomes so sensitive that I can hardly take it. He reaches up with his free and grabs onto my breast, massaging me, his thumb lightly brushing across my nipple.

When he draws his tongue across my entire length, I can feel my orgasm beginning to well.

"Come for me," Guy says, finally coming up for air.

We lock eyes, and then he slides a finger inside me, hitting my spot perfectly as his lips find me again. Neither of us looks away, even as my eyes begin to glaze over. A few moments later I come, and I feel the sweet release spread across the entirety of my body, all the way up to my scalp.

When I'm finally able to look at Guy again, I find him standing up, his athletic form silhouetted in the dim room, rolling a condom on his cock.

Holy shit is all I can think as I finally get a look at Guy completely naked. I've never seen anyone so ripped before. And I've certainly never seen anything *that* big before.

HELL YEAH! Emma screams.

"That was nice," I say, trying to play it cool. It was way more than nice—way more than anything any other man has done to me before. I'd give up scones if it meant he did that to me every day.

"Only nice?" Guy asks, sliding next to me on the bed. "I guess I'll have to work a little harder next time." His warm breath tickles my neck as he skims the surface of my arm with his palm.

I can feel his very stiff erection along the small of my back as he repositions himself. He slides the tip along my opening, pressing gently for a moment before pulling back the next. He's teasing me again. I try to push back against him but he grabs on tight to my hips, holding me in place.

He slides against my wetness again and I bite down hard on my lip, a frisson of excitement running up my spine. And then he pushes farther this time, inch by delicious inch until it seems like I can't take it anymore.

I groan.

"Are you okay?" Guy asks.

"More than okay," I say, inching myself into him.

He moans, deep and guttural, as his fingers dig even deeper into my flesh. I love that sound, sensual and satisfied as it rolls over me. Guy lets one hand wrap around me, massaging my breast as he begins to thrust. It's slow and methodic and everything I ever wanted him to do to me.

In and out. In and out. Christ, it feels so good as he fucks me. His hands dragging across my body. Gripping. Searching. Feeling. His lips find the crook of my neck and I'm losing it. His breath. His tongue. His lips.

I bite my lip again, trying my best not to make any noise, but it's no use. I can't stop this. I'm completely losing control and I'm liking every second of it.

"Is this better than nice?" Guy asks.

"Yes," I moan back at him, my hands fisting the bedspread.

I can feel his lips form a smile against my back before kisses me in between my shoulder blades.

"Again," I groan as he spanks me.

There's another loud smack as he brings his palm against me, stroking it gently afterward.

"That's it," I moan.

God, I'm so close. I'm so close. But then Guy stops, rolling over onto his back. I roll over to him, and he cups my face and kisses me harshly. I melt into him as we taste each other. When we finally pull away, he says, "I want you on top of me. I want to watch you come."

Oh. My. Guy.

I slip one leg over him and then ease myself onto him, savoring the feeling of him filling me completely. He grips the back of my neck as I rock my hips against him. With our eyes locked, I've never felt so close to someone else before. He pulls me even closer, kissing me again.

Guy lets go of my neck and then grips my hips. I rear back, letting my hair fall onto my back as I continue to grind against him. I can sense that he's close. He closes his eyes for a brief moment, pressing his lips into a thin line as he fights hard to hold on.

A few moments later, I feel myself clenching against him.

"I'm… I'm…" I mutter, letting my head rock back.

"Look at me," Guy says.

I do, and a few moments later, I come, right along with

Guy. I nestle against him, listening to the slow, rhythmic beat of his heart. There's no place I'd rather be. There's no other person I'd rather be with. And within a few moments, my body relaxes completely, and I fall fast asleep.

CHAPTER TWENTY-NINE

Guy

I WAKE UP to Charleigh giggling uncontrollably into my chest. I let her go on for a while longer because I enjoy her warm breath against my bare skin, and I don't want the moment to end. But my curiosity gets the better of me and I have to ask: "What's so funny?"

The giggling begins to wind down, and after a few deep breaths they finally stop.

And then start right back up again.

I roll over, bracketing her with my arms as I look down at her. Christ, she's gorgeous when she smiles and laughs. "What's so funny?" I ask again.

"I was—" *Giggle.* "I—oh my God!" More giggling. "I was supposed to put this—" she motions to me with her finger "—on hold until the renovation was over and you weren't my client."

"How'd that turn out for you?"

She thinks for a few moments and then nods. "Better than expected."

She wraps her arms around my neck and pulls me into her, our lips meeting again.

"I don't think I can kiss you enough."

"I don't think you could kiss me enough either."

I've never seen anything more beautiful in my life than Charleigh at this moment. She's let go of all restraint, of every wall she's had built up around her. There's a lightness in her eyes, a playfulness in her voice, and I can't believe how lucky I am to have her.

We continue to kiss, extending the moment for as long as possible until there's a loud knock on the door. Mortification would be an understatement for the expression on Charleigh's face when she hears Deanna speak to both of us through the door.

"Now that you two are done, get dressed and come downstairs for dinner. I made pasta with Italian sausage."

Both of us stare at each other silently as we listen to the thump of Deanna's feet as she walks back down the hallway and downstairs. The seconds seem to stretch into hours as both of our heads spin, reeling from what just happened.

"I guess we should be a little quieter next time," I say finally.

"No can do," Charleigh says. "It's impossible to be quiet with *this.*" I groan as she palms my cock, rolling it in her hand. "Or *this.*" She presses a finger against my lips.

"Then we'll just have to wait until she leaves next time."

Charleigh laughs. "Who'd have thought living with your mom at twenty-seven could be so complicated?"

"I don't think either of us minds a little complication."

I press my lips against hers, grabbing her wrist and pinning it above her head as we continue to make out. A few minutes later, Deanna calls out again. "It's getting cold!"

I break away from Charleigh, and it's clear from the look in her eyes that it's the last thing she wanted me to do. It's the last thing I wanted to do too. If I had the choice, I'd just stay in bed with her forever.

"I think I've had my fill of sausage today," Charleigh says. She bites her lips, trying hard not to laugh, but I can't show the same restraint and laugh enough for both of us.

"You're something else, Char."

I kiss her on the forehead and then roll out of bed. I glance at her as I lean over and grab my shirt off the floor.

"There's no reason to pout."

"I think there's plenty reason to pout. And plenty reason for you to keep that shirt on the ground where it belongs."

I pull the shirt on over my head. "We can pick this up again later. We live down the hall from each other now, remember?"

Charleigh rolls onto her side and then onto her stomach. Christ, it's hard to resist temptation when the most gorgeous woman in the world is lying naked on her bed, begging for you to strip down. I can't take my eyes off the curves of her body and the way her long hair rests gently on her back.

"So it's a promise that you'll sneak into my bedroom tonight?"

"I solemnly swear."

But as I'm looking at Charleigh on the bed, I'm not sure if I'll be able to last until tonight.

———

The metal bar smacks back into place, rattling the bench.

Maddox claps me on the back as I sit up. "Holy shit, dude! I've never seen you move that much weight before!"

I reach for my towel. "I haven't." I wipe the sweat from my brow as I try to catch my breath. I wasn't planning on lifting that much, but something was pushing me to go for it.

"Damn, dude. That must be a new PR for you."

"Smashed my old record by twenty pounds."

"Well, congrats." He smacks my back again. "Now get the fuck up and let me have a go."

I stand up, my muscles screaming from being pushed to their limits. I never thought I'd be able to push that much weight, but that's how it's been lately. Things that I thought would never happen, happened. Charleigh and me being the most unlikely. I still can't believe it, even though I've been spending every night in her bed for the past week. It feels too perfect, and I'm afraid that it could disappear just as quickly as it started.

"Let's fucking go," Maddox yells, clapping his hands loudly before leaning back against the bench.

"You sure about this?" Maddox hasn't lifted this much weight before either, and I'm afraid that he might be stretching his limits. I probably shouldn't have attempted it either, but with how invincible I've been feeling lately, I didn't want to stop the momentum.

"You afraid I'll smash your record?"

"No, I'm afraid you'll smash your chest."

"That's why I've got you here, bud. Quit yapping and help me get this shit off the rack."

I sigh, hoping to God that Maddox has it in him to move this weight, or else I'll be down a partner. I help Maddox lift the bar off the rack and let go.

He keeps his arms extended, prolonging the descent. He's beginning to shake and wobble and it's becoming clear that it's far too much weight.

"Dude, it's too much."

"Ffu—noo—pgh—" Maddox mumbles and spits, red-faced and straining as he holds the weight out. I grab the bar and force it back onto the rack.

"The fuck, dude? I had it."

I take off fifteen pounds on both sides of the bar, ignoring Maddox's swollen ego talking. "I know you did. I didn't want to see my record smashed so quickly."

Maddox nods. "Thought so."

I'm not sure if the sarcasm flew over his head or if he's taking the easy out I gave him. Either way, Maddox seems content with lifting a more manageable amount of weight.

As soon as he starts his reps, I catch a glimpse of Charleigh getting off her treadmill. And in that moment I give thanks to the person who invented yoga pants. Dear lord, she's a sight to behold. She's turning heads as she walks down the long rows of cardio equipment, ponytail bobbing with every step. She turns her head, a smile growing on her lips as she spots me. She changes directions and begins walking toward me.

I'm mesmerized, so much so that I completely forgot that I'm supposed to be spotting Maddox. I look down and he's writhing underneath the bar, leveling a murderous expression at me as he struggles out a few words.

I grab the bar, apologizing profusely as I rack it.

Maddox shoots up, trying to catch his breath before finally asking me what the fuck my problem was. Before I have the chance to answer, Charleigh appears in front of us, answering Maddox's question for me.

"Emma!" Maddox says, hopping off the bench. He tries to hug Charleigh, but she expertly dodges it by kneeling down to tie her shoelaces.

Emma? How does…

"Hey, Mattis," Charleigh says, looking up at Maddox.

"It's Maddox," he says, rubbing the back of his neck.

Finally, it comes back to me, so much so that I need to prop my body against the bench so I don't double over with laughter. I'd completely forgotten how Charleigh had dodged Maddox a few months back.

"I tried to email you, but I must've written down your address wrong. It was Emma bamma the slamma jamma at gmail dot com, right?"

Charleigh coughs and sputters, trying her best to maintain her composure. "Yup," she says. "How many M's did you put in slamma?"

Maddox counts it in his head as he holds out his fingers. "Two," he says, finally.

"Ah, it's actually three M's, two M's was taken."

"Oh." Maddox clears his throat. "Got it."

Charleigh and I catch each other's eye as she stands up. I motion to the water fountains behind us, and within a few seconds, she leaves and heads in that direction.

"Man," Maddox says, sitting back down on the bench, running his palm over his buzzed head. "I don't think she likes me."

I clap his back. "Don't worry about it, man. Plenty of other women out there for you."

"Yeah…" Maddox groans. "Yeah. Plenty of women who want to see the gun show." Maddox kisses his biceps and I roll away, cringing that my partner called his arms guns.

I find Charleigh waiting for me at the water fountains, but as I approach, she turns around and disappears into a hallway meant for employees. The moment I turn the corner, she leaps onto me, nearly knocking me off balance as she wraps her legs around my waist. She moans into my mouth as I press her against the wall, steadying us both.

She pulls away. "This is a nice surprise," she says as she plants kisses along the edge of my jaw.

"I had a break." I groan as Charleigh grinds against me. "And hadn't worked out—*fuck*—"

I'm doing everything in my power to restrain myself from ripping Charleigh's tank to shreds and rolling her yoga pants off her. Christ, what is she doing to me?

"I thought we worked out this morning. And last night. And the night before."

I laugh. These last few days have been amazing, to say the least. Both of us are insatiable.

"You're right. And if you keep grinding on me, we'll probably have another workout right here."

"Sounds good to me."

I pin Charleigh's hands above her head, kissing her harshly as she moans into my mouth.

"The hell's going on out here?" someone yells from down the hallway.

Charleigh releases me, sliding down from the wall and screams, "CPR. I passed out and this gentleman just saved my life."

"Get out of here," the man yells. "It's for employees only."

Both of us dart around the corner, and before we get too far I stop, pulling Charleigh back into me.

"Tonight?" I ask?

"Tonight," Charleigh responds.

I press my lips into hers again, savoring one last taste to hold me over, but who am I kidding? I'll never have enough.

CHAPTER THIRTY

Charleigh

"I COULD GET used to this," Guy says.

We just finished another walk-through, and now we're both enjoying the view of the forest from the newly expanded deck. The fresh-hewn cedar smells divine as it mixes with the smoke from the newly installed fire pit, the pines from the forest, and the damp soil after the rain. Fresh. Clean. Amazing. I never want to get used to this.

"Why would you want that?" I ask.

After removing my hands from the railing, I turn around and look at the deck again. I still need to have the furniture delivered to finish the space, but even without it, the space is wonderfully inviting. The deck is multi-layered and winding as it wraps around the house. Some of the larger trees have been incorporated into the design, rising through the deck. There's a pergola and small outdoor kitchen outfitted with stone, and the fireplace from the inside extends outdoors.

"What do you mean?" Guy asks.

I can feel his warm gaze on my cheek as he turns toward me, and the swell in my chest and fluttering across my skin screams the answer I already know. I never want to get used to the way Guy makes me feel. I want to feel like this forever. I never want to get used to it or take it for granted.

"Why would you want to get used to this? Why would you want to feel anything less than what you feel now?"

"I don't, but nothing ever stays the same. Everything changes, Charleigh."

"I guess, but I still don't like that phrase."

Guy laughs and pulls me into a hug. "And that's what I love about you. You're very clear about what you don't like. And if you remember, that was me at one point. But things change."

I pull my head back and make a face. "The jury's still out on you."

He kisses my forehead, and I'm melted chocolate in his arms. "Let me know when they're done deliberating because there's something I'd like to do with you once we're done with the renovation."

"And what would that be?"

"Christen each and every room."

His hands slide agonizingly slowly down my back until they rest firmly on my ass. He's got a half smile on his lips and burning embers in his eyes. Why did I wait so long for this?

I roll my bottom lip under my teeth. "I guess I might like that."

"Might?" Guy pulls one hand away and then the next. "I thought you might be a little more—"

I wrap my hands around the nape of his neck and kiss him.

"Better?" I ask, pulling away just a hair, our lips still brushing together gently.

"Much."

There's a throat clear in the distance, followed by a deep voice, which makes Guy and me break apart from each other. Ryder's boots thud against the wood as he approaches us. There's a ghost of a smirk on his lips. "Sorry to interrupt," Ryder says, his tone a little more playful than usual, "but I wanted to let you know I talked with the mason and electrician. Your issues will be no issue by next week."

"Great. Good. Thanks. Fannnnntastic."

Ryder smiles, glancing at me, to Guy, and then back to me. "Don't worry. I won't tell."

He tips his cowboy hat at us and then turns around. "I'll see you two at Jamie and Marissa's party this weekend."

"Yup, see you there!"

He's halfway to the house when I can finally breathe again. I'd talked with Guy about keeping our relationship secret because it's technically against Florence + Foxe policy to date any current clients. And it does nothing for my reputation if Andrea or anyone else at the firm thinks I'm stealing clients by sleeping with them.

"Shit," Guy says, turning to me. "I didn't mean to—I forgot Ryder was still here."

"Don't worry about it. Ryder's not Andrea. But we should probably tone it down for the bachelorette party because there's no way to know who will be there."

"That might be difficult," Guy says.

"Don't worry," I say, dragging a finger down his chest. "I'll more than make up for it later."

"I'm counting on it."

GUY

I know I promised Charleigh, but I'm not sure I'll be able to keep my hands to myself tonight. She'd spent most of the day torturing me by sending pictures of the dress she'd be wearing, and as much as I know it will look amazing on her, I think it will look even better pooled around her feet.

> **Guy:** What are you doing to me, Charleigh?
>
> **Charleigh:** What are you talking about? I'm just trying to get your opinion on my dress.
>
> **Guy:** By sending me pictures of your cleavage? I literally can't see your dress in half the photographs.
>
> **Guy:** Not that I'm complaining…
>
> She sends a shrug emoji back, followed by yet another selfie. Dear lord, she's gorgeous. She rarely wears makeup, but when she does…
>
> **Guy:** Keep it up and I'll drag you out of the party within a few minutes.
>
> **Charleigh:** Caveman style?
>
> **Guy:** Caveman style.
>
> **Charleigh:** I wouldn't mind that.

It's all I can think about for the rest of the day. Charleigh. The dress. Dragging her from the party and ripping that dress off her. I've never felt this way with anyone else before—so out of control. But I wouldn't have it any other way.

The day drags on at a snail's pace as I'm consumed with thoughts of Charleigh. Normally, I'd say nothing would be able to drag me out of my trance, but when I open the door to Deanna's house, I stand corrected. Judging by the foul odor permeating throughout the house, there's either a decaying animal in the walls or Deanna is cooking. Based on the whistling coming from the kitchen, it's the latter. But I can't rule out the former...

I say a little prayer in my head, force a smile onto my face, and head into the kitchen.

"Wow, what is that?"

Deanna turns around, wiping her hands against her red-checked apron, and beams at me.

"Tuna casserole surprise." The oven beeps and she grabs the mitts from the drawer. She opens the oven and then sets the casserole on the stove before turning to me. "Charleigh told me it was your favorite dish I used to make, and I thought you'd like something hearty in your stomach before the party tonight."

Did she now?

"Yeah, that would be great. Where is Charleigh, by the way? Has she left to meet up with Marissa yet?"

"She's still upstairs getting ready."

Deanna opens up the oven. The overwhelming scent turns into an overpowering one that forces me to turn around and block my nose before something comes up.

"Hurry back though. Don't want it to get cold."

No. We definitely wouldn't want that to happen.

"Make sure you give Charleigh a heaping serving. She told me she loves it more than sweets."

The sound of music filters into the hallway from upstairs. When I reach the second floor, I can't help but laugh. "MMMBop" by Hanson is blaring from Charleigh's room with her vocal accompaniment.

I creep down the hall, careful not to disturb the elusive creature in her natural habitat. And the closer I get to her room, the better the aural experience becomes.

Pitch: Imperfect.

Vocal abilities: William Hung.

And every lyric apart from the *mmm bop* is mumbled and butchered beyond recognition.

I reach the door and peek inside. She's bouncing around the room, performing what David Attenborough would describe as a bizarre but magnificent display of courtship.

Dancing? A mating ritual? Seizure? I don't know what I'd call this. Whatever it is, I can't take my eyes off her. She tilts her head back, letting her long red curls fall behind her. Her arms flail wildly above her as she spins around on one leg, the other raised precariously by her side. She's in the dress, and it's even more alluring in person than in the pictures.

We might not make it to the party after all.

"MMM BOP, doo pa bop a skibby a dooo wooo MMM BOP."

Charleigh breaks out the imaginary microphone as I settle against the doorframe. She's oblivious to my presence, and I'm not about to interrupt her performance.

GUY HATER

I'm not sure I've ever seen anything like it or if I'll ever see something like it again because I know she's going to kill me the moment she finds out I'm behind her. It's a shame I don't have my phone to document it for future generations. That anthropology dissertation will sadly go unwritten now.

She takes a running leap onto the bed just as the Hanson boys end their lyrical masterpiece. Charleigh sticks the landing like an Olympic gymnast, arms outstretched above her head and all. Perfect time for a slow clap.

She lets out a blood-curdling scream as she contorts her body like a cartoon character desperately trying to avoid a mouse skittering across the floor.

"Jesus Christ," I say, raising my arms to calm her down. "I didn't mean to surprise you."

I push off from the doorway and edge into the room. Almost immediately, a stuffed teddy bear connects with my face.

"Holy shit, Guy!"

I feel like I'm Neo in *The Matrix*, but instead of bullets, I'm dodging flying Beanie Babies and stuffed animals. I lean back just in time for a pillow to fly past me and into the hall, grazing my chest.

"What."

Duck.

"The."

Jump.

"Hell."

I catch Britannia The Bear, which is fitting now that "Wannabe" by the Spice Girls in blaring. Everything about this room is a blast from the past.

"You done, Charleigh?"

She rears her arm back, readying to launch the next assault. I hold out Britannia in front of me and take the tag between two fingers. "I'll rip it off. I heard Beanie Babies are worthless without the tags."

"What in the world is going on up there?" Deanna calls up the stairs.

"*Nothing!*" Both of us reply in unison.

I meet Charleigh's fierce gaze. She cocks her head to the side with parted lips as though to say, *your move.* The move I want to take doesn't involve surrender. I want to close the gap between us, flying Beanie Babies be damned, and kiss those lips because I've never been more goddamn attracted to anyone before.

I love Charleigh's fiery personality. I love her quirks. I love everything about her. I let go of the tag, and a few seconds later, the Beanie Baby hits the floor.

"Truce?"

She lowers her arm, eyes still narrowed on mine as she crosses the room. She smells like citrus, bright and sweet, the complete opposite of how she's looking at me now. I'd be a little more uncomfortable under her glare if it weren't for the Spice Girls telling us what they really, really want right now.

She tosses the Beanie Baby in the air. It smacks against the palm of her hand.

"Truce."

Just before she passes me, she shoves the Beanie Baby into my gut. Her eyes draw back up to mine. "For now."

She passes by me, but I snag her by the elbow and pull her back into me.

"Leaving so soon?"

Her lips, colored a deeper red than usual, spread into a toothless grin, and there's nothing else I want to do more than kiss them.

"We've got a party to go to."

"It's not for a few more hours. And I'm wondering how that dress of yours will look on the floor."

Charleigh blushes as she drags her teeth across her bottom lip. Her hand slides across my abdomen until it lands on my cock. She strokes me through my pants. "I'm sure you do," she says. "But you're going to have to wait until later."

The wind is knocked out of me as she spins away and heads out of the room.

"Enjoy your tuna casserole surprise," she says before waltzing out of the room.

She has no idea what she just started.

CHAPTER THIRTY-ONE

Charleigh

"I'M SURE CHAD'S going to propose to you, Becki. You're…"

Yikes. This is not how I envisioned this night going. I've spent more time with Marissa's friends than with Marissa. It wouldn't be so bad if it weren't for the fact that said friends have been drinking since dawn and each of their emotional states are in various stages of unstable.

Exhibit A: Becki

Age: Unknown.

Appearance: Disheveled. Her thickly applied mascara is bleeding down her face. And her cheeks are so puffy and red that it wouldn't surprise me to hear she'd been stung by a swarm of bees a few hours ago.

Issue: Chad (need I say more?).

"…wonderful and pretty and—"

Thankfully, I don't have to dig any deeper for more adjectives to describe this woman I've just met because she gets a phone call.

"It's Chad!" she squeals, tap dancing as she holds the phone in front of her. It's surprising that she's able to hold on to it.

"Are you sure—"

"Chad! Baby!" she squeals, spinning around so quickly that she nearly loses her balance and crashes to the floor. Although, given her current state of inebriation, I'm sure she wouldn't have felt it. "I miss you!" As she disappears into one of the stalls, I breathe a sigh of relief. My work here is done. I check my phone and find a message from Guy.

Guy: Where are you?
Charleigh: OH GOD PLEASE SAVE ME

It's been nearly half an hour since I walked into the bathroom. I intended to touch up my makeup quickly, but Becki cornered me before I had the chance to leave. Another girl bursts through the door and I have an overwhelming sense of *déjà vu*.

Nope! I'm not about to have a repeat therapy session, so I bow my head, ignore the tears, and rush through the door and smell the sweet smell of freedom. Unfortunately, freedom is smelling a whole lot like Axe body spray and it's making me want to gag. The culprit of the offensive smells becomes apparent when a strange older gentleman with a scraggly beard bumps into me and tips his fedora. "M'lady."

M'nope!

I press my lips into a hard thin line and bolt down the hallway and back to the main section of the bar.

I was a little surprised when Marissa and Jamie said they wanted to hold the party at The Lookout. There are plenty of bars to pick from in Boulder, but they were intent on keeping the party in Whispering Pine. I hadn't been back here since the night I ran into Guy. Sebastian, back then.

Speak of the devil. Guy's sitting in the same spot he sat in the night Emma and Sebastian met. He's even wearing the same outfit. I like it. I might have to call off our minimal touching rule we enacted for tonight. Everyone's drunk, so who'd even notice?

I weave in between throngs of men and women dancing to a mashup of '90s hits. It's more difficult than I thought. I pinball between groups of Marissa's friends as each of them drags me to dance with them. By the time I make it to the other end of the room, I'd danced to "Macarena," TLC's "No Scrubs," and a remix of Will Smith's "Gettin' Jiggy With It." And I'll have you know that no matter what Guy says, I've got some dance moves.

Out of breath, I slink into the same spot at the bar I sat in the last time, and the same waitress walks up to me to ask what I'd like to drink.

"Tequila and lime… And water."

She raises that same brow, wondering if we're going to have a repeat of that night.

"Hold the tequila and lime."

She leaves and a few minutes later there's a cold glass of ice water in front of me that I waste no time guzzling down. When I finally take a breath, I glance over at Guy.

My stomach drops for a brief moment when I see him laughing with another woman. She's twirling a finger into silky blonde hair as she leans into him.

I know I shouldn't be jealous, but it's hard not to be. Especially because the woman he's laughing with is Tilly, Marissa's English roommate from when she studied abroad in London. Who just so happens to be a fashion model and designer and multi-millionaire. Successful and gorgeous and the absolute last person I want Guy to be laughing with.

"Charleigh Holiday." The voice is deep and raspy, the type of voice you'd expect to hear in a commercial for bourbon. He sounds a lot like Ryder, but his tone lacks that arrogant edge. I turn around and see a near spitting image of Ryder, but instead of the trademark black hair of the King family, there's a shock of blonde.

"Reese?"

Reese King—Ryder's twin brother. They're not identical twins. Ryder used to joke that Reese was the blonde sheep of the family because he was the only one who wasn't born with a thick head of black hair. He was always a little more subdued than the rest of the King family, spending more time with his nose in books than on his family's ranch. But then again, subdued for the King family is gregarious in any other family.

Reese smiles and nods. "Can I sit?" He points to the chair next to me.

"Of course!"

He sits down and I can't help but breathe in his rich cologne. It's a little disorienting how good he smells, but then again he could be covered in manure and it would smell better than the Axe body spray that assaulted my nose earlier.

"I almost didn't recognize you," Reese says.

"If I didn't work with Ryder every day, I'd probably say the same thing. Apart from the blonde hair, you're the spitting image of him."

"You mean he's the spitting image of me, of course."

"Of course."

Reese smiles, his green eyes slowly appraising me. "How's it working with Ryder anyway?"

"He's not the whirlwind he used to be. Usually."

And as if on cue, there's a loud commotion behind us drawing our attention to the dance floor. The crowd parts and then rejoins, Ryder at the head as he starts reenacting the final dance from *Dirty Dancing*. Within a few seconds, he's lifting his partner over his head as "The Time of My Life" blares.

"Jesus Christ," Reese says, shaking his head. "He's definitely settled down."

I laugh. "Wow," is all I can muster as everyone else in the bar whistles, shouts, and claps, egging Ryder on.

"Some things never change."

I glance over at Guy again, and his eyes are searing a hole in me. Tilly's still chattering away, her hands wrapped around his bicep. I force the image out of my head and turn my attention back to Reese. After a few minutes of us catching up, my attention still drifting back to Guy and Tilly, the bartender places a glass of wine in front of me.

"A drink from the gentlemen," she says, nodding in the direction of Guy. I can't help but smile like a weirdo, giddiness bubbling in my chest. But that all but disappears when I turn and find that Guy's not there. Tilly's not there either.

"I have to go," I say quickly to Reese as I push away from the bar, glass in hand. He says something in response, but it's lost on me. I need to find Guy. I'm done with this whole pretend we're not dating thing. It's stupid.

I weave my way back through the crowd to the only place I could think he could be, and thank my lucky stars that he's sitting there. It's the same chair I sat in after he'd bought me a glass of wine. And he's alone.

"Is this seat taken?" I ask, pointing to his lap.

He glances up at me and smiles. "Not at all. Although I'm pretty sure we'll be in violation of rule number one— no touching. And rule number two—don't act like we like each other."

"Forget the rules," I say, dropping into his lap as gracefully as possible, which is to say not at all.

Guy coughs and sputters as my wine sloshes in its glass.

I take a sip of wine. "How was your chat with Tilly?"

Guy scrunches his brow. "Who?"

"Tilly. The British woman who was *so obsessed* with you," I say, affecting a terrible accent.

Guy laughs. "Tilly? I thought her name was Dilly." He pauses for a moment, his face scrunched as the gears begin turning in his head. "Which, now that I think about it, is a strange name for a woman." He shrugs. "I couldn't understand half of what she was saying."

Apparently, I was more enamored by Tilly than he was.

Guy snatches the wine glass out of my hand and takes a sip.

275

"I didn't take you for a white wine drinker."

"I'm not." Guy sets the glass down on the wood stump end table and then leans in close to me. "But I'll taste anything that your lips have touched."

I love everything about that. His warm breath tickling my neck. The raw, sensuous tone of his voice. But most of all, I love how it sends my body on edge. A surge of nerves flutters in my chest as I drink in his warm chocolate eyes and dangerous gaze. I roll my bottom lip under my teeth. "I like that. But I'd like it more if you used your lips on me."

"You sure? I bet Christiana's hanging around the bar, waiting for something uncouth to happen between us."

I smack Guy's arm. He's making fun of my paranoid thoughts about Andrea being out to get me.

"Shut up and kiss me." I wrap my arms around his collar and tug, but he won't budge. He brings his lips close to mine, so close that I can almost feel them.

"No," he says.

"What?" I breathe.

"Remember that time when you rubbed my cock through my pants before leaving me high and dry?"

I gulp. Oh dear. "That doesn't sound like something I'd do."

"Maybe it was Emma."

"Possibly. She's a wild one."

"And so is Sebastian."

"Can he come out to play?"

Almost instantly I'm thrown over Guy's shoulder, caveman style, and we're on the move. "Guy, what the hell?"

GUY HATER

"I can't wait any longer, Charleigh," Guy says, maneuvering through the crowd of drunk people who don't seem to notice the one-hundred-and-twenty-pound woman being dragged out of the bar by a caveman. A devilishly handsome caveman, but a caveman nonetheless.

We pass by Marissa and Jamie dancing. Marissa spots me and breaks away from him and shoots me a what-in-the-everliving-hell-is-going-on? look. I raise my hands—*I don't know*—but then smile and flash her a thumbs-up because, to be honest, I like everything about what's happening.

And even more, I like where it's heading.

CHAPTER THIRTY-TWO

Guy

AS I LIE on Charleigh's bed, stroking her hair as she lightly snores, I'm coming up short for a time in my life when I've been more content than right now. I'm hesitant to say it, but I feel that everything is perfect.

Of course, things aren't perfect. If given enough time, anyone could make a mile-long list of everything that's not perfect in their life. Finding what's wrong in your life is always much easier than focusing on the good. But right now, I'm focusing on the single best thing in my life: Charleigh.

Charleigh laughs softly, still fast asleep, and then a few seconds later she sleep talks about pancakes. I've learned the hard way that she's a very active sleeper. Hands in my face. Knees to the groin. Elbows to the ribcage. She's never once woken up in the same position she fell asleep in, and after seeing some of the odd positions she's found herself in the morning, I'm surprised that I haven't found her on the floor yet.

The best part about her sleeping habits, though, is her sleep talking. I've had brief conversations with her while she's been fast asleep. They've been very illuminating to her psyche.

"Do you want pancakes, Charleigh?"

"Mhmm," she moans as she grabs her pillow tighter. "Rainbow bear that's not—" She rolls over, letting go of the pillow as one arm dangles off the bed.

The moonlight cuts through a break in the curtains, covering her naked torso with a dreamy glow that makes her pale skin appear ethereal. Maybe I'm partial, but I don't think there's anything more beautiful in this world than Charleigh. I drag my fingertips delicately down her sternum and then pull the sheets over her.

I kiss her good night and fall asleep content, knowing that in the morning I'll wake up to the most beautiful woman in the world. Although the elbows to the ribcage throughout the night weren't exactly welcomed, Charleigh's smiling face when she finally wakes up makes up for it.

"Hi," she whispers.

I thread my fingers through her hair, brushing it off her face. "Hi, gorgeous."

Her face lights up, and I press my lips against her forehead. She wraps her arms around my neck and drags me down onto her. My cock, already hard, presses against her thigh as we make out.

"Keep this up," I say in between breaths, "and I'll make sure you never leave this bed."

Charleigh laughs, letting her head fall against the pillow, her hair fanning out around her head. I could look at her for hours. Her eyes. Her lips. Her smile. The freckles that spread across the bridge of her nose like dappled paint.

"That's the plan," she says, a mischievous smile spreading across her lips.

I kiss her smile and pull my face back just enough to see it reach her eyes before kissing her again, deeply this time. After a few moments, I draw back from her slowly enough that I feel slight resistance before our lips finally part.

"We'll starve," I whisper into her lips.

Charleigh presses her teeth against her bottom lip. "Delivery."

I lower my head, kissing her in a meandering line from her collarbone to the soft skin next to her ear. "I don't think they'll deliver to a bedroom."

"Maybe a couple of Washingtons would change their mind."

I pull back and watch as she rubs her thumb against her middle and forefinger as though she's doling out some cash, and I laugh. "Washingtons? Not even a Lincoln or Hamilton?"

She shakes her head. "Nope. It's more than generous if you ask me." A few seconds later, her stomach grumbles. "Speaking of food… I could really go for some—"

"Pancakes?" I interject.

She looks at me like I'm some sort of wizard.

"How did you—"

"Know?"

"Okay, that one wasn't that—"

"Impressive?"

"Okay, you need to—"

"Stop?"

She groans, rolling over onto her side as she pulls a pillow over her head.

I slide in next to her, big spoon to her little, wrapping my arms around her. "You know you love it." She *humphs* and grumbles and groans, but eventually, she relents.

"Maybe a little," she mumbles.

I kiss her in between her shoulder blades. "I'll get on those pancakes."

"Don't forget the chocolate chips."

"How could I?"

I've known Charleigh for a long time. There's hardly a single thing that I don't know about her. I know she chews the inside of her mouth when she's nervous. I know how she takes her coffee—not at all, unless she can't grab her usual decaf latte. I know that she prefers fall to any other season because, for her, pumpkin-spiced desserts and beverages are life.

But even though I know so much about her already, there's still more I uncover each day. And as long as she'll let me, I'll continue to do so.

After pulling on a pair of sweats and a white t-shirt, I step into Charleigh's unicorn slippers.

"Those look nice," Charleigh says, propping her head up with her hand as she lies on her side, watching me.

"I think they draw out the sparkle in my eyes."

She snorts. "Oh God, why do I like you so much?" she says, falling onto her back.

"So you admit that you like me?"

"Reluctantly."

I rap my knuckles against the nightstand. "I'll take it."

I head downstairs and into the kitchen.

"Morning, Guy." Deanna's sitting in her usual spot at the kitchen table. She's eyeing me over her magazine.

"Morning, Deanna. I thought I'd make pancakes."

"That sounds lovely. I made a fresh pot of coffee."

"Great."

Deanna bows her head, directing her attention back to her magazine. But as I rummage through the cabinets, grabbing all the ingredients for the pancakes, I can't help but feel like her attention's back on me.

"How was the party?"

"It was great," I say, measuring out the flour. "Everyone seemed to be having a great time."

"Then why did you and Charleigh come home so early?"

Well, shit.

We haven't told anyone that we're dating. Charleigh's been clear that no one should know until after the renovation in case something slips out and finds its way to Florence + Foxe. I've been fine with it because I don't want her to get in trouble for breaking company policy, no matter how much I disagree with it.

"We have an early morning today. There are a few things we both need to deal with at the house."

I feel bad about bending the truth. We do need to go to the house today, but it doesn't have to be early. I just can't tell Deanna the real reason why we both left so early.

She seems to be satisfied with the answer, and I go back to making the pancakes. Just as I'm pouring the batter into the pan for the first pancake, Deanna asks me the question she's clearly had on her mind for a while.

"When are you two going to stop pretending you're not dating?"

I fumble for a few seconds, trying my best to come up with an answer. Thankfully, I don't need to find an answer. When I turn around, I see Charleigh.

"Right now," she says as she crosses the kitchen wearing my flannel t-shirt and sleeping shorts. She stops right in front of me, rolls up on the balls of her feet, and kisses me.

"About time," Deanna says contentedly.

"About time, indeed," Charleigh says as her heels smack into the ground.

I can't even think of anything to say because my mind is racing. My heart is racing. I've never felt so much emotion for a person before.

"The pancakes are burning again," Deanna says.

"Shit!"

It doesn't take long for Charleigh to notice that I'm not helping her sweep dirt and debris from the kitchen floor.

"Are you going to help me sweep, or are you going to continue to stare?"

It's hard not to stare when your dream girl is standing right in front of you. The grin on my lips widens as Charleigh's expression grows more and more annoyed.

"Stare."

She huffs, shakes her head, and then resumes sweeping. "I can't believe Ryder hasn't cleaned this up."

I laugh, my eyes still fixed on Charleigh. "He's not finished yet. We haven't even done the blue tape walk-through."

She pauses, stares at me for a moment, and then resumes without a word.

"It's amazing, Charleigh. I wish you could stop for a moment and take it in."

Charleigh's design went above and beyond my wildest expectations. Even though the house looks nothing like the house I grew up in, she's been able to capture the essence that I felt when I lived here. It's cozy, inviting, and more of a home than it's felt to me in years.

I let my broom fall to the ground and head for Charleigh. Her head's down as she sweeps, so when I grab her broom, she jumps.

"Let go."

She frowns at me, tightening her grip around the broom. "Nope."

She tries to keep sweeping, but she can hardly move the broom a few inches with me holding on to it. After a few moments of struggle, I let go of the broom. She looks at me with a face that tells me she thinks she's won this one.

How adorable.

I take her face in my palms and kiss her. She's tense, but after a few moments, she lets go of the broom. Her hands move along my arms, onto my shoulders, until finally they reach my back and latch onto my back. She wraps her legs around my waist as I hold her up, moving slowly to the island behind us. We separate for a brief moment as I set her down on the island.

"Marissa and Jamie will be here any—" I silence her protests with my mouth, but only for a moment. She presses her palms against my chest and giggles against my lips before she pulls away again. "Just hold on."

I weave my fingers into the hair at the back of her head, tighten my grip and then pull. "As you wish." We continue kissing, our tongues crashing into each other. I could kiss Charleigh forever and it wouldn't be long enough.

"You need to stop," I say, pulling away from her.

Charleigh's out of breath and looking at me like I'm the strangest thing she's seen in her entire life. "Stop what?"

"Being so amazing."

It takes a few moments for her to register the off-the-charts level of corniness. But when it does, she bursts into an uncontrollable fit of laughter that takes more than a few minutes for her to come down from.

I don't mind it. I love it when she laughs, even if it's at my expense.

"Are you done?" I ask after she settles down.

She takes in a few deep breaths as she tries to calm her breathing. Finally, she says, "No," and begins it all again until I take the wind out of her sails with another kiss.

"Well, don't stop on our account."

The voice comes from behind us. Charleigh and I break apart and turn to see Marissa and Jamie smiling back at us. Well, Marissa's smiling back at us. Jamie's doubled over laughing.

"I told you," Marissa says, smacking him on the arm.

Charleigh hops off the island and does her best to rearrange her hair and dress. "Marissa! Jamie! So glad you could make it. Let me show you around."

Charleigh's a professional at pushing through awkward situations, and right now she's teaching a master class. I'm actually in awe over how quickly she switched into work mode. And she is in work mode because right now she's trying to win Marissa over on a vision for her wedding.

The whole reason why Marissa and Jamie are touring my house is to figure out if it would be a suitable replacement for their wedding and reception. Unfortunately, complications at their other venue made it impossible for them to have their wedding there. With their options for finding a new venue on short notice being limited, they nearly postponed the wedding until Charleigh swooped in and offered my house as a possibility.

I hadn't thought about it, but after listening to Charleigh's vision, I have no doubt she'd be able to make it work. And knowing Charleigh, she's going to go above and beyond what anyone expects.

"Just imagine standing in front of this soaring stone-faced fireplace, taking your vows—"

"This place is nothing like I remember," Jamie says, strolling back into the kitchen.

"Shouldn't you be taking the tour?"

Jamie shrugs. "Marissa's going to make the call. And from what I've seen so far, I'm pretty sure she's sold on it." He rubs the back of his head as he looks around the kitchen. "It's really amazing. I wish we knew how well it was going to turn out earlier. We wouldn't be in this whole mess."

I laugh. "Well, I hadn't even planned on renovating it back when you guys booked your first venue."

Jamie nods. "True." He walks over and runs his hand along the island. "Butcher block. Nice touch."

"All Charleigh. She went with it after deciding granite just didn't fit."

He snorts, and I know immediately what he's thinking. Charleigh and me. The look on his face is the same one Deanna wore when Charleigh finally kissed me in front of her. *I told you so.*

He doesn't bring it up. Instead, we talk about the wedding and go over the timeline for the finishing touches on the house. Eventually, I take him to my favorite part of the house: the deck.

The furniture is all in place and we take a seat on the Adirondack chairs circling the fire pit.

"I could get used to this," Jamie says.

I laugh, thinking about Charleigh. And no sooner than she popped into my mind, she appears with Marissa, who motions for Jamie to come with her.

Charleigh sits down next to me. "I think they're going to do it."

"Did Marissa like it?"

Charleigh rolls her head toward me. "Loved it."

After a few brief moments of silence, she says, "I just hope everything is done on time."

"It will be. It's not like there's much left to do."

I reach out and place my hand on Charleigh's. She's in her head, thinking about work. I'm a few seconds away from kissing her again to rip her out of her head, but before I have the chance, her phone rings.

She glances at it and says she has to take it, standing up and heading toward the other end of the deck. It seems like a fairly intense conversation from this vantage point, but it's hard to tell what's being said, so instead, I focus on the view of the forest.

Marissa and Jamie join me a few minutes later.

"Looks like it's settled," Jamie says, clapping my thigh as he sits down. "We're doing it."

"Yeah? That's great. Charleigh will be thrilled."

"I'm so glad we found a place," Marissa says. "I can't imagine waiting an extra month or two to be married to you," she says, nuzzling into Jamie's neck.

I sigh, turning my attention back to Charleigh. She's off the phone and heading back to us. Marissa tells her the news, and just as I expected, she's thrilled.

Once Marissa and Jamie leave, Charleigh turns to me and says, "I have good news."

"Yeah?"

"My landlord is offering me a new apartment to move into."

Is that supposed to be good news?

"Or you could move in with me once the reno's done."

Her eyes bug out. "Seriously?"

"Seriously. I'm not letting you go, Charleigh."

She lunges on top of me, and we both crash onto the floor.

"On second thought," I say through labored breaths, "maybe we could use a little space."

"Never," Charleigh whispers into my ear.

CHAPTER THIRTY-THREE

Charleigh

I'M AT LEAST fifty percent sure that I'm in the Star Trek universe because everything has moved at warp speed over this past week. All last minute issues with the renovation have been dealt with as quickly as they popped up, and after months of working tirelessly on this project, I'm finally able to take a few steps back and breathe. For a few minutes, at least, because the blue tape walk-through is in an hour, and I'm quickly becoming a nervous wreck.

This will be Christiana's first time seeing the house in person and not through my carefully curated progress pictures. I spent the night and then most of the early hours of the morning making sure that the house would be spotless for her.

Guy: Seriously. The house looks amazing. You

have nothing to worry about.

Charleigh: Could you put the cleaners and paper towels under the sink? I forgot to do that.

Guy: Already done.

Guy: Just BREATHE.

I lean back in my chair, close my eyes, and take in a deep breath. Okay. This isn't so bad. I lean back again, close my eyes, and try my best to relax. Apparently, I do a decent job at it because Andrea's able to sneak up on me.

"Sleeping on the job?" Andrea asks.

Her voice nearly jolts me out of my seat, but I quickly recover. "And even so I *still* get more work done than you."

I'm done playing nice with Andrea. I've tried ignoring her. I've tried befriending her. I've tried killing her with kindness. Barring *actually* killing her, I have no idea how else to approach her.

"Funny." A few seconds later, she adds, "Not."

Yikes. I forget what decade I'm in for a moment. Are "not" jokes back?

"What do you want, Andrea?"

She never comes over to my desk unless there's something she wants to rub in my face, so the quicker she's done, the quicker I can move on to more important things like figuring out whether I should have Guy light the sugar cookie candle or the pine tree candle. Mood is everything for these walk-throughs, and I'm not about to skimp on the ambiance.

"Take a look inside Christiana's office."

Andrea shifts to the side as I lean over and glance toward

Christiana's office. I'm not exactly sure what I'm supposed to be looking for. It all looks the same. There's someone I've never seen before sitting in front of Christiana's desk, but that's not unusual. There's always an unending stream of new clients coming and going from her office.

My chair creaks as I lean back. "I don't get it."

Usually, Andrea would have a self-satisfied grin on her face because she has information that I don't have. Instead, there's an expression I've seen on her face before: concern.

"She's interviewing for Lana's position."

I'm hoping I misheard Andrea, but the slow nod after I don't reply shoots that possibility down.

"I thought she was going internal."

Andrea shrugs. "I thought so too until I overheard part of the conversation Christiana had with her on the way to her office. She flew in from California."

Welp. This sucks. And here I thought Christiana would've at least waited until after the renovation to decide on whether she needed to look for an external candidate for Lana's job.

Andrea leaves me alone to stew. It's hard not to be annoyed. Even though these last few months have been draining and challenging, it was satisfying to have so much control over a project. And the thought that after it's all done I'll be returning to coffee duty is more than a little demoralizing.

I grab my phone and head to the parking lot. I need to call Guy. If there's anyone who can talk me down from this, it's him. After hopping into my car and shutting the door, I call Guy. It rings a few times before he answers.

"Hi there."

I'm trying my damnedest not to smile because I want to be angry right now, but after hearing Guy's voice, it's impossible to stop.

"Christiana's going with an external candidate for Lana's job."

"Shit." Guy sighs. "Did Christiana tell you? Was it announced?"

"Not exactly."

There's a small pause. "How do you know then?"

I tell him about Andrea and the woman interviewing for the job.

"And you trust Andrea? She could be trying to throw you off your game."

"It's possible." I hadn't thought of it, actually.

"She's more than likely trying to get in your head and make you second-guess yourself and botch the walk-through with Christiana so she could look better."

I wouldn't put it past Andrea to pull something like this, but I still can't shake the feeling that there's at least some truth to what Andrea's saying.

"Anyway, nothing's been announced. And remember that you've got a portfolio now. You can find a job at any other design firm in this city."

"It's one house, though."

"Harper Lee only published one book."

I snort. "We're hardly comparable."

"All I'm saying is that quality matters, and what you did with my house is quality work. It's exceptional and people will see that. Christiana will see that. Believe in yourself, Charleigh. You're more amazing than you know."

And with that, my faltering grin explodes into a wide smile, bubbling sensation in my throat and all. Guy knows exactly what to say to make me feel better.

"Thanks for that," I say.

"I mean it. I'll see you soon, okay?"

"Okay." I almost hang up when the thought hits me. "Sugar cookie."

"What?"

"There's a sugar cookie candle in the cabinet next to the sink. Switch out the pine tree candle for the sugar cookie candle."

"You've got it."

By the time I make it back to my desk, I'm already feeling better. I have no control over this process, so I'll let my design speak for itself. It will be up to Christiana whether it will be enough for the promotion. And if it's not, maybe Guy's right. Maybe I can look at other design firms because I know I'll be miserable going back to my old job now that I got a taste of what it's like to be a full-time designer.

My nerves of steel don't last long. I spend the next half hour rearranging my desk, desktop, and file folders because there's nothing on my plate for work except for the walk-through, which isn't for another hour.

I glance toward Christiana's office and find that same woman in her office. They're sitting together on the couch drinking coffee and laughing. Christiana is *laughing*. I don't think I've ever seen Christiana laugh. If this mystery woman is vying for Lana's position, then my chances are almost nonexistent at this point.

I grab my purse and leave. There's no point in me being here, especially when all it's doing is making me more nervous, so I head to my car and start for Guy's place. I call Guy on my way, and just like before, he's able to walk me away from the ledge and back into safer territory. I hate second-guessing myself.

When I finally make it to Guy's house, he's waiting for me on the porch. That overwhelming feeling of happiness bubbles up as soon as I'm close enough to see his smile.

"Hey there, Char—"

I knock the wind out of him as I wrap my arms tightly around him.

"—leigh," he finishes a few seconds later.

He slides his hand along the base of my skull, up to my crown, his fingertips gently kneading my scalp. Tingles spread from my head, down my neck, and throughout the rest of my body.

"You okay?" he asks after a few moments.

I smile up at him. "I am now."

***

"I'm impressed," Christiana says.

We've just finished our blue tape tour of the house, and even though there were a few minor issues that she brought up, it went far better than I expected, much to Andrea's chagrin. As it turns out, the woman Christiana spent much of the afternoon with was an old friend who was just visiting. She even came along to see the house.

"It's no easy feat to do what you did in this amount of time," she says as she looks around the kitchen once again. She clicks her tongue. "And you've got a real eye for detail. Everything flows seamlessly together."

GUY HATER

My heart is hammering so fast that it feels like it's going to burst right out of my chest. Christiana, always sparing with her compliments, is throwing them at me faster than I can keep up.

"It's more than I could've asked for," Guy says, seeming to sense that my brain is all sorts of discombobulated. He grabs my knee from under the table, and I instantly feel at ease. It's the first time we've touched since our hug a few hours ago. Even though the finish line is finally in sight, we've made sure to be on our best behavior in front of Christiana and Andrea.

"I couldn't imagine going with anyone else for this project. Charleigh has real talent. You're lucky to have her," he adds, his kind words melting every last part of me.

Andrea coughs, clearly annoyed that not only did her ploy to make me nervous fall like a lead balloon, but Christiana and Guy are both gushing over my design.

Today is a good day. And as I feel Guy's hand edge higher up my leg, I have a feeling it's going to be even better once everyone leaves.

"Yes, we are," Christiana says. "I think we're going to have a great one-on-one meeting next week."

Holy tap-dancing shit on a stick. Is she implying what I think she's implying because I sure as hell hope so. I glance at Andrea and she's bright red. Her hands are wrapped so tightly around her mug that I'm pretty sure she's moments away from shattering it.

I smile and thank Christiana for her kind words. And then a few minutes later, Christiana, her friend Livie, and Andrea leave.

As soon as I hear the front door shut I take a running leap at Guy and he catches me. I squeal with excitement.

"You killed it."

I'm so overrun with emotions that I can't speak. So instead, I do the next best thing: plant my lips on Guy.

"Fuck, it's been too long since I tasted those lips," he says as we finally break for air. He sets me down on the island, my hands still wrapped around his neck.

"Way too long."

I kiss him again, and soon his hands are moving across my body.

"Did I tell you how gorgeous you are today?"

I smile into his lips, our teeth gently touching. "I think so, but I don't mind hearing it again."

He kisses my jaw, trailing kisses down my neck. My skin erupts in goosebumps as he draws a line with his tongue.

"I think it's about time you make good on your promise."

Guy pulls back. "And what promise is that?"

"To christen every single one of these rooms, starting with the kitchen."

He lets out a guttural groan as I massage him through his pants.

"I think we can arrange that."

He kisses me roughly, gripping the back of my head as he pulls me closer. His taste is driving me crazy. His scent is dizzying. And I can feel his cock pressing against me as he leans into me.

"There's one problem though," he says.

"And what's that?"

"You're not naked yet."

He takes a step back, allowing me to hop off the island. I raise my hands in the air, and he kneels down, sliding his hands along the backside of my calves and up my thighs. He wedges the hem of my dress between his thumb and index finger, pushing my dress off of me as his hands run the length of my leg.

"I've wanted to do this since the moment you showed up today."

"Yeah? What else did you want to do?"

"I think I'd prefer to show you."

Just as my dress bunches around my waist, there's a cough from behind us. My blood runs cold as my eyes bulge. I look toward the sound and find Andrea staring at me with her phone pointed at us.

"Say cheese, Charleigh," she says, a wicked grin on her lips.

CHAPTER THIRTY-FOUR

Guy

I CAN'T BELIEVE it. They left. *She left.* What is she doing here?

"It's not what it looks like," Charleigh says, but it's clear from Andrea's smile that she knows exactly what she saw.

"I'm not sure the camera agrees, and I'm pretty sure Christiana will have a different opinion."

The air shifts immediately, as though I've been covered with a cold, wet blanket.

"No." Charleigh's voice is barely audible, her tone fractured by emotion. She tries to walk toward Andrea but I hold her back.

I turn to her and my heart feels as though it's breaking into a million tiny pieces. I've never seen Charleigh so small and sad. "Don't. I'll handle this." This is my fault she's in this position, so I'm going to get her out of it.

I turn my attention to Andrea. She's putting her phone into her purse, a smug look plastered across her face. There have only been a few times in my life that I've ever been this angry at someone, but the commonality between those situations is that they hurt the people I most love. My parents years ago, and now, Charleigh. And there's nothing I won't do to protect her.

"What's your plan here, Andrea? Do you really think showing Christiana this video will have any positive effect on your career? On your position at Florence + Foxe? Because I'm quite sure if anything, it will harm your reputation far more than Charleigh's. And to be clear, there's nothing wrong with what we're doing here."

Andrea laughs. "Please. I'll be doing Christiana a favor. She needs to know the real Charleigh. She's an untethered rule breaker who thinks she's better than everyone else."

Charleigh makes a noise as though to protest, but I push back before Charleigh has a chance. "That's because she is better. And that's why you're doing this. You know that you'd never rise as fast as Charleigh at Florence + Foxe, which is why you're turning to shady tactics."

I take a few steps toward Andrea, and for a few moments, her smug smile dissipates.

"You're jealous that you aren't as talented or driven as Charleigh. Just look around you."

I spread my arms wide and spin slowly around, taking in the phenomenal work Charleigh put into this place. Every detail shows her love and passion and dedication, and I could see why Andrea would be insecure. This is Charleigh's first project and it looks like a seasoned professional with decades of experience under their belt completed it.

"If you think showing Christiana this video will have a positive effect on your career, you're sorely mistaken. Go ahead, we'll fight this."

It takes a few moments for Andrea's smirk to return, and it's clear that everything I said went well over her head because she's still intent on telling Christiana.

"It's not going to work," I say.

She shrugs, and after a few moments of silence, she says, "But...I'd be willing to hold on to it." She pauses for a moment and then stares directly at Charleigh. "If you take yourself out of the running for Lana's position."

"She's not."

I move to Charleigh and grab her hand. It's freezing, and when I look at Charleigh, I hardly recognize her. She's downcast and refuses to look at anything but the floor in front of her. I squeeze her hand, hoping that it might jolt her out of her head but she doesn't squeeze back. And she doesn't look up either.

"We'll see about that," Andrea says. "Let me know soon or else I'll be having a chat with Christiana on Monday. And she'll be right. Your one-on-one meeting *will* be very interesting."

I'm so focused on Charleigh now that I hardly hear another word from Andrea. I kneel down in front of Charleigh, trying to make her look at me. I grab both of her hands and tug gently. "We'll get through this. Andrea's digging her own grave. You have nothing to worry about. *We* have nothing to worry about."

But I'm not sure if that's true. She's taking this hard, so hard that I'm not sure what to do or how to help her. Her lip quivers and then tears begin streaming down her cheeks.

"I should have known," she says weakly.

"Should have known what?"

I bring her hands to my mouth and kiss her fingers. They're like icicles. She rips them from my grasp as she gets to her feet.

"I should have known that this was a bad idea."

The effect of her words is immediate and brutal—a lightning strike that rips right through my soul. I motion between us as I stand up. "You don't mean us."

She mashes her lips and eyelids together as the rest of her body shakes. She spins around and braces herself against the island. I place my hand on her back but she shrugs it off.

"Stop. Just stop."

I take a step back, uncertain of what to do at this point because the person I care about most dearly in this life is in so much pain and I can't do anything meaningful about it.

"I know this is difficult, but I want you to think this through. I need you to think this through. We can take this straight to Christiana ourselves, cut Andrea off at her knees. I know it's against Florence + Foxe policy for employees to have a relationship with clients, but I think we can make a case for an exception. We can do this together."

Charleigh shakes her head, and after a few moments, turns around. She looks even worse, although hardly a few seconds have passed, and the pain in her eyes jabs me hard in the chest.

"I'm taking my name out of the running."

"No, you're not. You know why I know you're not? Because you're not a quitter, Charleigh Marie Holiday." There's a brief pause. Charleigh seems surprised that I know her name, but she shouldn't be. I know almost everything there is to know about her, which is why it's so heartrending to see her like this. This isn't the Charleigh I know. "I've never met anyone so driven and talented, and I'm not about to let you waste it. I'll take full responsibility for what happened in that video. I'll make my case to Christiana. She'll see it for what it is. Love." I can feel my throat beginning to close, hard lumps forming throughout it. I can't swallow. I can hardly breathe. I can't think about anything but this one point.

"I love you, Charleigh."

Charleigh wobbles and then again latches onto the island for support. She wears her internal struggle on her face. Her chin trembles as she opens and closes her mouth, words unable to surface. Finally, she closes her eyes, rivulets of tears streaming down her cheeks. And then she leaves. I watch her as she leaves, stunned.

When my mind finally comes to, I find myself on the floor, leaning against the island as I watch the last streaks of sunlight disappear across the kitchen floor. I don't remember the sound of the front door shutting. I don't remember how I came to this position on the floor. The only thing I can remember is the scent of Charleigh as she passed by me and the enormous empty feeling it left.

My body aches as I force myself to my feet and my skin feels feverish and clammy. I tamp the wick on the candle with my thumb and then leave the kitchen. I thought that

Charleigh and I would be sharing this home in a few weeks, but now I'm not so sure. I feel like I just jumped back a few decades when I'd lost everything in one fell swoop.

But I'm not going to make the same mistake this time around.

I hop into my truck and check my phone. There are multiple texts from Jamie that span a period of a few hours.

Jamie: Charleigh's here and she looks like a complete wreck. What the hell happened?

Jamie: She disappeared with Marissa into our bedroom.

Jamie: They're still in there…

Jamie: Still there…

Jamie: You're great at this whole texting thing.

Jamie: Okay, they just came out.

Jamie: Yikes, dude…just heard what happened.

Jamie: You okay?

Guy: About as good as you can expect.

Guy: How is she?

Jamie: I don't think I've ever seen her this distraught.

Guy: I'm coming over.

I toss my phone on the seat, turn on my truck, and peel out, rocks spraying behind me as I gun it out of my driveway. My phone beeps incessantly as I'm driving toward Marissa and Jamie's apartment. Right before I make the turn onto the highway, I answer Jamie's call.

"What?"

"Don't come over. It's not a good idea right now."

"Why the fuck not?"

Jamie sighs. There's dead air for a few moments and I swear I hear Charleigh on the other end. But then Jamie speaks again. "I know your heart's in the right place, but Charleigh's head isn't. She just bawled her eyes out for hours, and seeing you right now won't help either of you. She passed out on the couch and from the looks of it, she won't be up until tomorrow anyway. I think it's best if you hold off for now. Give her a call tomorrow when both of you have had some time to think."

"But—why can't I—" It's taking every last effort inside me to hold back. I want to argue. I want to plead my case. I *want* to see Charleigh again, but I know Jamie's right.

"Fine. I'll let her recharge."

But I'm not going to let her run away again because if we can't face this together, what hope is there for our future?

⌒⌒⌒

"Open up!" I yell, banging on the door to Jamie and Marissa's apartment.

I've waited long enough. I'm done waiting. I need to figure out what the hell is going on with Charleigh. She's been silent over the last few days, and I can't deal with it any longer.

I bang on the door again, and finally, I hear some movement behind the door. Both Jamie and Marissa open the door, concerned looks on their faces. I know I look like hell. I haven't shaved. I've hardly slept or eaten because all I can think about is Charleigh.

"Where is she?" I ask, pushing by them. "Charleigh?" I call out as I move through the apartment. Jamie tries to grab my arm, but I shake him off.

He says something but I can't hear him as I duck into a bedroom. I run into him as I turn to leave the room.

He grabs me by the shoulders. "She's not here."

I shake my head as I stare at him. "What do you mean? Where is she?"

"For one," he begins, "I'm pretty sure she's at work. And two, I helped her move into a new apartment this weekend. She's not staying here."

The realization hits me hard, and nothing Jamie or Marissa say penetrates my consciousness as I move on autopilot out the door and back to my car.

CHAPTER THIRTY-FIVE

Charleigh

YOU KNOW THE gut feeling you get right before you jump off a tall diving board? Anxiety. Nerves. Call it what you want. It's the feeling that either pushes you to take the leap or reels you back in.

I've been constantly living with that feeling for the last few days. It doesn't get any better or worse. It wraps itself around me like a coat that I can't remove. And as I'm sitting here in Christiana's office, it's cinching tighter and tighter with every passing second.

I can hardly lift my head, I'm so ashamed of what I'm about to do. I can't bring myself to look Christiana in her eyes as I tell her that I want to be taken out of consideration for Lana's job.

It feels like I'm having an out of body experience, or watching someone else's life being played out on screen.

I'm staring at them, screaming for them to make a different choice but they can't hear me. It continues to play out until finally, Christiana speaks, and I'm sucked back into my body.

"I'm shocked. I really am."

She leans back in her chair. I glance at her for only a moment because I can't bear to look at the combination of concern and disappointment on her face.

"Help me understand because there has to be something I'm missing here. Do you not want to be a lead designer?"

"I do, but I think it might be too soon for me."

"And why's that?"

Because if I take this job, Andrea will show you the video, and then I'll be out of a job and a reputation.

"I'm not sure I can handle the workload."

Christiana sighs and leans forward. "I know you can handle the workload because you proved that you could with this last project. The work you did on Mr. Finch's home is some of the best work I've seen out of someone so young. You have a bright career ahead of you, but it seems like you're your own worst enemy."

The lump in my throat grows larger by the second. Pretty soon I won't be able to breathe.

"I was going to offer you the job, Charleigh. And I'm still willing to offer you the job, but it seems like you've already made up your mind."

I nod because I know if I try to speak now nothing will come out.

Christiana presses her lips together into a thin line and shakes her head. The disappointment in her face tells the story she doesn't want to speak. She thinks I'm making a terrible choice. She thinks I'm throwing my career away. And at this point, I don't think she's wrong.

"Send Andrea in," she says, turning her attention back to the papers on her desk.

I don't have to look for Andrea because she's already waiting for me at my desk. "You look rough," Andrea says as I pass by her and collapse into my chair. "So am I going to have to show Christiana this—"

"Just go." I point to Christiana's office. "She wants to talk to you."

"I knew you'd come to your senses." She leaves a few seconds later, gloating in self-made misfortune.

I try to bury myself in work, running through the checklist of tweaks that were brought up during the blue tape walk-through, but it only helps for a brief moment. My mind keeps returning to what happened. And then to how I treated Guy. That's the worst part about all of this. He told me he loved me and I ran away without saying anything.

I've never felt so much regret in my life. It's so heavy and painful and it follows me everywhere. One second I'm crying, the next laughing—no rhyme or reason to the swift, unpredictable change in emotion. There's a constant pain in my chest and moments when I can't breathe and think I'm about to die. It's terrible but nothing less than what I deserve for deserting the person I love.

I love Guy, but I let him go.

He deserves better.

"Charleigh, dear. Could you run out and grab me a triple Venti, half-sweet, nonfat, caramel macchiato?"

Okay. It hasn't even been one week since I removed myself from the running and Andrea thinks she's my superior. I don't even dignify her request with a response or even a glance.

"Charleigh. *Dear*." She taps on the top of my cubicle. "Are you alright?"

I look at her for a brief moment and then turn my attention back to work. I'm finishing up one last email before I head out to Guy's house to look at a few minor details that Ryder's finishing up. I text Guy to see if he wants to join, but just like the last messages I've sent him, he hasn't responded. I don't expect him to either.

"Well?"

I hit send and then glance one more time at Andrea. "What?"

"My coffee."

I stand up and grab my purse off my desk.

"That's better," she says as I pass by her.

I come to an abrupt stop, wondering whether it's worth my time. It takes only a split second to come to the conclusion that yes, yes it is.

"Oh," I say, turning around. "I'm not getting your coffee. I'm not doing a single thing for you because you're not my boss. And you never will be."

Andrea scoffs, folding her arms. "Is that so?"

"Yeah, because do you really think Christiana is going to pick you for Lana's replacement?"

"Why wouldn't she?"

A scrolling list of reasons unrolls in my head, but I

choose to go with this simple observation. "I'm no longer in the running. Who else in this office is up for the job? You. There *is* no one else, so if she was going with you, she would've tapped you for it already. Right?"

The look on her face is a mix of shock, anger, and a touch of fear. It's a good look on her and makes me feel a tad better as I head to my car. But that miniature high crashes to the ground when I see a one-word text from Guy.

Guy: Busy.

I throw my phone into my purse, turn on the radio, and blast it as I try to drown out the noise in my head.

Busy.

The single text I received from Guy this past week. Coincidentally, it's exactly what I've tried to be in order to keep my mind from wandering back to him, but it hasn't worked whatsoever.

Work has been a mess. Now that my first and possibly final project is done, I'm back doing grunt work for Christiana. Back to doing everything she doesn't want to do. Back to being on the lowest rung of the totem pole.

One look at my apartment makes it clear that my life is a mess as well. Empty pints of ice cream, pizza boxes, and Chinese food containers decorate my floor like some modern art interpretation of my depression.

The only thing that's kept me going is helping Marissa with her wedding. Now that it's at Guy's house, she's enlisted me as a quasi-consultant. But it's still not enough to keep my mind from drifting back to Guy and where I left things with him.

It's my fault that I'm in this mess, figuratively and literally.

I wade through the mess of filth lying around my living room and head into my bedroom. With throwing myself into other work, I'm exhausted by the end of the day, so I still haven't unpacked everything. Half-opened boxes are strewn haphazardly across the room, but I somehow manage to make it to my bed without tripping over something and breaking my neck.

The only comfort I've had is looking over photos of the renovation. Every now and then there's a picture of Guy, and it makes me smile. But only for a moment. It's happening again right now. I'm looking at the first photo he sent me: him shirtless and sweating as he poses in front of the load-bearing wall he eventually took down without my permission.

Even though I was so mad at him for it, I secretly liked that he took the initiative. I wish I could go back to that. I wish I could go back to the time when things between us were fine.

Marissa: Stop moping.

I stare at the screen for a while. It's strange how Marissa seems to know exactly what I'm doing at any given moment. As though she's bugged my apartment with cameras.

Actually...

Charleigh: I'm not moping.
Marissa: Have you finished unpacking yet?

I glance around and then respond in the affirmative. It's a test to see if she really has bugged my apartment.

Marissa: Send me a picture, I want to see.

I send her a picture of the only finished room in the apartment: the bathroom.

Marissa: Wow. Nice shower curtain. Spacious too. How about the rest of the apartment.

A period instead of a question mark. I know she means business.

Charleigh: Low battery, my phone's about to die. Maybe tomorrow!
Marissa: Don't make me come over there.

I take another look around the room. It really is a complete mess. I can't believe I let this happen. Even though these past few weeks have been extremely painful, I should've never let it come to this point.

Charleigh: Why don't you come over tomorrow? You can see the place and we can get some ideas I had for the decorations.
Marissa: Okay!

I need something to jolt me out of this, and plans with Marissa will do just that. I get to work, and in a matter of hours, the apartment is beginning to look like an adult lives here and not a caveman and/or a litter of pigs.

I start in on the unopened boxes. The first one is packed with some of my stuff from my room back at home. CDs and notebooks filled with random stuff I wrote when I was a teenager. After flipping through all of them and reading a select few entries, I come to the conclusion that it would be in my best interest to burn them in their entirety to spare any unsuspecting victim from cringing to death.

I set the box aside and open up another. Sitting at the top of the box is the sign that Ryder salvaged from Guy's house. I'd had it framed with a picture I'd found in my mother's scrapbook that showed Guy and his parents out in front of the house. I was going to give it to him once we finished the project, but I completely forgot about it until now.

I take it out along with the card I was going to give him and set them both down on the floor in front of me. I pick up the card and a picture falls out. It's a picture of Guy and me at the end of kindergarten. We're both smiling wide, and I'm holding the painting that he'd torn up.

I can't help but tear up as I look at it. Even at that young age, we were able to mend our relationship. Why not now? He gave me that picture, and I forgave him.

Now it's my turn to do the same.

CHAPTER THIRTY-SIX

Guy

Charleigh: Can we talk? I'm sorry.

ISN'T THAT WHAT I tried to do? I tried to talk with Charleigh and work through the problem with her together, but she shut me out. And now she wants to talk? It's like a slap in the face, and I'm not going to entertain such a small gesture.

I slide the phone back into my pocket and glance at the highway in front of me. It's almost midnight and the road is quiet. We've hardly seen a single car pass in the last five minutes. But to be honest, I haven't been paying attention.

No matter how hard I try, I can't stop thinking about Charleigh. Even now, after stowing my phone, there's an urge prodding me to take the phone out and call her. *She's coming around,* it says.

That might be true, but after the dead air between us, I need something more than a flimsy apology through text. I'm tired of chasing someone who doesn't know what they want. I know exactly what I want: Charleigh. And I've pursued her relentlessly. But I'm tired of running on this treadmill and getting absolutely nowhere.

I turn to Maddox. He's inspecting the speed gun like it's an alien object, turning it over, tapping on different parts. I'm a little surprised he hasn't tried to take a bite out of it yet. "You up for a drive?" I ask.

He looks at me silently for a moment, still fiddling with the speed gun. Then he nonchalantly says, "Fuck yeah." He blinks a few times and then drops the speed gun in his lap.

"Good, because I can't sit here any longer."

"Where are the speeders and drunk drivers? I need some action."

"It's a good thing we're this bored."

He nods his head. "Yeah. I guess you're right." After a few moments, he slowly turns his head to look at me sidelong. "But we could pull someone over. Tell 'em they were drifting. Could give us something to do."

I stare at him blankly as I put the cruiser into drive. He shrugs, leaning back into his seat as we head out. We cruise for a while, taking random exits and circling back onto the highway. There's been absolutely nothing to distract me from my thoughts. Charleigh still owns the inside of my head, and there's nothing I can do about it.

"Where the fuck are we?" Maddox asks.

Maddox's voice jolts me back to reality. Shit. I'd been so focused on Charleigh that I have no recollection of driving here.

"I zoned out, I guess."

We pull up to a stop sign, giving me a few moments to look around and gather my bearings. It's a rural road with a four-way stop that looks vaguely familiar.

"Shift's over. Let's get out of here already."

I hold up a hand to stop him as I look around. He shrugs and then pulls out his phone. It takes a few moments, but when I see the white cross, it hits me hard. The cross is new, freshly painted. Someone's been maintaining it. There's a fresh bouquet of vibrant flowers resting on the ground in front of the cross.

I've done everything in my power to avoid this intersection even though it's the shortest route back to my house. I hop out of the car and Maddox says something, but it rolls off me.

The distance is short between the car and the cross, but seconds seem to dilate into minutes as I walk. It's hard to breathe, and my vision narrows into focus, the bright white cross the only thing I can see.

When I finally reach it, I collapse onto my knees, the damp soaking into my pants. My throat constricts and it feels like I'm being slowly choked. I reach out and trace the letters of my parents' names etched into the wood. It's been nearly fifteen years since that night, but the feelings flowing through me make it feel like it's just happened.

Distant memories wash over me in no apparent order. Birthdays and outings. Playing catch with my dad in the back yard. Family dinners and holiday events. Memories that I've not thought about in years flood back with such ease and with so much force that it's difficult to process it all at once.

"Dude, you okay?" Maddox asks. "You've been here for like fifteen minutes."

"Yeah," I say, clearing my throat as I stand. "I'm fine."

I walk past him, but he doesn't follow, standing in the same spot, no doubt making the connection between the names on the cross and me.

I make it back into the car and start it up. Maddox is silent for once when he hops in. I make a U-turn and just after we pass through the intersection, a white truck whips past us in the opposite lane, blowing through the stop signs.

It hits way too close to home.

Maddox pops the sirens and then smacks the dash. "Let's fucking go!"

The tires squeal as I make another U-turn and then smash the gas to pursue the truck, which is already just a white dot in the distance. It takes nearly a full minute to catch up to the truck and when we do, it's clear that the driver's drunk. He's drifting from the shoulder and then into the opposite lane.

He's completely oblivious to the sirens and flashing lights behind us as he drives for another couple minutes, slowing down, speeding up, drifting and swerving.

"About time," Maddox says as the driver pulls onto the shoulder. The car is hardly in park before I'm out of the car and charging for the driver. And when I see the driver's face, everything blurs around me.

I see *him*. I see the face of the driver who smashed into my parents that night.

I leave my supervisor's office and head to my desk to grab my things.

"What's the damage?" Maddox asks me as I approach.

"One month unpaid leave."

"Unpaid? Shit, man. No admin duty?"

I shrug. It's a light punishment for what happened, even though I don't remember any of it. Apparently, I forced the driver's side door open and ripped the driver out of his car and tossed him to the ground. Thankfully, Maddox pulled me off him before I could do any physical harm to the man.

"Where are you headed?" Maddox asks.

"The guy's still here, right?"

"Monty? Dude, bad idea."

"Relax. I'm apologizing."

"You know the sarge is going to lose his shit if he catches you talking to him."

"I'll take the risk."

Maddox shrugs. "Your funeral, bud."

I know this is the last thing I should do right now, but it's the only thing I can think of that will make me feel less like a piece of shit. There are four people in the drunk tank, all of them in various stages of inebriation. One of them is having a conversation with himself in the corner, two are asleep, and the last is sitting on the floor with his head in between his knees.

I tap on one of the bars with my knuckles. Neither of the sleeping drunks moves, while the chatty drunk in the corner glances at me in the way drunks do when they're trying hard to concentrate on something, usually not throwing up. He stumbles toward me.

"They're poisoning us, man. The chem-trails. MKUltra. The reptilian overlords are trying to control our minds." He taps his skull as his eyes grow wide. "Do you have any weed, dude?"

"Seriously? I think you've had enough for all of us."

About halfway through my sentence, he gets enthralled with his previous conversation with the wall and heads back to his corner. I look back at the guy who had his head between his knees, and he's staring at me. I motion for him to come over, and after a few moments, he struggles to his feet and walks toward me.

He's got the telltale physical signs of a long-term alcohol abuser. Redness the extends across the bridge of his nose and under his eyes. Puffy and bloated and overall just rundown. I see his kind a lot, but there's something about him that's familiar, and it's not because of our interaction earlier.

Neither of us talks. I'm trying to figure out why I have this strange feeling in my gut and chest while he's waiting on me. He won't make eye contact with me as he sways slowly, trying to maintain his balance. I move my head to get a better look underneath his dirty, ragged hair that frames his patchy beard. Even now he still reeks of alcohol.

Finally, he turns, and when I see his eyes, the realization hits me. I'm looking into the same set of eyes I kept seeing every night for years after my parents' accident, but now they're set in a younger face. The man's son. Monty.

"I'm sorry, man," he says, grabbing the bar. He bites down on his lip. Shakes his head. "I'm a fuck up. Plain and simple." He snorts. "Like father, like son. This shit's in my blood. There's no escaping it."

I don't even know what to say at this point. I'd always wanted to confront the man who killed my parents, but he died long before I had the courage. And now that I'm face-to-face with his son, I don't know what to think.

He looks at me for a brief moment before looking back down at the ground. "I don't know, man. I'm sorry." He turns around and heads back to the same position he was in when I arrived.

I stare at him and can't help but see a part of me. I was angry and lost and incapable of escaping the downward spiral brought on by my parents' accident. He's in the same spiral, but it's lasted his entire life. It's all he knows.

"It was Charleigh's idea."

"How long has she been maintaining it?"

"Since you left Whispering Pine."

"Really?"

Deanna nods. "She makes sure it has fresh flowers each month and repaints it almost yearly."

"Why?"

Deanna looks at me as though I should know the answer. "Because she loves you, Guy."

"She had a weird way of showing it when I came back here."

"Charleigh has her own way of doing things. She might have a tough exterior, but deep down she feels everything."

I sit there, mulling it over for a while. Eventually, Deanna speaks, but this time Charleigh's not the topic. She starts talking about the man I pulled over tonight. The whole reason why we're sitting at the kitchen table at nearly 2 a.m. She's telling me his story. The story he alluded to.

"Monty's parents divorced shortly after the accident. His father left town and never returned. His mother was so torn up about the whole incident that she turned to drugs. He never really had a normal childhood after that.

"But you had a support network. Monty was left to fend for himself because his mother retreated into her own world. There was a time where it seemed like he'd make it through the other end somewhat normal. He started working on his grades. He started playing sports. He did all the things his father didn't do. He didn't want to become him.

"He went to college. The first person in his family to do so. But with him gone, his mother started drinking, and every time he came back during breaks she was a little more gone. It wore him down, and soon enough, he started drinking too. Partying. That led to harsher drugs. More alcohol. He stopped taking responsibility for his life. And eventually fell into all the same traps his father did."

There's a long pause. I'd only ever considered how that night affected me and no one else. It never crossed my mind that the man who killed my parents had a son, a wife, a family. How he'd affected their lives that night and every night leading up to it.

"It's a sad story," Deanna says. "It's what happens when you live your life based on the past. If you can't let go, it will take control and you'll never be able to move on. Progress, Guy. That's what this whole thing's about. Keep moving forward."

She doesn't say anything else after that. It's late. Or early, depending on how you look at it. She gets up, wraps her robe tightly around her, gives me a kiss on the head, and then heads upstairs.

I sit in the same spot long after Deanna leaves, thinking about Monty and what Deanna said. I can't help but feel like I'm doing the same thing in some way. A part of me is holding on to the past. It's holding on to my parents and that night. And if I let it, that part of me will lead me down the same road as him.

Progress, Guy. That's what this whole thing's about.

I need to move forward.

CHAPTER THIRTY-SEVEN

Guy

WE FINISHED THE renovation a week ago. It's done. I never thought I'd say those words, but it's finally here. I should be happy about it, but I'm not. All I can think about is what else is done and over with.

I don't care about losing out on my dream job. I don't care about the prospect of working for Andrea. None of that matters. I could get all of that back in time. The only thing I can't get back is the only thing that's important to me: Guy.

I glance at the old photograph of us. It hasn't left my pocket since I found it in my old things, except, of course, when taking it out to glance at it. I've glanced at it approximately a thousand times in the last few days, and it still has the same effect: a jolt through my core, goosebumps, an intense high followed by an extreme low.

I slide the picture back in my pocket and then try to turn my attention to my inbox. There's a slew of emails from Christiana asking me to do the same tasks I had to work through before my project: boring, mind-numbing administrative tasks that she doesn't want to do.

I'm done with it. I'm tired of being dragged around by other people. I'm tired of running when things get tough. I've made some terrible decisions lately, but no more. I look once more at the picture in my pocket before I head to Christiana's office.

She's in the middle of a meeting with someone, but I don't care. I open the door without knocking. Instantly I feel two pairs of eyes on me. An uncomfortable feeling rises in my gut, but I push it right back down.

"Charleigh, what are—"

"I want to be considered for Lana's job again. I know I can do it, and I know I'm the best candidate for the job."

The woman seated in front of Christiana's desk mumbles something incoherent, and it's clear that she's interviewing for the same position.

"I know this is abrupt, but I wanted to let you know."

"Oh—okay."

I've never seen Christiana so flustered, and it feels good. I turn to leave, but just before I do, I look back at Christiana. "Also I slept with Guy—Mr. Finch. I hope that doesn't change my standing, but I wanted to be transparent."

So, fuuuuuuuuck you Andrea.

Christiana and the interviewee both flush bright red, and without another word from either of them, I leave the office. I run into Andrea on my way back, arms folded across her chest.

"What do you think you're doing?"

"Exactly what I should've done. You're a horrible person, Andrea, and I'm not going to give in to you. Show Christiana the video. I don't care."

There are a few whispers around us, but I ignore them and head to my desk to grab my purse. I'm in my car and heading to my mom's house in a few minutes. I'm not running anymore. I'm taking everything head-on. I might be jobless by the end of the day, but I don't care. Everything will be okay if I have Guy. But I have no idea if he'll take me back after how I treated him.

I take the steps to my mother's house two at a time. I don't bother knocking, I just push through the door with so much force that I'm surprised it doesn't fly off the hinges.

"Guy!" I scream as I survey the entryway. I head upstairs and rush down the hallway, but when I reach my bedroom the wind gets knocked out of me. Guy's stuff is gone. Guy's gone.

I nearly slip and fall on my ass as I rush back downstairs, and when I get to the kitchen, my mother looks at me with the expression that I remember seeing often growing up. *What. Are. You. Doing?*

"Sorry," I say, pausing for a few seconds to catch my breath.

"No need to be sorry. I'm just glad it's you and not the herd of hippos I'd envisioned rampaging through my house."

"Where's Guy?" I ask, ignoring the light dig.

"He moved out a few days ago. Back at his house. I thought he'd have told you."

"It's complicated."

She gives me another familiar look. "Probably less so than you believe."

I turn around and head back to the front of the house. "And Charleigh," my mom adds. I pause at the doorway. "He's had a difficult week. Take it easy on him."

I'm not sure what to make of her comment, but I don't have time to think about it. I leave the house, hop into Franny, and head straight to Guy's.

I pull into the driveway just as Jamie and Marissa are pulling out. I stop in the driveway and roll down my window. "What are you guys doing here?"

"Dropping off some wedding stuff," Marissa yells over Jamie. "What about you? Shouldn't you be at work?"

"Long story. Is Guy in there?"

Marissa tries to hide a smile but does a poor job of it. "Yes. He's upstairs in his old room."

"Really?"

She nods.

"Sorry to break this up, but we have more wedding appointments to get to," Jamie says.

We say our goodbyes, I roll up my window, and then park right next to Guy's truck. I almost break into a sprint, but I'm stopped by nerves. I don't have the same urgency I had at my mother's because my brain is catching up with my heart.

I've never done anything like what I'm about to do, and it's nerve-racking.

The nerves swirl in my gut like a hurricane, increasing with intensity the closer I get to Guy. Eventually, I make it to his room. The door's open and I can hear him moving inside, but I'm frozen in place, trying my best to breathe.

Every muscle in my body is clenched tight, as though I've been swaddled like a baby. You could push me and I'd tip over and hit the floor without any resistance or ability to stop myself.

"Are you going to hang out there like a weirdo or come inside?"

Gulp. Everything tingles. "Oh, um." I pop into the doorway and get my first look at Guy in weeks, gulping yet again. Dear lord, this man gets even more handsome by the day. "Yeah, I was just inspecting the work Ryder did on the wall out here." I drag my finger along the edge of the doorway as though I'm pointing something out.

I can feel Guy's eyes on me the entire time, and when I finally look back at him, I'm right. He's staring directly at me. "What's going on in here?" I ask, glancing at all the open boxes on the ground.

Guy maintains his gaze on me for a few more seconds that seem to stretch out for far too long. "Something that should've happened a long time ago. I'm packing up all my old stuff. Donating it all. I've held on to it long enough. It's time to move on."

I walk over to Guy and sit down next to him on the bed.

"Are you sure you don't want to keep anything?"

He shakes his head. "I've got it all in here," he says, tapping his temple and then his heart. "It's safer in here than out there."

After a few moments of silence, I say, "I'm sorry for everything I did. I should've taken your advice. I should've taken Andrea head-on and gone straight to Christiana."

My eyes water as my lips tremble. The lump in my throat is growing, and I know it will be difficult to swallow in a few seconds. "I didn't listen to you. I shut you out. I don't know why. It's just what I do. I know I do it and I hate that I put you through it." I look at Guy, my vision blurred from tears. "You don't deserve it."

Guy looks at me but doesn't speak. I can't read his expression, but it doesn't matter. I need to get this out. I pull out the picture from my pocket and hand it to him.

He takes it in his hand and looks at it with the same expression. I don't know what to say. I don't know what to do. And the seconds seem to turn into minutes as Guy stares at the photo without saying a word, his expression unchanging. My throat feels like it's about to close in on itself as tears begin to well in my eyes.

"Where did you find this?" Guy finally asks, a smile beginning to form on his lips.

"I found it when I was unpacking." I sniffle a few times and then clear my throat. "You were always the one to fix things between us. I always stewed. I always ran. And I'm not going to do that anymore. I told Christiana about us. I have no idea what's going to happen. I might be out a job, but I don't care. The only thing I care about is you. If I lose—"

I close my eyes, feeling the tears roll down my cheeks and my neck. A few seconds later I feel Guy's hand on my knee. The warmth from his touch radiates through me, and I feel the strength to keep going.

"I know I haven't made it easy on you, but I want to make things work between us. I want to be friends again. I want to talk and joke and—"

"Sleep?" Guy asks.

"Yes. And sleep together. I want to do everything with you."

I choke out a choppy laugh as I finally force myself to look at Guy through watery eyes. And as soon as I see that smile, those eyes—the Guy I've come to know so well—I feel every warm and beautiful feeling bubble up inside of me.

He drags his fingertips softly down my cheek, pressing his thumb against my lips. He wraps his warm palm around the base of my skull and pulls my face close to his.

"I want to do everything with you too, Charleigh. I always have. I always will."

My body feels electric, pulsing with so much energy, it's almost too much. I've never felt so happy before. I never felt *anything* like this before, and the only possible thing I can think of doing is lunging at him and holding on to him with all my might. We topple backward and Guy groans and moans, but I don't care. I'm not letting go of him again.

"Can't. Breathe."

Okay. Maybe just this once.

I let him up and he takes a huge breath of air. "I forgot how powerful your hugs are."

I'm smiling so hard that my cheeks hurt. "I have one more thing. I was going to give it to you once the house was finished. It sort of got lost in everything that's happened. I'll be right back."

Guy looks at me suspiciously but only says, "Okay…"

I grab the present from the car and then rush back upstairs to hand it to him.

"So what is it?" he asks, bringing it to his ear and shaking it.

"That won't tell you anything. You'll have to open it."

When he finally rips the paper off the present, he sits there, staring at it for what seems like hours without saying a word. Finally, I ask him if he likes it.

Guy looks at me, tears beginning to well in his eyes. "I love it, Charleigh."

He reaches over and hugs me and then kisses me. I suck in my lower lip, relishing his taste when he finally lets go.

"Where'd you find it?"

"Ryder found it during the demo, and then I put it in a case with the only photo I could find of you and your parents together."

"You kept it a secret this entire time?"

I nod. "Are you mad?"

"Mad?" Guy asks. He laughs. "I'm not mad at all. I love it. Now we have to find a place to hang it."

"There's a spot right next to the door that I thought would be perfect."

"You think of everything, don't you?"

"Sometimes."

I move to stand, but before I can get to my feet, Guy grabs me. "You're not going anywhere," he growls.

"Is that so?" I say, making a faux struggle to get off the bed.

Guy pulls back, a half smile on his lips. "Unless, of course, you don't want me to make good on my promise."

I raise an eyebrow, thoroughly confused. "And what promise is that?"

"To christen every room in this house with you," he rasps.

The effect is instant—tingles everywhere as his gruff voice rolls over me.

"You remember what happened the last time you said that," I say, trying to pretend as though I don't mind if he doesn't make good on that promise but failing horribly.

"I don't give a damn," he says just before he kisses me.

And neither do I.

CHAPTER THIRTY-EIGHT

Guy

I SHOULD BE paying attention to my best friend getting married five feet away from me, but it's impossible when Charleigh's sitting in the front row. She's teasing me with that dress she's wearing, hugging her in all the right places, the hem pulling higher on her thigh as she crosses her legs.

Even though both of our professional lives are a mess—I'm still on leave, and Christiana hired someone else for Lana's position—things have been amazing between us. Whenever Charleigh isn't working, we're joined together at the hip. And lips. And other places. There's no one else in this world that gets me the way that Charleigh does.

There's a sharp jab in my sternum. I rub my chest and look up and find Jamie's death stare leveled directly at me. "The. Ring," he whispers out of the corner of his mouth.

Oh. Right.

I glance at Charleigh one more time as she tries her best not to laugh. Her cheeks are bright red as a playful smile spreads across her lips.

I pat my pockets, coming up empty. I can feel myself beginning to sweat as the realization hits me—*where the fuck is this ring?!*

My eyes bulge as I look at Jamie and then Marissa, who looks like she's about ready to kill me. I continue digging through my pockets as whispers spread throughout the crowd.

Psst! "Guy…"

I recognize Charleigh's voice and glance at her. She pats her left boob, and I shake my head, not understanding. She makes a gesture, pulling something out and then placing it on her finger.

Oh, right.

I check my front pocket and sure enough, there's the ring. I hand it to Jamie, who snatches it out of my hand. I mouth a thank you back at Charleigh and she shakes her head.

I turn my attention back to the ceremony. I've never seen Jamie and Marissa so happy. It's so radiant that it's contagious. When I glance back at Charleigh, I can see she's affected just as much—eyes watering, smile as big as I've seen on her. I don't think I've ever felt so in love like this before. It's overwhelming and all-consuming, and when Charleigh looks at me through teary eyes, it feels as though I might explode.

I drag my attention back to Jamie and Marissa just in time for their vows, but if I'm being honest, they hardly register. Most of the ceremony doesn't register. The only thing I remember about the wedding is my time with Charleigh. I remember feeding her mini cupcakes. I remember dancing with her and drinking with her and sneaking off to my old bedroom for a quick makeout session.

In other words, the wedding was amazing, even though I don't remember much except for Charleigh. Or to put it another way, the wedding was amazing *because* of Charleigh.

"And there's another one!" Charleigh says, holding her phone out to me.

I laugh. "I told you everyone would love your design."

Earlier in the week, the social media manager for Florence + Foxe posted photos of my house on Instagram, and almost immediately, Charleigh began getting emails from across the state and even country requesting her expertise in various projects. She'd forwarded the requests on to Christiana, but once they found out that Charleigh wouldn't be working on their projects, they bolted.

"I'm telling you, I think you should branch out. Open up your own firm."

"I don't know. It's a lot of work. A lot of money. It's a lot."

"And you can deal with a lot. You dealt with me on this project. You dealt with Andrea and Christiana. I mean, you love this work, and it may be years until you do it again now that Christiana hired someone else for the lead designer position."

Charleigh groans. "I know…"

I stroke Charleigh's hair as we rock back and forth on

the porch swing. The party's still raging on, but it feels like Charleigh and I are in our own little world out here.

"Give it some thought. It will be easier to start now since you have so much demand."

"But I need money. Offices. Employees."

"Money? That's easy. Offices? There's plenty of room here. Employees? I'm not working for another month, so I could help. And Ryder would be more than happy to help with the construction site."

Charleigh sits up and gapes at me. "I can't take your money. It's way too much."

I turn to meet her. "I'm in this for the long haul. And I want the best for you. I saw how much you loved working on your own, and if there's something I can do that would help you do that, I'm going to do it. I love you."

The last sentence comes out without even thinking about it. It rolls off my tongue so easily and I follow it up with, "I mean it. I love you, Charleigh."

Charleigh's lip trembles and tears begin to stream down her cheeks. "I love you too."

She wraps her arms around my neck and pulls me into her. Even though my lips are nearly raw from having kissed her so much tonight, I kiss her again. Again and again and again. I'll never have enough of her.

"Just think about it," I say after we finally break apart. "I know you can do it."

She hangs her head and then shakes it. I reach out and nudge her chin up. "What's wrong?"

"Nothing," she says, smiling through the tears. "No one's ever believed in me as much as you do. No one's loved me as much as you do. And I've never felt as much as I do right now."

I wipe a few of her tears away with my thumb. "So these are good tears."

She nods her head, taking in a few choppy breaths "Very good tears."

"Move in with me," I say without even thinking. Charleigh seems to be almost as surprised as I am. I hadn't planned on asking her officially, letting it happen more organically, but it feels right. And if I'm being honest, I'm being selfish. I want her all to myself.

After a few agonizing minutes of Charleigh not saying a word, her face alternating between smiling and utter confusion, she finally says, "Okay. But on one condition."

"And what's that?"

"You've got to keep baking me those brownies. Every. Day."

"Every day?"

"Every. Day."

I laugh. "If it means you move in with me, you've got it."

"Good." She plants a chaste kiss on my forehead. "Now we're heading back to the dance floor. I hear the Spice Girls and I'm not about to miss my jam."

She hops off the swing and I watch her as she hurries off in direction of the Spice Girls. Everything around me seems to blur and slow down as I watch Charleigh. I don't hear anything. I don't see anything. The only thing that rises into my consciousness is her. The love of my life— who is now showcasing some of those same dance moves I first glimpsed in her bedroom.

And that's what I love about her. I love how she dances to the beat of her own drum. I love how passionate she is—

even though that passion includes terrible '90s pop music. I love how she doesn't back down from a challenge. She's kind, loving, and more than I deserve.

And even though I rarely know what to expect from her, there's no one else in the world that I would rather spend my life with than her.

EPILOGUE
FIVE YEARS LATER

Charleigh

"OH MY GOD, Charleigh. You've outdone yourself again," Deirdre says.

I smile. "I'm so glad you like it."

Deirdre was my first client when I struck out on my own years ago. Since then I've remodeled her kitchen, reworked the landscape, and now I've just finished my last job for her—a complete overhaul of the old barn on her property. It used to be a working farm, but there haven't been any animals, other than her herd of huskies (seven is my last count…), for years so the barn was left unused and derelict.

But that's no longer the case. We converted the barn into a gorgeous multi-level apartment with soaring ceilings and thick transverse beams.

"I don't know how you do it," Deirdre says.

I smile. "With a lot of help."

It's true. I couldn't have done any of this without Ryder's crew. He takes my vision and turns it into reality. But more than that, none of this would've been possible without Guy. He gave me the push to strike out on my own, even when Christiana told me I was making a mistake by quitting the firm. He gave me the financial backing to take the risk. He even quit his job to help out full time. I told him he didn't need to but it was what he wanted. His job had been wearing him down mentally, and he needed a change. Both us did. That first year was full of changes and challenges and setbacks, but we somehow made it through, much to Andrea's chagrin I'm sure.

Sometimes I wonder about her—where'd she end up after I left Florence + Foxe. But then I look at my husband and the life we've built together and realize that I don't care in the slightest.

Husband.

It feels so weird saying that. Guy is my *husband.* It still gives me a chill a year later. A good chill. The *best* kind of chill.

Guy: You ready to see your new home?

Oh. My. God.

Charleigh: Seriously? It's ready?!
Guy: I'm over here now if you want to see it for yourself.

We closed on a house months ago. We spent five wonderful years at Guy's home, but we both decided we wanted to start a new chapter in our lives. We wanted a new place to create new memories, free from the past. And to be honest, it was just too big for us. Our new home isn't very far away, but according to my mother, it's not close enough. But then again, anything that's not next door isn't close enough for her.

It's a ranch-style farmhouse that sits on a few acres of land—the perfect size and location and style for us. But it needed work. Guy spent the last few months working on the renovation for me, making sure everything's moving forward, because I've been inundated with so many projects that I didn't have the bandwidth to work on it.

There were times when I tried to inject myself, but Guy forced me to stay out of it and focus on my clients. He wanted the final project to be a surprise—no peeking of any kind allowed. It was basically the most difficult thing for me to do, but I made it without a single peek.

I'm ready to be surprised. In a good way, I hope. And I hope Guy's ready to be surprised too because I have something up my sleeve.

"I've got to go, Deirdre. Let me know if there's anything else that you need from me."

"Oh, I'm sure I'll find something for you. I can never get enough of your designs."

I rush to my car and speed over to my new home. Guy, Deanna, Jamie, Marissa, and their baby girl, Aubrey, are all waiting for me.

"Welcome home," Guy says as I approach.

"Holy shi—" Marissa clears her throat just before I finish. "Ship."

"What's a holy ship?" Aubrey asks, tugging at Deanna's pants.

"Oh, that's just the Titanic," Deanna says.

Aubrey then launches into a series of "what" questions as I walk straight to Guy and give him a massive hug.

"I'm so glad you made me wait. It's absolutely gorgeous."

"Well, it was designed by a talented woman."

"I should hire her."

"I'm not sure she's available. I hear she's pretty busy these days."

"I bet."

"Ready for the tour?"

"Hell yeah."

As soon as I open the large cedar door, my jaw drops. I'm completely blown away by how everything has turned out. Even though I knew exactly how it should look based on my plans, I'm still shocked to see it all come together. It's even better than I'd imagined.

The once enclosed entrance is open and sprawling, the tall angled ceiling accented with large, richly colored timber beams. The large resurfaced fireplace and reclaimed wood mantle has me drooling, and when I see the kitchen, brownies stacked high on the counter, I know I made the right choice by putting Guy in charge.

Once we finally finish the tour, Guy asks me what I think, and I tell him, "It's wonderful, but it's missing something."

He looks nervous—so, so nervous. "What? Is there something wrong with—"

"No," I say, raising my hand.

Time for my surprise. I reach into my purse and grab the thick piece of wood I'd been hiding.

Guy looks at me strangely. "I'm not going to ask how you fit that in your purse…actually, I am. How did you?"

I tap my purse. "It's enchanted. I'm Hermione Granger," I say with a smile, turning around and heading for the front of the house. Everyone follows me outside and when they're behind me, watching, I hold the wood against the door.

The etching of the wood reads:

The Finch Family est. 2018
Charleigh, Guy, Karina, Carter.

It takes a few moments, but eventually, I hear Marissa gasp, followed by Aubrey asking who Karina and Carter are.

I look back and see Guy. There's an expression on his face that I've never seen before, but it's the exact expression I never knew I wanted to see. I can feel my legs get a little wobbly as I feel myself giving way to the overwhelming emotions coursing through me. And before I have the chance to wobble more than once, Guy lunges for me, grabbing the etching and me at the same time.

He kisses me again and again until he finally pulls away, kneeling to set the wood on the ground. He places a hand on my stomach as he rises back up. "Is this for real?" he whispers, his voice wavering.

I nod, tears beginning to well in my eyes.

He hugs me, his cheek brushing against mine. "I can't believe it," he whispers.

"Believe it," I whisper back.

"What did I tell you?" Marissa says. "I don't know about that last name though."

"I had to veto that one. Finn Finch. Too much alliteration."

"I think it's perfect," Guy says.

"I think you're perfect. I think our family is perfect, although I might be a little biased."

"I'm okay with that."

"Who's Karina and Carter!" Aubrey yells.

"Your new cousins," Deanna says, tapping Aubrey on her nose.

"Can I meet them?"

"In a few months."

"I guess we're going to have to add a nursery into the plans," Guy says.

I nod. "Yes, we will."

And for the first time, I see tears stream down Guy's cheeks. My heart swells, and every nerve ending on my body begins to fire. There's no question that I married the perfect man.

"I love you, Charleigh," Guy says.

I smile, so wide it begins to hurt. "I love you more."

ABOUT ETHAN

Ethan Asher writes romantic comedies and contemporary romance. He lives in Texas with his wife and dog. When he's not writing, he enjoys hiking, reading, and cooking.

You can find out more about his life on Instagram: @authorethanasher
www.authorethanasher.com

Made in United States
North Haven, CT
16 June 2023

37815627R00211